Matilda of Flanders

= Edith of Scotland

Stephen
of Blois
= Adela

STEPHEN d. 1154

Henry of Blois
Bishop of Winchester

Eustace
d. 1153

William
Earl Warenne d. 1159

1

/ of Germany = Matilda
the Empress
= Geoffrey Plantaganet
of Anjou d. 1151

Hamelin

HENRY II

Geoffrey
d. 1158

William
d. 1164

Geoffrey (Hikenai's son)

=

Matilda
b. 1156

RICHARD I
b. 1157

Geoffrey
b. 1158

Eleanor
b. 1161

THE LION OF JUSTICE

THE
LION
OF
JUSTICE

Margaret Butler

Coward, McCann & Geoghegan, Inc. New York

For my husband

Author's Note

This book, which takes up once more the fortunes of the characters in *The Lion of England*, is concerned primarily with Thomas Becket's elevation to the Archbishopric of Canterbury, and the famous quarrel between Henry II and himself that resulted from it.

I have adhered strictly to the facts of the quarrel itself (most of their public utterances are taken from the records), but the remarks and actions of minor characters which go to explain their somewhat arbitrary behaviour are entirely my own. There is no factual basis for Leicester's help in Thomas's eventual escape but since his sympathy for the Archbishop was manifest throughout, it seemed reasonable to attribute what help was given to him. Where the records are incomplete imagination has supplied links, as in the case of Thomas's rather feeble attempts to force the King to allow him to return to England in the spring of 1160. That he did make some devious but unsuccessful moves towards that end are obvious from the one-sided correspondence of John of Salisbury which is all that remains.

Eleanor the Queen has only a minor role to play; she was little more than an onlooker during these years though doubtless her attitudes to Henry were shaped further by the events she witnessed.

It is more than likely that Henry first met Rosamund de Clifford in the mid-1160s – some historians have it that her son by the King, William Longsword, was born well before 1170. However, the height of Henry's affair with her comes later and thus cannot enter the present book. The date of his entanglement with Roger de Clare's sister is also in doubt but it could hardly have begun later than 1163. Her

Christian name is unknown (at least, to me); the only certainty being that she was a woman of extraordinary beauty.

Although the Fitzurse family, with the exception of Cicely, were all historical figures (the holders of Dunster Castle down to the present century are descended through Robert Fitzurse), their story is wholly a work of imagination.

My thanks are due to the Assistant Keeper of Manuscripts British Museum, London, and also to the staff of Enfield Central Library for their help in my quest for facts.

Margaret Butler

I

January–March 1161

ON THE DAIS the King shifted restlessly; it was apparent
that his heart was not in the Twelfth Night festivities. He
had hardly spoken since dinner and the wine he had drunk
might have been water for all its effect on him. Nor had he
joined the games as he had always done in past years but sat
on between his Queen and his Chancellor as though it were a
day like any other.

The noise and laughter in the hall swelled louder. They
had set the Lord of Misrule's beard on fire now and he ran
bellowing about until someone doused him with a jug of
wine. Even that raised only a momentary flicker of interest
before he sank his chin once more on his hand.

A stranger, knowing nothing of his private concerns,
might have thought Henry FitzEmpress had everything he
wanted. Here he sat in Le Mans, the seat of his ancestors;
young, personable enough, and surrounded by his family
and friends; King of the English, Duke of Normandy, Count
of Anjou and Maine; and Duke of Aquitaine in right of his
wife who was renowned for her beauty and her wit. By her
he had three living sons and a daughter, and an acknowledged bastard son besides. But the mother of that boy was
dead and that was the only thing that mattered to him now.

Five months she had been dead and still he grieved against all reason. The young courtiers witnessed such enduring sorrow with awe. But the older statesmen and officials were growing impatient; bawds were easily enough come by, after all, and such a display of heartache for such a cause was unseemly in a king. Not one of them dared say a word to him, for all that; the most they had done was to approach his beloved friend the Chancellor in private. And it seemed that even he, for all his influence, was unable to help this time.

A group of them eyed the King now, casting veiled glances among themselves as they talked. 'Those fools will go too far,' de Luci said as a further burst of merriment broke out. 'Can they not see he's not amused? They should have waited till he'd retired before they brought on the Lord of Misrule.' Disapproval sounded in his voice. He was a very correct man.

Cornwall, the King's bastard uncle, answered him. 'The Chancellor's still here, and the Queen. They'll want to see the fun.' He turned his head, grinning, as the Chancellor's infectious laugh echoed along the table.

Henry heard it too. It no longer seemed strange to him that his friend could laugh while he mourned for his mind knew now what his heart had known from the beginning: Thomas was glad Hikenai was dead. It had shown in so many ways – the halting, awkwardly delivered words of condolence and the over-hasty urgings to submit to God's will with humility, the fine and specious reasoning used to point out that all was for his own ultimate good. . . . And the embarrassed silence which had greeted the news of his intention to build a leper-house in Caen to her memory.

He clung to his grief, feeling it treachery to forget. Every trifling reminder brought her before his inner eye. This time it had been the holly and the ivy that decked the walls – in honour of the little Christ as some would think, but he knew better. They were in fact symbols of an older belief,

2

as was the great Yule log which had taken four men's strength to carry. If Tom knew, he would get rid of the lot; even that innocent greenery would be an affront to his fierce orthodoxy.

As for Henry, he no longer knew what he believed. Very little, he thought in the depths of his heart. He only knew he would be very glad to see the last of this Christmas.

He heard Thomas laugh again. The Lord of Misrule was capering before the dais. He did not recognise the fellow they had chosen for the part but by custom he would be a man of no position to illustrate how the last should be first in Christ's Kingdom. This was his night, on which he might do and say as he would and none gainsay him. He was dressed in an odd assortment of finery; a lady's gown of green, full and old-fashioned, once fine and now very dirty, and over that a cape of marten skins. As he danced he lifted the skirts and old, trodden-down shoes with thick clumped soles showed underneath. Servant's shoes. On his head he wore a tinsel crown.

'Ho, up there!' he shouted, 'you're in my seat. I'm king tonight! Come down from there, you varlet!' He was very drunk.

Well, they would have their games. Even in church on this day the boy bishop would be enthroned with mitre and crozier. Henry smiled grimly, seeing all their eyes on him, suddenly anxious.

'Come up, come up, my lord,' he said, rising, 'and sit beside your queen.' He saw his wife's eyes widen and stared at her with a malice he did not try to hide. The proud bitch needed humbling. 'Come, kiss your queen,' he said. 'I mean, I pray your grace do her that honour.' He waved to his vacant chair.

All the lords were listening, amazed. They had waited for the King to let fly with his hanap, instead he was actually offering the fellow his place. They felt a lack of fitness in the

3

proceedings, even for Twelfth Night.

Fortunately the Lord of Misrule felt it too, dimly through his drunken haze. He stood on the step of the dais, swaying and blinking, and tried to focus his eyes on the speaker. He took a step forward, staggered, and fell upon his knees.

Eleanor the Queen sat quite still. If that greasy creature attempted any familiarity—

He fumbled forward, still on his knees. She looked down at the tinsel crown, tipped all askew, and felt a touch on her foot. 'God keep you, my lady,' she heard him mutter, then he was backing off. He had kissed her toe. She kept her chin high and did not look at Henry. He had sought to humiliate her and failed. It was enough for now.

She stayed just long enough so that people might not say his behaviour had driven her out, and gave him good night as pleasantly as ever. But still she did not meet his eyes. She did not think she would ever wish to look into them again.

When they had disrobed her, she was glad to sink into the feather bed and be alone. She did not want to think of what had happened but sleep would not come, and in spite of herself, her thoughts kept going back to Henry. That they were outwardly reconciled was true but she knew as no other could the barriers that were between them. Henry would never forgive her the blow to his self-esteem when she had lost her temper and stated her true opinion of him, and for her part, she could not forget that he had put her away for two long years while he carried his English whore around with him. And she knew that he had re-established her only because of the slut's death – yes, shun the idea as she might, she could not deny it in the silent reaches of the night.

Was it true then that he had never had any feeling for her? Had he married her only for her Duchy? – and to spite Louis of France? She recalled how he would never miss a chance to score off Louis – she had always supposed that was pique because Louis had been her husband first, but perhaps

4

the feeling had antedated their marriage. She had, it appeared, been wrong about so many things. She had pretended to herself that this reconciliation was a new beginning, had duped herself into believing that with his strumpet dead he would become a different man. . . .

Now she knew that none of it was true. The brazier winked its red eyes at her in the gloom and she shivered suddenly and looked around. But the night candle burned straight and clear; there were no demons lurking in the corners. Prayer was difficult, all the same. And it did nothing to dispel the bitterness that corroded her heart.

The scene had made little impression on Thomas the Chancellor who took it all as part of the spirit of Christmas. It did not strike him as strange that a Christian king should offer his seat to a subject on a feast which celebrated God's birth in the lowliest of places. Perhaps part of the explanation lay in the books he had been reading.

During the holy season he had pored over the two books he had only skimmed when he first received them nearly a year ago. He had more time to himself now that the King and Queen were friends again, and Henry did not call upon him quite so often.

Policraticus and *Metalogicon* had been dedicated to him by their author, his old friend John of Salisbury. John had not sent them directly to him, however; they had arrived only after having been perused by their friend Peter, Abbot of Celle, who had been asked to withhold them from Thomas unless he approved the contents. As Thomas read the arguments set out in the books, he was not surprised at his friend's lack of boldness; after all, John must suppose the Chancellor epitomised the humour and attitudes of the Court, and the contents would certainly arouse anger in one who upheld the royal prerogative above all else. Thomas began to wonder how well John really knew him.

5

They had been friends for years in the Archbishop of Canterbury's household where both had begun, but inevitably they had drifted apart after the King had raised Thomas from the humble position of Archdeacon to be Chancellor of England. Yet Thomas knew that luxury and worldly success had not changed him; he was grateful for the benefits the King's deep attachment to him had brought, but it was Henry's love he thanked God for. He had been Chancellor for five years and could truly say that in the main he had kept his honour and his ideals intact. An old, familiar grievance against John moved in him. Clever, virtuous and far-sighted as he was, why did he not see the same qualities in Thomas? Why did he feel that a go-between was necessary? So far, Thomas had agreed with every word he wrote.

Now, with the evening's festivities over, he took up the book again. He would read for an hour before he retired.

John wrote of the kingdom as an analogy of the human body, the King its head, the judges its eyes and ears, the warriors and officials its hands, the serfs its feet and the priests its soul. That was natural and acceptable; the discomfort (and Thomas did feel discomfort) lay in the author's insistence that spiritual power must be superior to secular power.

John pointed to the famous story of the Emperor Constantine who, saying he was not worthy to sit among priests, took the lowest seat at the Council of Nicaea, and burned all petitions of accusation against them – for, he said, 'it was not permissible for him as a man and one subject to the judgment of priests, to examine cases touching those who cannot be judged, save by God alone'. John also stated that a prince ought to be chaste and moderate.

Thomas sighed at that. Chaste and moderate Henry certainly was not. But as he went on he found much praise of Henry and of his grandfather, old King Henry on whom he modelled himself, though even here John could

6

not leave well alone. He wrote of the royal power: 'but if it resists and opposes the Divine Commandments and wishes to make me share its war against God, then with unrestrained voice I answer back that God must be preferred before any man on earth'.

Thomas read that many times. He knew it was the truth, for himself as well as John; it echoed from his heart. All his years with Henry had not altered it. But Henry would not understand, particularly now that his temper seemed to have changed permanently for the worse. Thomas decided to postpone all mention of John of Salisbury's works until he was in a kinder humour.

February – March 1161
As soon as the day's official business was over, Thomas took Theobald's letter in his hand and set out to visit Henry. It was a wet afternoon, the sort of day on which spirits are at their lowest. But he could put off his request to the King no longer; this was the last of many letters he had received during the old Archbishop of Canterbury's illness, first begging, then commanding him to return to England.

Thomas found Henry alone. A book lay open near the hearth; it was the one which Wace, the poet, had presented to the Queen as a coronation gift. He sprang up and Thomas saw the welcome in his grey eyes, he looked much more like his old self. 'Tom!' he said. 'God's bread, but I'm glad to see you. I've read my eyes away in this poor light. Come – come and sit down.'

After they had talked a while, Thomas brought out the letter and showed him. Henry flicked it with his thumbnail, scowling. 'What does he want you for?'

'He is gravely ill, perhaps dying. It may be the last time I shall see him.' Henry began to shake his head and Thomas rushed on. 'Apart from that – we have been long away from England. It would be well in any case if I returned.'

7

Henry was shifting restively. 'You want to go – to leave me.'

Thomas looked at him quickly. It was true, he did. France was not home to him as it was to Henry. He longed to see London again, even more than he longed to see Theobald. Henry continued in an accusing tone, 'John of Salisbury wrote that letter.'

So the old jealousy was still there: he must have no affections beyond those for Henry, no desires that did not coincide with his. He said, 'It is chiefly on your business that I would go.'

'No,' said Henry. 'No, it is unnecessary. Besides, I need you here.' He spoke in his royal voice. All at once, Thomas felt trapped. Henry had parcelled him up in strands of love and duty as neatly as any spider. It was useless to argue when the King spoke like that. He dropped the subject.

Days passed, but Thomas's discontent did not. Henry's flat refusal even to consider the last request of his faithful old Archbishop had shocked as well as disappointed him. He had heard Henry described as thankless often enough; never before had he been faced with such clear evidence of it. It awakened thoughts in his mind that had not been there before.

The uncertainty of Henry's temper had frequently obliged Thomas to indulge in mild conspiracies against him, but always for the sake of others. It had never before been necessary for himself. Now he sat and wondered what he could do to gain his own ends.

The idea came to him one night in bed, and he set about putting it into practice the very next day. He wrote to John of Salisbury, warning him that he, Thomas, would be responsible for the rumours that Archbishop Theobald wished to consult with him about the succession to Canterbury – 'and to this end only, that the King will send me back into England. I would have you persuade our lord the Archbishop to write again strongly reproving me for not obeying his summons, and let us hope that rumour will do the rest.'

A letter, couched in the severest terms, did arrive but to no purpose. Henry was adamant that the Chancellor remain with him. And John's own secret letter to Thomas made it plain that he was puzzled. 'For common report suggests that you and the King are of one heart and mind, and in view of such intimate friendship your desires and dislikes ought to coincide. The Archbishop has asked if there may not be some collusion between you in this matter.'

Thomas sank his teeth into his lip. If they but knew his true feelings. . . . It seemed that John had misunderstood and told Theobald what was afoot. Surely they did not really believe that he was plotting to gain the Archbishopric? He read the letter again uneasily – but no, the tone was friendly, even mildly conspiratorial – 'I think I have an inkling of the truth and realise your situation almost as vividly as if I were on the spot. . . .' Thomas was puzzled in his turn – and vexed. His plan had misfired and there was an end to it; he would not get back to England by that means. And eventually he would be called upon to explain his devious behaviour to John.

Towards the end of February came the news that Theobald had taken a turn for the worse and following hard upon it, another message from John of Salisbury. John wrote that everyone around him was extremely worried by the Archbishop's symptoms which seemed to point to his imminent departure from the world, and now that it appeared likely he would not see Thomas again in this life, he, John, must impart to Thomas the old man's wishes.

Thomas stopped reading at that point. He felt real bitterness towards Henry for disappointing the kind old man. He returned his eyes to the crabbed script but it was a little while before he could take in the sense of the words. Even when he did, he had to read it several times before the full import

9

struck him.

'... that it is his dearest wish that you should sit upon the Archiepiscopal Throne when he vacates it ... that your approval of the arguments in my books has finally set the seal upon this hope ... knows that you will guard the Church against the King ... that even when it was not apparent, he has never doubted your loyalty to the Church' – Thomas made a wry mouth at that – '... and your loyalty to Her will be the more whole-hearted and not so beset with difficulties when all spiritual power is yours. ...'

Thomas was aghast. To have his machinations recoil upon him thus! In his wildest dreams he had never expected such an outcome. And yet – he let out a short, sharp breath of wonder – deep in his heart, had he not always known that this was Theobald's intention? What he himself intended was another matter. As far as he was concerned, the only inclination to accede to Theobald's wishes lay in that last line. To have God's business as his sole responsibility seemed to him the greatest good a man might desire.

And to leave Henry now would be no hardship. Thomas had reached the heights in his office; he stood next to the King in the hierarchy of secular power – and it was not enough. He knew himself to be capable in the worldly sense of filling the Archbishop's seat and there, indeed, he would listen to none but the Pope and his own conscience. It was a heady temptation, yet even as he hovered between doubt and certainty, he knew he could not do it. The plain fact was that he was unworthy.

The dreadful loss of self-confidence he had suffered after Toulouse had left him; he was not worse than other men, yet neither was he sufficiently better. And the man who would be Primate must be better. Thomas did not mistake his self-knowledge for humility of spirit; he saw the truth too well for that. He loved fine apparel, warmth and good food. He loved fighting, too – all things unfitting for a simple priest, let alone an Archbishop. Nay, he could not do it; to give up all he held dear would be too great a sacrifice. And he would not be Archbishop unless he felt himself able to be an Archbishop *ne plus ultra.*

Anyway, Henry would never hear of it. He would not be parted from any of his possessions without a struggle and Thomas knew his own value as the King's chief servant.

But when he finally brought his attention to the King's official correspondence, he found there a private letter to Henry from the Archbishop. He tapped the seal with his thumb nail, frowning. Had Theobald made the same suggestion to Henry? Surely he did not think that the King would agree. . . .

Thomas put the private letter on one side and continued his work but in an abstracted state of mind. Theobald's idea had unsettled him and the vague discontent of the last few months was hardening into a determination to get away for a time at all costs. He must have time to think. But first he would write to John telling him why he could never be Archbishop. Complete honesty was the only course.

He motioned to the clerk to sharpen a quill for him and his eye fell upon a little group in the corner, ostensibly busy with some documents, but actually tittering and whispering among themselves. Walter Map, the student he had recommended to Henry two years earlier, was with them. He looked up at that moment. Thomas caught his eye and nodded to him in greeting. An astute and subtle young man, that, he thought, and then looked again for he seemed put out – indeed, much like a schoolboy caught by the master in some foolish prank.

Thomas rose and went towards them and did not miss the way Walter slid a scrap of parchment from his sleeve to the bottom of the pile before him. He passed his hand across his face to hide his smile and spoke to them all with the chaffing good humour that had always earned him the affection of his underlings.

They talked earnestly for a few moments while the young clerk sharpened Thomas's quill with a concentration that furrowed his brow and caused the tip of his tongue to protrude, then Thomas said, 'I think you are privy to a jest that I might share?' He glanced slyly from one to another and riffled the pile of documents with his forefinger.

Walter had the grace to colour slightly. 'It was but a foolish line of verse,' he said with some reluctance. 'I do not normally waste the hours of business—' He drew forth the scrap and handed it to the Chancellor.

Only two lines of Latin were upon it and Thomas smiled ruefully as he scanned them.

> *Meum est propositum in taberna mori*
> *Ut sint vina proxima morientis ori.*

Swiftly translating, he murmured, 'For on this my heart is set when the hour is nigh me, let me in the tavern die with a tankard by me!' He shook his finger at Walter. 'I cannot have you corrupting my clerks,' he said with mock solemnity. 'Away with you, back to the King's offices where your ideas may meet with more approval.'

Walter gave a shamefaced grin. 'I cannot take all the credit for the sentiment,' he said. 'I have but added to a poem that came out of Germany with the goliards. But some Religious are so mealy-mouthed that one is forced in the opposite direction.'

'Especially the Cistercians, eh, Walter?' said one of the clerks.

'They're a fraudulent breed—'

'Tell our lord of thine oath!' with a high, nervous giggle.

'Nay,' said Walter, 'no more. I would keep his good opinion of me.' He looked at Thomas with something like appeal and suddenly saw the twinkle in his eyes.

'Tell me,' said Thomas.

'Well ... It is only that I have vowed to except Jews and Cistercians from my oath to do justice to all, since it's absurd to do justice to those who are just to none.' He grinned at the Chancellor. 'For some reason, these dullards think that the height of wit.'

Thomas laughed indulgently, then noticed the disapproving eye of William Fitzstephen, his senior clerk and jealous admirer, and pulled a face of feigned dismay at Walter. He dropped his voice as he said to him, 'No harm – no harm as long as they do not take you too seriously. And now – you to your tasks and I to mine! Give you good day, Master Map.' He leaned forward and kissed the young man's cheek and then turned him firmly in the direction of the door.

He smiled to himself as he sat down again. He could not help liking Walter but his mischief was infectious, and discipline in a crowd of very young men was difficult. William would keep them in order though.

Still, Walter's remarks about the Cistercians (one of whom had probably offended him in some way) served to confirm Thomas's own opinion that spiritual men must be beyond reproach. He began to compose his letter of refusal.

Rohesia, the Queen's chief lady-in-waiting had retired to a convent in Poitou soon after Christmas. Now Mabille de St Valéry had her position, yet in spite of the long-standing friendship between herself and Mabille, Eleanor regretted old Rohesia's going. Mabille was deferential when Rohesia would have been forthright, silent when Rohesia would have expressed open disapproval and she never proffered unasked advice. Eleanor felt she should be delighted with her and could not understand why she was not; in fact she was missing the nearest thing to a mother she had known. It was because of this she found it difficult to talk openly to Mabille

13

of her condition and of her feelings about it. However, there was no one else.

It was one of those cold March days when a high blustery wind sends sharp particles of grit flying to sting hands and faces, so the Queen had elected to stay within doors; but she was restless, and had paced about the solar watching the occupations of first one, then another of her ladies. Somehow nothing seemed to catch her interest.

'Come Mabille,' she said at last.' 'Come within and you shall read to me the tales of King Arthur from the *Roman de Brut*.' Mabille followed her into the bedchamber.

But when the lady-in-waiting had fetched the book from the press the Queen made no move to open it, merely laying it down beside her while she gazed abstractedly into space, idly tapping her foot on the floor. Mabille watched her hesitantly for a moment. She believed herself to be genuinely fond of her mistress and would have been indignant had anyone suggested that she had stepped so readily into Rohesia's shoes for the sake of material benefit, but it was so and everyone knew it except herself and Eleanor. She thought, this post is not the sinecure I expected. She shows a different face to me now that I am committed to her service, and began to wonder how much of the Queen's situation with her husband, over which she had condoled with her so often in the past, was due to her own moping humours.

'You know that I am pregnant, Mabille?' the Queen said suddenly.

Mabille looked at her quickly and nodded. The intimacy of her duties around the bedchamber precluded physical secrets between them and she had already considered and dismissed the possibility that the Queen was entering upon the change of life. 'I had thought it must be so,' she answered.

'No doubt you have wondered why I have not mentioned

it before.... It was because – because I feared it might come to nothing. I have not spoken to the King either – I would not have him disappointed.'

'Do you feel unwell, madam? Should we not call the physicians?'

'No,' said Eleanor rather sharply, 'I am not unwell. Say rather that my bodily feelings are unusual.' Deep in her heart, though, she knew that her different emotions about this pregnancy stemmed from the mind rather than the body and that the fear she had mentioned would have been more truthfully described as a hope. She did not want this child. But that was a fact she would not face, and so she thought – these feelings are only spring-fret and will pass in a month or two.

Mabille was thinking, perhaps the change is beginning then; but she did not voice that because she knew the Queen did not like to be reminded of her age. She must be close to forty though, and has borne seven children.... Outwardly she smiled sweetly.

'I'll rub your head,' she offered. 'Come, lie down on the couch,' and she set to work to unlace the Queen and make her comfortable, tut-tutting under her breath in the gentlest manner possible as she removed the leather corset that confined Eleanor's waist.

Oh, to have Rohesia about me now in place of this fawning fool! thought Eleanor, with a sudden pang. Can she be happy in her convent cut off from Court and all her friends? But she was at least in her homeland, surrounded by familiar soft accents and the slow-paced life of the warm south. Surely she was happy? An abrupt wave of longing for her own duchy swept over Eleanor. To see Poitiers again, and the tower William the Troubadour had built for his mistress, the Countess of Chatellerault! In her mind's eye she saw the view from that high place of her ancestors; the walls enclosing the small Merovingian city with the suburbs strag-

15

gling down the slopes beyond, the encircling streams and sunlit valleys ebbing away into blue distance. There the vines would be putting out new leaves, exquisitely fresh and green against the darkness of ilex and pine, while she was trapped here in a bleak and draughty castle with straw-littered floors, pregnant by a man she hated.

Yes, I do hate you, Henry FitzEmpress, she thought viciously; it was a bad day for me when first I looked on you and mistook your greedy lust for love. Even Louis Capet knew better how to treat a woman. Mother of God, that I, the greatest heiress in the world, serenaded and adored by poets and troubadours, should come to this!

Mabille was holding up the corset. 'Do you not think it would be wise to discard this?' she was asking in the conciliatory tone she always used now.

Eleanor did not answer her. In her mind she could clearly hear Rohesia's downright accents. 'Loosen your bodice, child! And throw away that contraption till after the babe be born! Pretty figures, like flowers, are but a lure to set the seed.'

April – August 1161

In Canterbury, Archbishop Theobold had lain weeks a-dying. Yesterday the Infirmarian had given his word the old man would not last the night, but he had said that before and still the strong heart had beat on in the shrivelled frame. Today, though, the air in his chest rustled with a sound like dead leaves underfoot. The end would not be long.

The young monk who watched him thought that judging by his looks he should have died a week ago, but he was conscious still at intervals and even now was stirring again, the withered eyelids fluttering and the small, purplish lips puffing out with every difficult exhalation. When he had gathered himself for the effort, his voice was surprisingly loud. 'I have bepissed my bed again,' he said.

16

On the other side of the room, the Infirmarian jerked his head around and so far forgot himself as to lay his hand on the arm of the bishop with whom he was quietly conversing, cutting him off in mid-speech. The bishop closed his half-open mouth with an injured air, but followed his companion to the Archbishop's bedside. As he approached the young monk drew back respectfully, hands clasped and head politely bowed.

'Fetch clean sheets,' whispered the Infirmarian. But the old Archbishop tried to raise himself, muttering, 'Nay, nay, do not disturb me now – it will but happen again.' He paused and groaned, trying to gasp in more air. 'Stay back lest the stink incommode you.'

'There is no unpleasantness,' the Infirmarian assured him. 'Is there anything else we may do for you?' He turned to the bishop. 'No man ever took harm from lying in his own water,' he murmured with rare delicacy.

The other nodded. He was Gilbert Foliot, Bishop of Hereford, who had been visiting London and had come at once on hearing of the Primate's imminent end. From his large, pale face down to the long, bony feet encased in shoes of coarsest leather, there was nothing of softness or gentleness in Gilbert Foliot, and universally respected as he was, few loved him, for his irresistible likeness to the Prophets of old had a chilling effect and his fierce asceticism separated him from the frailties of his fellows. About him was an aura of violence long repressed, as of a banked fire smouldering still under many layers of the ash of rigorous self-discipline. God spoke often to Gilbert Foliot; he heard and obeyed as Samuel did, with a simplicity that made him invincible.

Now he watched the dying man with sombre, deepset eyes, unconsciously drawing his own breath a little deeper each time Theobald gasped as though his efforts might benefit the other. He was prone to attacks of breathlessness himself in times of stress so that he found it wellnigh un-

17

bearable to watch the Archbishop's struggles. He dragged his eyes away and almost immediately his breathing eased to a slower, more comfortable rhythm.

He inhaled deeply with relief. 'How long has he lain thus?' he asked softly.

The Infirmarian misunderstood. 'He can but only just have soiled himself,' he said quickly. 'He is never left alone. All through the night John of Salisbury was at his side – he is sleeping now, but Brother Gervase has watched these two hours past and I within call.'

'Nay, I meant his difficulty in breathing. How long has he suffered thus?'

'He grew a good deal worse at Prime this morning. We thought then that he was ready to pass into God's keeping but when he received the Sacrament he revived somewhat and has been since as you see him now.' The Infirmarian's voice trembled a little and Gilbert felt a sudden shock of surprise to see his eyes fill with tears. 'Where shall we find another such? *Miserere Domini!*'

'God will provide the shepherd for his flock,' said Gilbert, and in spite of himself a little thrill of anticipation passed through him. 'Fear not, my son. He will answer your prayers and those of your brethren, do you but choose a successor honestly, without fear or favour.'

The Infirmarian wiped his eyes quite openly upon the hem of his sleeve. 'I had not got so far in my own thoughts, my lord Bishop. I was but grieving the loss of our dear father in God.' He gave the bishop a quick, considering look and Gilbert was left wondering if he had betrayed the true reason for his swift coming.

Yet it did not matter if he had. It was no sin to be ambitious for high preferment in God's service, and with objective honesty Gilbert had weighed the merits of every possible candidate for the Primacy and found none more deserving than himself. He was not swayed by self-love or

18

vanity and he knew he would make a good Archbishop; his life was beyond reproach and he was an able administrator. So he had readied himself for the call he was convinced must come, and it had seemed like a sign from God to be so near when Theobald died.

He knew that the Archbishop's own choice of a successor would carry great weight with his monks, that was why he had been eager to bring himself to his notice at the last. And he was thankful for John of Salisbury's unwonted absence – that one was altogether too acute at penetrating the motives of others. But now that he was actually at the death-bed, he had misgivings – not of his own competence, but of Theobald's discernment. Was he perhaps too far gone to realise that God's will might be read in apparently fortuitous events?

Just then the old man groaned again and stared un-seeingly in their direction. 'Is he come?' he said feebly, 'Is that he?'

Gilbert closed his eyes upon a surge of relief and gratitude.

'Is he come at last? Thomas!' cried the old man, his voice cracking. 'Thomas!'

Gilbert stiffened. The Infirmarian sighed. 'Nay, your grace, nay. Here is the Bishop of Hereford, come for your last blessing.' He peeped at Gilbert's still face. 'Go forward,' he whispered.

Gilbert knelt beside the couch and felt the hand of the dying man fumble at him. 'Not Thomas?' he muttered. 'Why will he not come?' And he turned his head towards the wall and seemed to sleep.

Gilbert stayed there on his knees as if in prayer. It was very quiet in the high, vaulted Infirmary; the only sounds were the dry rustling of the Archbishop's breathing and the soft undertones of the Infirmarian as he instructed Brother Gervase in the furtherance of his duties; being a man of more than usual tact, he would not watch the Bishop of

Hereford take leave of his lord. He stood with his back to them, blocking the young monk's view so that they might be private.

There were curious, unfamiliar smells in the big room; Gilbert distended his large, hairy nostrils and snuffed at them; part of his mind was trying to identify them but without conscious thought, neither was he conscious any longer of the Archbishop's agonies. He was trying to decide whether to attribute this disappointment to Theobald's lack of perspicuity or to—

But how could that be possible when he had searched heart and conscience both, and knew himself to be, of all men, supremely fitted for the office which for God's sake he so earnestly desired?

Tonight the King had dined with those of his lords and barons who were at present in Normandy, and now that the main dishes were being cleared, they lounged about the board in desultory conversation.

Thomas the Chancellor sat next to the King but he did not have much to say because his heart was heavy still with the news of Archbishop Theobald's death. He had just realised, too, that the administration of Canterbury would pass into his hands as did all vacant sees, adding to a burden fast becoming intolerable. And Henry would certainly wish to sequestrate the large revenues to pay for a defensive war against Louis who, enraged by the precipitate haste of the marriage which had deprived him too soon of his daughter's dower, had taken the field in the Vexin. It seemed to Thomas that all his ploys to benefit his master ended in despoilment of the Church, and this time he could not quiet the nagging of his conscience.

'*Nemo potest duobus dominis.*' 'No man can serve two masters.' The Vulgate text sprang to his mind with an aptness that was frightening. Only this morning his eye had

20

fallen upon it and blinded by long familiarity, had passed on unregarding. Now it was as though Our Lord had spoken those words to him alone and Theobald's almost inexplicable desire took on a new meaning. For it seemed it was impossible to serve both God and Caesar.

Yet think around the problem as he would, he could not get past the inescapable fact of his own unsuitability. Had poor old Theobald – and John of Salisbury – imagined that they knew him better than he knew himself? For John had not taken what Thomas now feared were excuses rather than reasons for refusal as an end of the matter. He had written again asking Thomas not to be hasty in his decision but to leave room for the operation of God's will.

Suppose he put aside thoughts of his own unworthiness and accepted? Henry might be persuaded to release him in the hope of gaining an Archbishop who understood his problems. And he would go back to England!

But only at the price of giving up all he held dear – surely too much to ask of one who had enjoyed the sweets of worldly pomp for only six years. In the depths of his mind the memory of an aphorism concerning gain and loss moved and tried to surface, then was gone. The difficulty of disentangling his own motives was proving too much for him; his head ached with the effort. He wrenched his thoughts back to the present and began to listen to the lords about him.

They were talking mainly of women – their wives and daughters, and the trouble they caused through wilfulness or affectation, and in one or two cases, through a tongue as barbed as any serpent's.

'Ut, ut!' chided Cornwall, who while scarcely recognising his wife's existence, loved his daughters to the point of weakness. 'Treat them with kindness! Grant them their trifling wishes without argument. A man should rule his house as God the world – with benevolence. Then, if you must thwart them on some matter of importance, surprise will keep them silent!'

'Nothing will silence my wife,' observed someone gloomily. 'Let the Archangel Gabriel himself appear and she will have it he has got the message wrong.'

'You should beat her regularly—'

'Have you seen her? Easier could she beat me!'

'Females are like horses,' said Cornwall, now well into his stride. 'Beat them and they'll turn vicious – but gentle them along and they'll be your faithful servants. Give me daughters any day sooner than sons – always quarrelling and fighting and jostling for precedence – aye, and longing for your death that they may step into your shoes—' He leaned forward and raised his cup towards the King. 'I drink to the hope that God will grant you another fair daughter, nephew. Sons you have aplenty!'

Henry smiled and accepted the toast, but Thomas could see something had pricked him; he thought he did not wish to be reminded of the Queen. He had suspected she was again with child but Henry rarely mentioned such matters to him; he wondered how Cornwall knew. Through his women, most likely; begetting and breeding was a source of abiding interest to them.

He saw that de Mandeville's small, sharp eyes were fixed upon the King with interest; evidently Henry saw it too, for he said lightly yet with an undertone of menace, 'And do you, too, wish me a daughter, de Mandeville?'

'I wish you what you wish yourself,' answered de Mandeville quickly but he dropped his eyes as soon as he had said it and played with his wine cup with a nonchalant air that deceived no one except Cornwall.

He, sensing nothing, blundered on, glowing and cheerful, over conversational ice that grew increasingly more fragile until some of the younger men began to bait him in the hope that that would silence him. But far from improving matters,

22

the King's sudden unaccountable irritation was vented upon them, and what had bade fair to prove a pleasant hour threatened to become uncomfortable for everyone.

Thomas thought it time to interrupt and started to talk to the King quietly of Louis's preparations in the Vexin; after a while the King's high colour died away and he and Thomas sat with their heads close together, shutting out the rest of the company from their talk.

My lord of Leicester drew a long sigh as he contemplated them; he considered, like many others about him, that it would be an ill day for the rest of them if the Chancellor got his heart's desire and returned to England. He was the only one who could smooth down the King by his mere presence and direct his wrathful impulses away from his courtiers and towards his true enemies. Already he had the King in a good humour again. He smiled to himself, looking along the board at them, because he loved them both and was happy that they loved each other.

Thomas looked down, toying with his knife, and then up suddenly so that he met Leicester's eyes, and Leicester was put quite out of countenance by the expression on his face. For it said, as plainly as if he had spoken, that all his cheerful badinage was done from necessity, nothing else, and to him it was an onerous task.

What first gave Henry the idea of metamorphosing his worldly Chancellor into an Archbishop would be hard to say, but most certainly it did not occur to him that God might have moved his heart to consider so extraordinary a proposition, and Thomas's one essay into rumour-mongering had been marked by so conspicuous a lack of success that the whispers had never percolated high enough to reach the royal ears. Nor did the thought come from Theobald; his last letter to the King was concerned only with 'commending to you the holy church of Canterbury from which you received the governance of the realm by my ministry, and begging you to guard it against the attacks of evil men'.

Whether, then, it was by some curious transference of thought, whereby the minds of different men begin to work along the same lines at the same time, or whether a chance mention of the Archbishop of Mainz, who was also Arch-Chancellor of the Empire, sowed the seed, Henry himself did not know; but it came to his mind fully formed, perfect and entire, a picture of Thomas as Archbishop of Canterbury and Chancellor of England; or rather, as Chancellor of England and Archbishop of Canterbury, for there was no doubt in Henry's mind as to which role was the more important. The idea cheered him as nothing else had done since Hikenai's death.

As a native, Thomas understood English customs and administration, and if anyone could end the traditional hostility between the royal and ecclesiastical hierarchies it was he. It seemed to Henry that the Chancellor's undoubted love and loyalty to his interests would bind Church and State into an harmonious whole, and so, certain that the ingenious notion was all his own, he was quite prepared to take all the credit for it.

But he was in no hurry to impart his thoughts to Thomas. (Besides, while Canterbury lay vacant, its revenues accrued to his Treasury.) The plan went on working in his mind as he weighed the pros and cons. He did mention it to a few intimates, testing the wind, as it were. One of them was his mother whose opinions on political matters he always valued.

He was dashed when she advised against it, but since she could give no concrete reasons for her dislike of the idea, merely confining herself to Cassandra-like predictions of disaster, he discounted this. She had grown old suddenly, he reflected; perhaps the continual fine tremor that was now affecting her hands was similarly affecting her judgment.

24

Certainly, none would have recognised the haughty young Empress in this frail, tremulous old woman. She had also become very devout; it was even possible that she imagined he should leave the choice of Archbishop entirely to the Canterbury monks. In the end her apprehensions only hardened his resolve.

Since he had not taken the trouble to swear his confidants to secrecy, rumours about the King's choice soon flew about the Court, and the faithful William Fitzstephen, ever alive to his beloved master's interests, carried them to Thomas.

To the Chancellor it appeared that pressures on him were building up on all sides. He put his hand to his forehead in a gesture of weariness. William looked at him with concern.

'Have you the headache?'

'Nay . . . nay. What would you think, William, were I Archbishop?'

'Oh . . . my lord —'

Thomas looked into the young clerk's shining eyes and saw the answer with a sinking of the heart. His voice was sharper than he intended when he spoke. 'Set me not so high, William!'

He softened his tone with an effort. 'I have no wish to be Archbishop, nor would it be fitting. There are men who are bishops already who are worthier than I.'

There was an obstinate set to William's lips. 'In your own words lies the proof of your pre-eminence,' he said in a low voice and then, greatly daring, 'Let me remain in your service, my lord, whatever you may become. Archbishop or beggar, I ask only to serve you.'

A harder man than Thomas would have been touched and a softer one might have shown it. Thomas only looked at him sideways with a rueful expression. 'Beggar? You would not care to be the companion of such – in your own word lies the proof of your inexperience.' And then, almost as if speaking to himself, 'But I have sometimes thought a beggar may come closer to God than such as I. Let it rest in His hands then – if it be His will that I become Archbishop, you shall stay by me. For I think that if that happens, I shall have need of all my friends.'

He gripped William by the shoulder pleased by the young man's evident gratification and the dog-like devotion in his eyes; yet it could not quell his heaviness of spirit.

'Speak not of this matter to others,' he said slowly, 'for my mind is not settled on it – and what you have heard is only rumour.'

But within the next month or two, the story that the Chancellor would be Archbishop was on everyone's lips so that Thomas could no longer pretend ignorance of it. Until Henry made a formal offer, though, he could say nothing and the necessity for discretion irked him almost beyond endurance. They were in the Vexin now, fending off Louis's attacks, but somehow, Thomas's heart was not in the task.

All he could do was to pray for guidance and he got little comfort from it for an aridity of spirit had come upon him. What he did get was a painful, badly swollen knee which made walking impossible, so that when Louis decided to concede the victory to Henry, the consultations for a truce took place around Thomas's sickbed. It was by now the end of June and still Henry did not mention the topic which occupied everyone's mind. Instead, he bade Thomas good-bye and took his mercenary army into Gascony where a minor rebellion had flared up.

Gradually, the fluid on the knee dispersed, helped or hindered by compresses that ranged from the merely herbal to messes so revolting that Thomas had to pinch his nostrils together when they were applied.

At last, the blessed days of convalescence came. Thomas could get as far as the garden, and to sit in the open air after a month within doors was a foretaste of Paradise. His knee still pained him but he could make shift to walk a little with

26

the aid of a stick. A chair and a small trestle board were carried outside and placed beside the bench for his convenience. Here he could meet his friends to converse and play chess, and here he could read in peace, were he alone. It was a pleasant spot with a low wall behind it, and in the crumbling mortar grew all sorts of tiny, clinging herbs; they were in flower now, yellow, blue and mauve. Thomas did not know their names, or indeed whether they were too lowly to have any, but he examined them with care, reflecting upon their minute perfections and the infinite care which God had lavished upon all His creation, be it great or small.

He was playing chess one day with William when a visitor, who had come straight from Court, was announced. Both men looked up, William, young, fresh-faced, clad sombrely in black, and the Chancellor, handsome still though thinner, very fine in an expensive cape of Watchet blue that turned his eyes to sapphire.

'Aschetinus!' he exclaimed (and aside to William, 'It's the Prior of Leicester'). 'How do you do, my old friend? You see I cannot rise to greet you – but come – come, sit here by me!'

The Prior threw up his hands in mock horror. 'What are you wearing? A long-sleeved cape! You, a cleric! That is more fitting for men who carry falcons than for one who is Archdeacon of Canterbury, Provost of Beverley, Dean of Hastings, and Canon of here, there and everywhere! And this is the man who, if all I hear be true, will be Archbishop of Canterbury!'

Thomas's smile was wry. 'I assure you, my lord Prior, I know of any number of poor priests in England, any one of whom I should rather see Archbishop than myself – for if I should be so promoted I would either lose the favour of the King or neglect the service of the Lord God.'

Aschetinus's look was quizzical. 'You – to lose the favour of the King?'

27

'I know him – I know him from his skin to his soul.'

William glanced quickly from one to the other. He knew the visitor only by sight but it was evident that he and the Chancellor were very close friends; even to William, Thomas had never been as frank as this. And plainly, this Prior of Leicester who had come straight from the King, not only knew of the rumour but accepted it as truth. . . . Gathering up the chessmen, William gazed at Thomas with a burning love. Who would grace the Archiepiscopal throne as he would? In him the kindness and tenderness of a woman were mingled with the firmness and strength of a man; he was the epitome of virtue.

A slow indignation took fire in him against this stranger who had dared to criticise his master's love of finery. How should this drab and ordinary monk presume to sit in judgment on one who out-matched him in every possible way? He blushed when the Prior spoke kindly to him, being lost in a dream of Thomas the Archbishop, tall in the jewelled copes of Canterbury, gracious in his splendour. . . . His answer was abrupt to the point of rudeness as he excused himself.

Aschetinus stared in some perplexity after William's retreating back. 'It seems I have given some offence to your clerk,' he murmured.

'He is overhot in my defence at any time and has been worse since my illness,' Thomas answered; William's curtness to his guest had discomfited him, the more since he knew the reason very well and felt some guilt because of it. William's devotion to him had its absurd side but it was pleasant to be idolised; it was like lying in a feather bed instead of on bare planks. He tried to explain this to Aschetinus; at the end of his rather rambling discourse the Prior said drily that he, a monk, had little experience of feather beds and too much by far of bare planks.

Thomas said abruptly, 'This is why I would not be Arch-

28

bishop.'

Aschetinus grimaced. 'Because of your feather beds?'

'Because of the manner of man I know myself to be. I am disabled by my very nature. Tell me, good Prior, should an Archbishop love the things I love? You have remarked my fine dress, and it were idle to deny I love the things of the world.'

'Our lord the King cares nothing for such things. Would a man like him make a better Archbishop?'

Thomas looked sharply at the Prior and said that that was not all, he had other reasons besides.

'Reasons? Or fears?'

Well, fears, then, if he would have truth, chief amongst them being collision with the King upon matters of principle.

'Ah! You are not so easy a man that you will bend to any wind for comfort's sake? That is as I thought. What, then, makes you think you are unfitted for this appointment?'

But Thomas only frowned and shook his head. Wine was served the Prior. After Aschetinus had drunk deeply, he gave a long sigh, and wiping his lips with the back of his hand, began to speak as though the Chancellor's refusal were an accomplished fact. Thomas listened for a while in silence, but somehow the Prior's ready acceptance of his unsuitability for ecclesiastical honour grated upon him and before long he found himself putting forth arguments in his own favour.

'All these things are true,' he told Aschetinus, 'but if I may come at the dilemma from all sides, God will open my eyes to the path I should take. If He would but send me a sign —'

'You are an honest man, Chancellor,' said the Prior, 'and for my part, I now know what I came to learn. I shall not try to move you in one direction or the other – but I will tell you why I think you feel yourself unqualified for this honour. On the one hand, the standards you set yourself are too high; beware the sin of pride! You forget we are all sinners in the sight of God. You have no right to judge – even yourself. And on the other – you desire this appointment with a passion that you hide from yourself because you fear that your motives will not bear scrutiny.'

He leaned forward and put his large, square hand on Thomas's. 'Let God lead you where He wills. And be not so fearful of losing that which you love. Give to God and He will return an hundredfold!'

Thomas lay long awake that night. He was certain now that Henry would offer him the Archbishopric. Men spoke of it too openly for him to doubt it any longer, and thinking back, he wondered why he had been so positive of the King's refusal to part with him. After all, he had known for a long time that Henry took less and less notice of his advice. That he would eventually be his own master had been obvious from the beginning to a discerning eye.

And he was beginning to believe that this whole matter, so unimaginable at first, had indeed been prompted by God. Only God, who knew his heart, could know what a sacrifice it must be for him to give up all his fine, rich living and his gorgeous attire. To become a priest! For in Thomas's mind, the priesthood, that holy state to which he never had aspired, was the stumbling block. To bring down God to earth again and hold Him close between these hands. . . . That was a thought that lay between awe and terror. It would indeed mean the forfeiture of all that he held dear, for he could never accept God's commands half-heartedly; if he gave, he would give his all.

But uppermost, if he were honest, was the fear of losing Henry's favour, and he knew instinctively that he would certainly lose it if Henry discovered his fealty was given to

God. Draw back then, said his heart, persuade Henry that you are not the man he needs. Remain as Chancellor and keep the friendship of the King.

Yet ought he not to say, 'Thy will be done'? Unwillingly he remembered that the One he followed had no where to lay his head and had been tempted on a high mountain by the glories of the world. He twisted and turned, tormented by indecision, by dread of the direct choice, and when finally he slept, his slumber was fitful and broken by troubled dreams.

II

August 1161

REYNOLD FITZURSE, FREE for a time from his duties as
one of the Chancellor's knights, had ridden into his father's
manor of Williton with a great train of servants and followers. Though more than a year had passed since that
mysterious affliction had fallen upon his mother, this was
the first opportunity he had had to come and see for himself. Convinced that the sight of her granddaughter would
restore her to health, he had transported the major part of
his Household to Somerset. This time Beatrice, his wife,
had offered no objection although she had before con-
sistently refused to accompany him on his short visits.
Reynold did momentarily wonder whether that was because
Will de Tracy was going along with them on his way home
to Devon, but in spite of the careful watch he kept on her
he never caught them alone together. Nor did he have any
real reason to suspect Beatrice except that he felt her un-
welcoming attitude towards him was in itself suspicious.
She had not always been thus.

Of course, it might be due to the two miscarriages she
had suffered since his return from France last year, but she
surely owed him something for the loss of his heir while he
was away at the wars. Little Maud was all very well and

Reynold still adored his child, but his wife must accept his need of sons. Not once had he beaten her nor even openly blamed her for the losses, but she showed no gratitude. Quite the contrary, but she evaded her marital duties whenever she could, excusing herself by saying that the custom of women was upon her, or was about to be, or that it was a day proscribed by the Church.

He bitterly regretted introducing his cousin, Ilaria de Boullers, into his household for he was certain she put Beatrice up to many of these excuses. She had been repudiated by her own husband at least ten years ago and it was only latterly that he had begun to wonder how she had avoided either remarriage or the cloister. Yet at the time, with Beatrice for ever complaining that she had no lady of her own degree to bear her company, it had seemed a good idea to take her in; besides, he had expected her to keep a sharp eye on Beatrice on his behalf. But it had not worked out like that. Instead, Ilaria, forgetting the ties of kinship between them, had become closely attached to Beatrice. She was not with them now. Reynold was too sick of the sight of her swarthy face with the dark line of hair on the upper lip to bring her. He had packed her off back to her brother for a time, but her absence had not improved matters between his wife and himself.

His friend Will de Tracy might have given him a clue had he felt so inclined. He had watched Beatrice's affair with Hugh de Morville from the beginning with detached amusement, and he had a strong suspicion that Reynold's so-called heir had been de Morville's by-blow. Not that Hugh had ever mentioned Beatrice by name. But then, he would not do that. He was deep – as deep as a deep well, and as cold, thought Will. When he recounted his seductions one could sense the icy contempt he bore his victims. It was clear that he did not like women, and remembering the cruelty which was meted out to his adoring young pages,

Will concluded that he liked boys very little more.

Will himself was a short, fair, thick-set fellow in his middle twenties, remarkable for only one thing, his insatiable appetite for women. But unlike Hugh, he really liked the creatures, liked their idle empty chatter, their warmth and softness; and they, sensing this, made much of him. He was thinking about women now as they came into Williton; the shape of the little rounded tree-crowned hills reminded him of a damsel's breasts. Perhaps there would be a serving wench. . . .

He stared around with interest as they rode over the plank bridge across the moat; it was the first time he had visited Fitzurse's chief seat. Though small, it looked prosperous under the summer sun, neat and well-tended. There went a likely looking maid – you could always tell when they cast those eager, sidelong glances in the men's direction. He kept his eye on her as she ran up the steps into the hall – a house serf, most likely. She'd do, unless he saw a more handsome one.

Smiling his wide unchanging smile he knelt before his host, was lifted up and kissed and passed to another younger man for greeting. This would be Reynold's bastard brother, he supposed, though there was but little likeness between them; and the lady Beatrice was kissing would be his wife. . . . He ran a practised, appraising eye over her but looked away quickly when he saw her front teeth were missing. Too skinny anyway, and some sort of cripple to judge by her ungainly movements. Some fellows had no luck with their wives. He remembered his own plump little pigeon with satisfaction, and not listening to the chatter about him, ran his eye around the hall in search of the wench who had attracted his attention.

Ysabel, Robert's wife, nudged Beatrice. 'Is he a friend of Reynold's? De Tracy's heir?'

'Oh yes, a great friend,' said Beatrice. 'Do you not re-

34

member that he and Robert had their knightly training at de Tracy's? Though they are not to be compared with many that we move among—' She began to talk about the great men at Court in the most familiar way to let Ysabel know that she and the other Fitzurses were of little account. This made her feel so much the better that she thought she might even enjoy herself here for a short time. Ysabel, who had not seen Beatrice for more than six years, thought she had not changed much.

But Reynold was right; Beatrice had changed, just as Ysabel herself had, though the difference was not so obvious. Hugh de Morville's treachery had killed any small spark of softness in her and she had discarded much else along with her dreams of romance and Courtly love. The woman who had spat on Jehane's grave was a realist who knew that talk of love had but one end in view and all it led to was pain and sorrow. Beatrice would not be taken twice in the same trap and many a young squire was taken aback at the hard-eyed stare with which his well-meant compliments were received. She turned her attention instead to other matters of more material moment and schemed endlessly to further her social ambitions. After discoursing upon that topic for a time and then commiserating with Ysabel on the loss of her looks, she remembered to ask after her mother-in-law.

Ysabel looked distressed. 'She is no better,' she answered in a low voice.' We are all hoping that the sight of Reynold will work some improvement.'

'Is she truly mad?' Beatrice whispered eagerly. 'What does she do? Does she shriek and tear her hair? She is locked away, is she not? In truth, I always thought her odd. . . .' She nodded to herself with some satisfaction, and then as though struck by a different thought – 'They will not expect *me* to visit with her, will they?'

But Ysabel seemed reluctant to talk much on that subject

35

and went away to oversee the cooks, so that it was not until after dinner that Beatrice's ghoulish curiosity was given full reign. Then the old baron, Reynold's father, who throughout the meal had questioned him closely about the Chancellor, carried him away with him to see his mother. The baron came back before Reynold and sat alone, staring into the fire, but Beatrice thought he did not look very troubled and she watched him covertly while she gossiped with Ysabel who sat under a branch of candles with her sewing.

'Should my lord leave Reynold alone with her?' she said with another glance at her father-in-law.

'He has come to see his mother, has he not?' said Ysabel. 'She will not harm him.'

'Harm? I do not speak of harm; but is there not a contagion in madness?' Beatrice looked at Ysabel sharply. 'Why else is she locked away?'

Ysabel kept her eyes on her needlework. 'For fear she might harm herself.'

'Oh, God forbid such a thought. Poor lady; poor soul! But tell me all.' And Beatrice shifted up a little nearer on the bench, her face filled with expectant relish. 'I have ne'er seen a madwoman. Is she much altered in appearance? One hears such things—' She began to tell Ysabel a tale of the strange and gruesome behaviour of an elderly nun whom her mother had once known.

Ysabel listened in silence and answered as briefly as she could for she found Beatrice's assumption of concern as offensive as her prying questions. Carefully she arranged the long loose cuff of her sleeve at the wrist that the visitor might not catch sight of the scar on her forearm. She did not know whether Beatrice had heard of Lady Maud's attack on the baron's natural daughter when she got that injury but she had no intention of retailing the story to her. Mold, Lady Maud's only ally, had been sent off to Worle (ostensibly to prepare her quarters there) and Beatrice was not likely to hear the tale from anyone else.

'She is well enough if she is kept quiet,' she said cautiously, 'so the baron will not have her troubled with the cares of the household. I am mistress here in her stead,' she concluded, and turned her eyes away from the long, distrustful look Beatrice gave her.

Sir Richard Fitzurse, Reynold's father, had been silently watching the scene, and felt the considerable dislike he already had for Beatrice grow stronger. But he trusted Ysabel's discretion as he now trusted her in everything; Beatrice would not be diverted by tales of family scandal from her lips. And for some reason, it still seemed important that Reynold should not know he had acknowledged the child of his mistress Beta as his own. He had kept the secret from him too long, and it was too inextricably intertwined with Maud's deranged behaviour to admit to it now. He hoped his son and his wife would not stay here long.

In bed that night Beatrice and Reynold aired their thoughts about the situation at Williton and drew closer in their disquiet than they had been for many a long month. Both were uneasy but for different reasons; Beatrice because her suspicions had been aroused concerning her husband's eventual inheritance here, and Reynold because of the wild tales his mother had told him. He recounted them to Beatrice who, while secretly disappointed that her mother-in-law did not howl and foam at the mouth, had enough sense to realise that they too were evidence of insanity. She told him so.

He sighed then, and putting out his hand, tentatively touched her breast. When she offered no immediate objection, he heaved himself over on top of her. Beatrice did not allow that to interrupt her train of thought; she twisted her head to one side and said, 'You do not think that those two plan to edge you out of your patrimony here?'

But Reynold's mind was on other things and he did not

37

answer. Beatrice continued her speculations throughout the performance and was so engrossed by them that even Reynold's staccato farting, a common accompaniment to his exertions, escaped her notice.

During the next week of fair weather Reynold and Will rode out daily about the manor with Robert, the baron's bastard son, who acted as his steward. Robert held a grudge against Reynold because he was heir to Williton; he minded very much that his brother should have the fruits of his hard work. Reynold knew nothing of this; he only remembered their comradeship as boys. They had both been brought up at de Tracy's and since Robert had admired Will's parents, he was prepared to like him. He had met him once or twice when they were young but did not know him well because Will too had been educated among strangers, as was fitting.

Yet despite all their efforts to be easy together there was a gulf between them. Robert thought they found him steeped in rustic ignorance and suspected them of laughing at him behind his back and, though he reminded himself that his blood outmatched theirs through his mother, he felt himself a yokel in their presence. They had travelled abroad while he had never been further than Wiltshire; doubtless they had enjoyed ladies of high quality while his bawd was nothing but a serf.

In fact, they thought no more of him than that he was a surly killjoy. He objected to their riding through the villeins' unharvested corn and to their horses fouling the stream where the people drew their water; consequently when a small white dog persisted in darting and yelping round their horses' hoofs, they were in a mood to show him that they cared nothing for his strictures.

Reynold sawed at his horse's mouth and turned back; out came the dog again, barking and running to and fro.

Reynold put the horse to a gallop but the cur leapt aside from the thundering hoofs. 'Come on, Will,' he shouted. 'run the little whoreson down. One kick in the skull'll finish him!'

Robert compressed his lips watching them trampling back and forth, hallooing and urging each other on. In the end they tired of it and came up with him. 'We'll get it sooner or later, Will,' promised Reynold, 'I'll have a dog-skin bag of it for little Maud.'

'That's no villein's dog,' warned Robert. 'It belongs to Leofric the cottar. He says it's a good ratter.'

'Well, he shall have his price for it, eh, Will?' said Reynold, 'I would I'd a mace in my hand! I'd have splattered its brains.'

Will nodded. He had previously decided to stay until Manor Court, two days hence; now he thought he would extend his stay until the dog had been suitably dealt with. He also decided that he would do the splattering. 'I'll wager you three marks,' he said, 'that I get it.'

Court Day dawned as fair as those that went before but about mid morning a little warm breeze sprang up, blowing out of the west, and low on the southern horizon a range of pure white clouds went along before it like the first banners of an advancing army.

In the hall the house serfs scurried in and out, making all ready for the Court. They set up boards on trestles in the shape of an open-ended oblong so that the accused might come up between those who were the pledges for the tithings (and so formed a kind of jury) and stand in front of the baron and all the local knights who held fees of him. Herluin the bailiff was there already, rattling his rolls and parchments, and watching Reynold with a jaundiced eye as he strode importantly to his place at the High Table.

Sir Richard Fitzurse came at last and sat on his seat which

39

was the great oaken chest where he kept his treasure; it had a back and arm rests for comfort. Will found a position against the hearth, filled now with fresh green boughs from the barren pear tree in the yard, where he could get a good view of the proceedings. Robert sat with Herluin.

The jurors presented, as it appeared they always did, that old Hilde the breweress had brewed against the assize and sold sour beer. She was declared in the baron's mercy and fined two pence, and Will saw Robert, with a wary look at his father, catch her eye and nod vigorously. Will grinned behind his hand and wondered what else he got there besides ale that he should be willing to pay twice for the privilege of drinking in her hovel.

The door in the screen at the end of the hall began to bang to and fro in the rising wind and Herluin raised his voice as he read a presentment against the cart of Ernulf Ape, a freeholder, which running backwards down the meadow full of hay, had struck him down and killed him. Now his son Thurstan, who would inherit, owed a relief to the baron. Thurstan came forward.

'It is a good cart, my lord,' he said, 'and ill can I afford the loss of it – but it is a bane, the slayer of my father. So will you take it, lord, for the relief of my inheritance?'

The baron frowned and clicked his fingers towards Herluin and they put their heads together and murmured. But at length the baron looked up and said that a bane was unacceptable as a relief and that his judgment was that Thurstan should give the cart to God – that is, to the monks at Sutinstocke. As to the relief, he would take a good work horse if Thurstan did not wish to pay in silver.

Thurstan scowled, and Will thought that he grieved more for the loss of his cart than of his father, but then he concluded that the fellow probably knew his own business best.

Grave-faced, they listened to the tale of a scolding wife, several fornications, and then to a number of cases of assault and abusing among the villeins. Towards midday Sir Richard called for ale and meat which turned out to be smoked legs of mutton, jet black and shiny, for the knights, and some kind of anonymous pasties for the lesser folk. Will watched hungrily as the meat was carved, each slice shading from dark brown at the edge to succulent pink near the bone, and affected not to see Reynold's signals to join him at the High Table; he stayed where he was and ate his meat from the point of his dagger with no ceremony.

Later they came to more serious business. Helias Attewelle, a freeholder, had lost a calf and wished to accuse Godric, the baron's serf, of stealing it. Godric denied the charge, saying that his cow had not calved until the day after Helias's calf had disappeared from the common pasture, and that it was his opinion that a wolf had had it. But this idea met with fairly general condemnation; wolves rarely came out of Exmoor in summer.

While several of Godric's neighbours were prepared to swear he was a man of good repute, an equal number shook their heads and expressed doubts of him; in the end they were wrangling nearly as fiercely as the chief participants. Finally the baron demanded a recapitulation of events, but even here no two were agreed and Will could see he was fast losing patience. For himself, he could not make head or tail of it.

'It must have been stolen,' cried Helias, 'else why did it not return when I sang it back home?'

'What is this singing?' demanded the baron.

Herluin muttered something and Sir Richard frowned. 'Tell us what you sang.'

'Thus I sang,' cried Helias, and burst into a loud and tuneless dirge. 'Bethlehem was hight the borough wherein Christ was born; it is far famed over the earth. So may this deed be in the sight of men notorious, *per crucem Christi.*' He swung sideways. 'May the cross of Christ bring it back from the east.' He turned again. 'May the cross of Christ bring it back from the west.'

The baron waved him to silence but Helias sang on to each point of the compass—' the cross of Christ was hidden and is found. The Jews hanged Christ, they did to him the worst of deeds, they concealed what could not be concealed. So never may this deed be concealed, *per crucem Christi.*' He stopped a moment, panting, and drew a deep breath. 'Thus I sang, and besides – Peter, Patrick, Philip, Mary, Bridget, Felicitas; in the name of God and the Church, he who seeketh, findeth.'

An old man further down the board spoke up. 'It is said that when this singing is done, wax from three candles should be dripped in the hoof track. That will be why the calf came not back.'

'Where could I get wax candles?' cried Helias indignantly. 'But within two days I saw my calf again, along with his beasts!' And he pointed accusingly at Godric.

'One newborn calf is much like another,' observed the baron.

'He must be put to the ordeal of fire as is the custom,' said Helias, and the old men along the board nodded solemnly.

'Nay, nay!' cried Godric shrilly. 'My neighbour Osmund will bear me witness that my cow calved.'

'Aye, but how may he say whether the calf in question dropped from your cow or another? God will decide the issue,' said the baron, 'Make all ready.'

Outside a warm wind was blowing, and Wihtgar the farrier stood by the fire while flames roared round the iron bar. Two of the baron's men held Godric; Will had to laugh at the way his eyes rolled in terror. The priest stood nearby and the villagers clustered round, some avid, some aghast. In his great chair which had been carried out into the open sat the baron with Reynold and Robert on either

42

side.

Slowly the colour of the iron changed from black to darkest crimson, and then cherry red as the wind blasted the fire into incandescence. Godric was praying now, his eyes tight shut. Robert, who knew him well, felt a qualm until he remembered that God would certainly protect the man, were he guiltless.

At last the baron nodded and Wihtgar pushed the cooler end of the iron so that the other end which now glowed a pale clear orange stuck out from the fire. Godric was hustled forward. As his hand closed on the hot metal he gave a wheezing howl and staggered a few steps before he dropped it. Then he fell on his knees and rocked backwards and forwards. His mouth was wide open as though he thought he screamed but no sound came.

Will did not watch the serf; he watched his hosts because their expressions told more about them than he would learn in any other way. The baron's face was still and closed, and he had turned away his head a moment before Godric grasped the iron. Will followed the direction of his eyes as they fell upon Reynold. He, quite unaware of their scrutiny, gazed on the scene with a look of fascinated relish, wet lips drawn back to show the small yellow teeth pressed hard together. Both heard the hissing intake of his breath as Godric fell and saw him rub lips suddenly gone loose with the back of his hand. Will looked back at Reynold's father but could read nothing in his blank and empty face.

The baron had kept his countenance with the greatest effort of will for in that instant his attitude towards his heir hardened beyond alteration. This one would never have power over his people if he could help it. He watched Godric writhing on the ground without seeing him but at last his fists unclenched.

'Bind up his hand,' he called, and a moment later, 'All is done. Back to your labours,' without further ceremony,

43

he rose and walked off alone into his hall.

Although Godric's hand did finally heal cleanly so that he was adjudged innocent, it was thereafter no more than a useless claw for he could never again stretch out his fingers. Robert thought that God had probably punished him thus for some other sin which had gone undetected. Godric himself, with better reason, thought so too; but his wife, from being a cheerful, garrulous woman turned cold and disagreeable: she thought it a great injustice that a man without a strong right hand should be as able as ever to get her with child every year.

Very early the next morning, the baron's natural daughter Cicely crossed the hayfield towards the water meadows. Already the aftermath was showing green through the sharp, yellowish stubble and she skipped and hopped as she went along, partly at the pricking of her ankles and partly for sheer joy in being alive. It had rained heavily in the night but the weather had gone over and the day was brilliant. Up in the blue sky larks were singing and she kept a sharp eye open for a nest, but none was here where the mowers had been so recently. Before she came down to the greener meadows she heard the honking of geese and knew the other child she sought was there.

He sat with his back to her among patches of daisies that had sprung up almost overnight where the geese had cropped the grass, and she crept up softly behind him and put her hands over his eyes.

Dropping her voice in an effort to mimic an adult, she said, 'Wherefore are you not driving the geese, you knave? Up and down they should go, filling their crops and making all neat at the same time!'

'Cicely!' he laughed, 'I had but sat to breathe awhile. The geese do very well down here. They drive me, not I

44

them.'

'Let us go down to the stream and look for minnows.' She pulled at his hand. 'I am sent for cresses so we may spend an hour together – they will not miss us yet, Robin.'

He grinned at her, a brown faced boy with thick eyebrows which would meet across his nose when he grew older, and a dimple in his chin. He was Weaver's second son, two years her senior, and they had been close from babyhood for Weaver's toft adjourned the mill. Always, whenever they might play truant from household tasks, they had spent their time together but that was not so easy now since Miller's death and Cicely's translation to the manor house. He had not looked for her to come today and had set his ambitions upon the capture of a newt of gigantic proportions which he had glimpsed occasionally in the pool the children thought was bottomless. He renounced him now without a second thought.

'I can't stay longer,' he said, 'or my father will be after me with a willow switch' – mentally he marked the position of the sun in the sky – 'but for an hour—'

Along the edges of the stream the grass grew tall, interspersed with the last straggling buttercups and yellow ragwort, and here and there a clump of meadow cranesbill, still carrying a few purply-blue flowers above its masses of brown seed heads. The children knelt on the bank, peering into the clear water in which minnows darted aimlessly, disappearing into the cresses and flickering forth again, and all so swift that the eye could not follow. They dabbled their hands among them for the joy of putting them to flight but with the stilling of the water the dancing mindless shoals were back once more.

Tiring of fish, they moved slowly along the bank, watching for the kingfisher which Robin had seen once and no more thereafter. Nor did they see it this time but startled a water rat which paddled frantically to escape Robin's clutching hand and gain the safety of a hidden hole.

'I'd have had him,' he cried, 'but that my knee slipped on that tussock!' and with his sleeve sopping to the shoulder, flung back over the low bank and rolled helplessly into the stretch of wet, churned earth where the cattle came to drink. 'Sweet Christ!' he said. 'Now I'll be beat! I stink like a midden!'

But when they examined the extent of the damage, there was only one patch of the buttery mud on the side of his tunic and that might crack off when dry and escape detection. So he washed hands and legs in the stream and then lay in the sunlight on the short sward well away from the wallow, picking at the mat of tiny purple vetches near his head.

'Does not the baron mind that you come still to the common and the meadow?' he asked her unexpectedly.

'Why should he?'

'My father says you are the baron's own get and I should keep away from you,' he said.

She stared at him with round blue eyes. 'How can such be? My father is – was – the miller.'

'Your mother was Miller's wife,' he said, and picked assiduously at the vetches.

Neither of them was unaware of how young creatures came to be conceived; they lived too close to animals to be ignorant of obvious facts, and since whole families shared the same sleeping quarters, they learned early of the commerce between men and women. But it was too large an assumption to suppose that humankind followed exactly the same pattern as the beasts, and if Robin, who had younger brothers and sisters, was prepared to believe it, Cicely was not. She sat in silence for a while until comprehension slowly came.

Then she said, 'St Joseph was not the true father of the little Christ either. It is called foster father. The miller, then,

46

was my foster father.'

'Aye – mayhap,' said Robin.

Cicely sat quiet and let the thought take shape. She could not grasp it very clearly but to her child's mind there was little relative difference between the power of the baron and the power of the Holy Ghost. Somehow she had been conceived of the baron and born of her mother. . . . It was very like the story of the little Christ – and it had somewhat to do with lilies. Not that she had ever seen one in reality, only a picture in a beautiful book that the monks had made for the baron. He had shown it to her after the priest had told her the story of the Annunciation.

Presently Robin said that he must look to the geese and Cicely went along the stream and gathered a big armful of cresses; they dripped water all down her skirt but she did not notice that because her mind was too full of the wonderful thing which Robin had told her. Indeed, for years afterwards she thought Robin had said she had been conceived by a miracle.

When she came back to the house she made for the kitchens to leave the greenstuff with the cooks, but Madam Ysabel was there and a glorious smell of new baked bread filled the place. It was dark inside and very hot for the fires were going full blast to heat the ovens.

'What have you there?' asked Ysabel who was stirring maslin in a wooden bowl to make the thin, flat cakes that were the villeins' dole when they worked the demesne fields.

'Cresses from the stream, madam. They are for you,' and Cicely presented them to her with a dazzling smile and the air of a great lady bestowing her guerdon on a knight.

Ysabel smiled faintly. She could not help feeling some fondness for the child who was both pretty and polite but a curious sense of loyalty to her mother-in-law whom she did not even like had made her keep Cicely at a distance.

'A big girl like you should not waste her time in the

47

fields,' she said. 'It's time you gave some help around the house.'

'Oh, madam,' cried Cicely, 'will you teach me to make bread? Only maslin, I know I cannot waste the wheat flour. Will you, madam?'

Disarmed by the child's eagerness, Ysabel said, 'Not so hasty! Do you be still a moment while I finish this. Then we will see.'

Behind her, the cook who did not like women in his kitchen except to wash the pots, sniffed loudly. Was he to put up with children too?

Cicely sat down on a stool and watched the bubbles rising as Ysabel beat the batter. 'Let me try, madam,' she begged, 'I will not spill a drop.'

'Not this time. Tomorrow, if you are good, I will show you from the beginning.'

Cicely began to clap her hands and bob up and down on the stool so that the batter in the bowl heaved and swayed like the sea.

'Hush now – if you behave like a little one, you shall learn nothing,' cried Ysabel.

Cicely sat still as a mouse for a full minute until a sudden recollection struck her. 'Madam, there are those who say the baron is my true father,' she announced.

The cook gave a loud snort which made them all jump. Ysabel was nonplussed and rounded on him, ordering him off to the other end of the kitchen to begin preparing the meats.

'Methinks I was made as the little Christ was made,' continued Cicely. 'Do you think it, madam?'

'Hush!' said Ysabel sharply, 'you must not say that. It's not true nor must you think it! It was – it was more like the story of Abraham and his handmaiden.'

'I know not that story. Will you tell it to me?'

So keeping her voice low, Ysabel told the story of Abra-

48

him, Sarah and Hagar, though it was a somewhat garbled version for all she knew of it she had learnt from mummers who were not noted for accuracy with Holy Writ. Cicely listened with interest and thanked her prettily; then she said, 'I think it was not like that, though. The baron did not turn out my mother and me into a wilderness of desert. What is a desert?'

Ysabel sighed and began to explain that it was a waste like Exmoor, wishing not for the first time that she had a child of her own to explain things to.

Over by the ovens the cook spat on the baking sheet to see if it were hot enough with more vehemence than was strictly necessary. It summed up his opinion of clack-tongued females very neatly and he felt so much better for his gesture that he began to sing a doleful song which quite drowned Ysabel's reply. That pleased him more and when the spittle had bubbled and boiled away, he poured on the maslin batter with a generosity he had cause to regret immediately for what should have made two score cakes would not stretch beyond twenty-five.

Two cakes apiece was the villeins' portion – well, today it would be one of nearly double thickness – and with a swift glance behind him he deftly knocked five off the sheet. Five maslin cakes could be added to the portion of beef he had reserved for Weaver against the price of his new hosen. Even cooks must live.

That afternoon Reynold and Will did not come straight back from Doniford where they had been visiting one of Fitzurse's military tenants but rode up into the foothills of the Quantocks and so came into Williton from the east. They were in high spirits for William de Reigny had plied them with wine and listened to Reynold's shouted boasts of their exploits in Toulouse two years ago, though now and again his tufty eyebrows had risen and his lids drooped as if he were weary. But he excused himself by saying that he had lost sleep the night before with the earache to which he was subject; when they were ready to go he took leave of them with the utmost politeness and stood looking after them a long time when they rode away.

So they were feeling pretty well pleased with themselves and with the impression they had made as they came down the hill towards Williton. At that moment they remembered the dog. Perhaps Reynold put his big bay horse to the gallop a fraction earlier but Will had the short stave he kept at the side of his saddle swinging in his hand as they rounded the bend by the cottars' huts. The familiar shrill yelping broke out and Reynold overshot the flash of white; he pulled violently on the reins so that the horse's head jerked up and it slewed sideways. Will, hard on his heels, leaned from the saddle and struck out with the stave. They both heard the sharp crack as it connected and gave a yell of glee but as Will glanced back over his shoulder, his horse, still at full gallop, put its hoof in a hole and pitched forward. He kicked free of the stirrups just in time and hurtled over the horse's head to land with a bone-jarring thump on the stony track where he lay like one dead. Reynold wheeled his horse and came up beside him.

'Will! Will, are you hurt?'

Will groaned. 'Christ, something's broke.' He breathed in quick, open-mouthed gasps. 'I think it's my shoulder. Christ! I can't move!'

Reynold dismounted hastily and bent over him. 'Put your other arm round my neck.'

'No – wait, God damn you!'

'Let me feel it. Aye – you've put the shoulder out. I can't get that back on my own. Can you mount the horse? God's blood, Will, you look bad—'

Will groaned again. His face was the colour of parchment and little beads of sweat stood on his forehead. 'No,' he muttered. 'No, I can't. Fetch someone.'

Reynold was staring back down the track where a little knot of naked children, none above five years old, had gathered. 'Wait,' he said, 'I'll see if any there can help.'

He came back within a minute or so, his face almost as pale as Will's. 'They're all off harvesting.' He crouched beside Will in the dust and spoke hurriedly. 'It wasn't the dog you hit, Will – it was one of those brats.'

'Is it dead?'

'What do you think? Thanks be to St Decuman none was here to see.' (It was only in moments of greatest stress that Reynold remembered St Decuman.)

Will began to groan again. 'Get rid of the stave. And for the love of God get someone here to me instead of worrying about some villein's get!'

'Aye,' said Reynold, 'Aye. . . . I'll not be long.'

Eventually a litter arrived and Will was transported to the manor house. Reynold had not mentioned the dead child and his preoccupied look was attributed to concern for his companion, but he knew the reckoning with his father was to come and his mind was more upon that than Will's frenzied bellowing as they attempted to set his dislocated shoulder. They had made him pretty drunk before they started but he refused to lose his senses so they did it while he was still conscious, and one of the serfs who held him down got a kick in the face which blacked both his eyes.

Afterwards though, he and Will hatched a story that blamed the dead child for the whole incident, and since its injuries were quite consistent with having been kicked on the head by a horse, the whole affair passed over more quietly than they had dared to hope. Robert, who might have remembered the dog and been suspicious about the site of the accident, made no remark on it, and Will was prepared to have his horse tried as a bane, providing

51

Reynold recompensed him later in secret.

But during the next week when they sat and talked together, it became obvious to Reynold that Will would not be fit to ride into Devon for at least a fortnight. He was already like a bear with a sore head because his mishap had put an end to his nocturnal sporting with the serving wenches. As for Reynold, although it had been his original intention to stay at least a month, it irked him to be thus constrained to wait upon the convenience of another. Now he was eager to be gone.

Nothing had worked out as he had expected. In the beginning he had made light of the reports on his mother's strange malady; then half-buried memories of a servile leman had revived and he had become suspicious of his father's reasons for shutting her away. Now he could see for himself that his brother's wife, rather than some mistress, kept the keys, much to his own wife's irritation. His conviction that the sight of himself and his little daughter would restore his mother's senses had come to seem sheer folly. On the one occasion he had taken little Maud up to the tower chamber she had buried her face in his shoulder and started to cry, and the old woman had talked so wildly and irrationally that he had begun to believe she was in truth possessed of a devil. . . .

Still, he continued to visit her every day until she started to look askance at him and hint that he too might wish her out of the world, and in response to his indignant denials, let loose a torrent of filthy invective that matched anything he had heard among harlots. He came away that time shaken and disturbed beyond measure. The next day, Court Day, she would not speak to him at all.

There was some vague talk of taking her to be blessed by a holy man nearby, an anchorite who would not leave his cell, but he did not think the baron would permit that in view of her unpredictability. . . . Lacking any further ideas himself, he fumbled doubtfully around the problem for several days and finally took it to Beatrice who disposed of it summarily in one sentence – 'There is nothing we may do for her save pray and that we can do elsewhere as well as here!'

He nodded, marvelling afresh at her capacity for going straight to the point. She was right, of course; they were doing no good here. So he would wait until Will was recovered and then they would go. Nor would he ever come again; it would not help this stranger who had been his mother. He would pay for Masses for her soul's health – and with that thought he felt released; it did not strike him that deep in the core of his mind he had dismissed her as one already dead, nor that in her lucid moments she might know it.

His father was agreeable to all the arrangements Reynold proposed to make and on the first Sunday in September all the Fitzurse kin (with the exception of the subject of the exercise) travelled to St Decuman's to hear the first of nine monthly Masses for the deliverance of Lady Maud from the devil who possessed her.

Cicely, lurking by the kitchen door with her mother and some of the serfs' wives who had come to bake their bread in the manor ovens, watched them all ride out. 'Do they go to pray for her?' she said, nodding towards the tower. Beta, who had been ordered to keep the child close for the period of the visit, smiled grimly. She spoke, half under her breath, to one of the women. 'Let them play their mummers' games! She'll not walk this hall again for all their Christian prayers—'

Cicely did not try to listen to the rest. She was used to mysterious asides concerning the Lady, and although her mother never spoke openly, she knew already that there were stronger Powers than any that the baron dreamed of when he knelt in church. As long as they confined the Lady

53

in invisible bonds, she would be safe. For Cicely remembered that this Lady (or the devil who inhabited her) had once ried to kill her, and feared her exceedingly in consequence.

And then, as though brought about by the fact that they had spoken of the madwoman, a loud screaming was heard from the tower, and all the women ran towards the steps and clustered at the bottom, staring up and calling to the two of their number who had been told off to wash her and ict as tiring women in Mold's absence. After a minute, one of them stuck her head out of the door. She was laughing. 'Come up!' she yelled, 'Come up and see how fine we've made her!'

Cicely crept up the stairs at the tail of the procession and hovered fearfully at the door while the rest went in. 'Faugh!' they cried, 'What a stink! What's she done now?' Cicely peered round the jamb. 'Shit on the floor again, the dirty old sow! And Goda here has served it up for her' – the woman went into a fresh burst of hysterical mirth – 'for breakfast! Look at her!'

Cicely looked with shrinking distaste. The Lady's face was smeared with excreta; she thrashed and screamed at the end of her chain in her efforts to reach her tormentors.

Cicely crept away and crouched by the kitchen door. For at least an hour afterwards she could hear them up there, goading and jeering at the Lady. It made her feel sick until she recalled that it was not really the Lady but the devil within her they were maltreating.

In church Beatrice listened with growing impatience to a long, impassioned sermon directed, it appeared to her, chiefly at the sins of women – sins which invited visitation by demons – the punishments for which were dwelt on with satisfaction and at great length.

So that when Ysabel, moved to tears by the priest's eloquence upon Christ's suffering and sacrifice, turned to her

54

with an impulsive clutch of the hand, whispering, 'Shall we not at least love each other as we should love Him who so endured and died for us?', she could only stare at her. She had undergone the hellish pains of premature child-birth twice in little more than a year, and she had good reason to suspect she was pregnant once more.

'Pah!' she said, 'he should have tried being a woman!'

III

September 1161–April 1162

IN SEPTEMBER THOMAS had sufficiently recovered his health and spirits to travel to Domfront where Henry, his affairs in Gascony settled to his satisfaction, was to meet him. The Queen was lying-in there with a newly born daughter. Thomas thought that a fortuitous circumstance for the presence of the royal children would dispel any constraint, and he felt what amounted to a dread of meeting the King with his mind still unresolved.

But he looked forward with eagerness to seeing the little ones for he loved children and they, almost without exception, adored him on sight. It had been arranged long ago that he should foster Young Henry in his household when the boy was old enough to leave his mother; he hoped that he should be able to take him soon. The younger ones he hardly knew but to him there was only pleasure in the prospect of hearing their endearing childish prattle.

Nor was he disappointed. In the company of these innocents, he could lay down the cares of office and romp freely as once he had done with their father. Young Henry was between six and seven years old, and a fine manly little knave who did not weep a tear when he knocked out his first loose milk tooth but smiled a wide blood-stained smile and presented it proudly to his diminutive wife. She was thin, dark and shy, as conspicuous among the sturdy golden Angevins as a poppy in a wheatfield.

All of his children, with their varying shades of reddish fair hair, bore a strong resemblance to Henry; even that cuckoo in the nest, the elder Geoffrey, betrayed no evidence of the difference in his parentage, no look as yet of his dead mother that Thomas could recognise. They seemed, one and all, to have the same easy, open friendliness as the younger Henry whom Thomas had loved. Only Matilda, who was quieter and more solemn than the boys, wore a different port; she reminded him of someone else. It nagged at him until, quite suddenly, he saw the Empress in the disdainful glance she bent upon her brothers' horseplay.

They quarrelled fiercely over who should enjoy the coveted position on Thomas's lap until the King, worried by their increasing boisterousness, ordered them to have a care of his Chancellor's weak knee and carried Thomas off with him to his own apartments. It was the first time they had been alone for nearly three months and Thomas found himself tongue-tied.

'You should have had children of your own, Tom,' said Henry. 'How you can bear with them. . . .'

Thomas shook his head. 'Nay – that happiness was not for me. I love all young things but I have never wished to marry. And without a wife—'

Henry grinned. 'It's not difficult without a wife. But enough – I did not bring you here to torment you, but to talk of serious matters.' He paused a moment and Thomas felt his heart thump. 'I have been considering the question of the succession as I must for I am close to thirty. I know that you would uphold Young Henry's right to my crown if I should die, but I fear that not everyone has your loyalty. So I have decided that I must see him crowned in my life-time as kings do in France and Germany.'

57

He stopped and looked at the Chancellor as though waiting for a comment. Thomas nodded and dropped his eyes swiftly as if he feared the King might read his thoughts. Only an Archbishop of Canterbury could crown a king in England. He said nothing.

Henry continued, 'First he must go to England to receive the homage of the magnates—'

Thomas was remembering that Stephen had attempted to have his son Eustace crowned in his lifetime and Theobald had opposed him. Here, then, was the reason why Henry wanted an Archbishop who served his interests, and it was a reason he could accept as valid. He was relieved. Why had he suspected that Henry's motives might be disreputable?

'You must take him now, Tom. Train and advise him as a future king – he will be very willing to go with you. And you must take him to England in the spring; I would not have him find his heritage as hard to win as I did.'

So he would go home at last! And, oddly, now that he had been given what he had longed for all these months, it signified little – quite overshadowed by the choice that loomed before him.

Afterwards, they returned to the children's quarters to tell young Henry that henceforth his place was with the Chancellor. Thomas noticed that the Queen was quiet; she said nothing but drew the small boy, Richard, closer in the circle of her arm. He appreciated for the first time that women found it painful to give up their children to the care of others and looked at her with sympathy.

'When may I go with the Chancellor?' cried Richard, and she hushed him quickly, trying to keep his attention on a woollen ball she dangled before him.

'I don't want that!' he said. 'That's a babe's bauble!'

'That's what you are,' said young Henry with condescension. 'You're but four years old and still a babe!'

Richard evaded his mother's grasp and flew at his brother. He was a big child, and heavy, and the suddenness of his attack surprised young Henry so that he got in several kicks before his brother retaliated. They rolled like puppies in the rushes, clawing and biting at each other, until the King leaned over and grabbed Young Henry by the scruff of his jerkin, forcibly separating them.

'Let me down,' screamed the child, beating at his father's arm. 'He kicked me; I'll kick him back. Let me go.'

Henry glared at the small, struggling boy. 'I had thought you old enough to leave the womenfolk,' he said. 'Truly you have much to learn. What will my lord think of you – fighting with teeth and nails.' He put the child across his knee and beat his buttocks soundly, then stood him on his feet. 'There's your first punishment from a man. Your brother shall have his from a woman as is fitting for a young child.'

Young Henry's face was very red but he did not cry. 'He'll get no punishment,' he said, 'not Richard. But I'll thump him when I see him alone.'

Thomas picked the boy up. 'But you're coming with me,' he said, 'and if you'll be good, you shall ride on the front of my saddle.'

The child was stiff in his arms. 'I shall kiss my wife goodbye,' he said, 'and then I'll come. I shall not kiss *him* nor bid him goodbye.'

Nor would he in spite of all his mother's cajoling but thrust out his lower lip and glowered, so like his father that Thomas had difficulty in keeping a straight face.

'Time he was taken from his mother,' Henry muttered darkly. 'You'll not spare the rod, Tom. He must learn obedience.'

If the Chancellor felt an inward qualm at the task before him, his face did not show it as he took young Henry from the Queen's embraces and carried him towards the door.

59

The child was warm and heavy on his shoulder, his breath moist and sweet-smelling on his cheek. As they went out, he heard Richard address his mother: 'I can read better than he can, can I not, mama? I can add numbers, too, and make them come aright. A babe cannot do that, can he?'

He felt young Henry move to look back at them over his shoulder and turned his eyes towards the face so near his own. Young Henry's tongue was protruded to its fullest extent at his brother. Thomas transferred him to his other arm and donned his most forbidding expression.

Young Henry chuckled infectiously and dabbed a kiss at him. 'I am happy to go with you, my lord Chancellor,' he said airily. 'Women are good for babes, but I would be a man. Richard is a mama's boy, but I shall be a king.'

Later Thomas felt that his meeting with Henry was an anti-climax. He had wrought himself up to receive the offer of the Archbishopric (though still not knowing whether he would accept) and Henry had not so much as mentioned it. He could not help feeling disappointed. It was absurd that everyone spoke of him becoming Archbishop as a foregone conclusion when the matter had never been brought up between the two principals. He went remorselessly over the old arguments but the words of Aschetinus worked in him, harsh with truth.

He knew his standards were high, but not from pride. It was rather that he saw, right down in the centre of his soul, the shivering weakling which dwelt there, which must be forced with whip and spur to tread the path of valour. But no one else should ever know of it. It was that which had put forth the excuses of unworthiness in order to evade the hardships and difficulties of the spiritual life. He would listen to it no more.

Henceforward, he would go where God led, no matter how great the sacrifice, should Henry make the offer....

60

But still within him something cowered and whined with fear and would not be quieted.

The winter passed uneventfully except for the difficulties with young Henry whenever his father came to see him. Seemingly, he had transferred all his affections to Thomas who was embarrassed by the child's insistence on his presence during the King's visits. Henry was impatient with his self-willed son and annoyed to see no marked improvement in his behaviour, and Thomas found it impossible to tell him that the boy was as happy and amiable as he might wish at any other time.

The King's visits usually ended in a beating for young Henry so that finally he greeted his father only with sulky looks and unwilling service. 'For it is not right that I should serve him thus,' he confided to Thomas. 'I am a king's son and he only the son of a count.'

'Who told you that?' asked the Chancellor. 'I do not believe you thought of it yourself.'

'The Queen, my mother, told me. But it is true, is it not?'

Thomas said somewhat grimly, 'Do you remember that if your mother is a Queen, your father's is an Empress. And fathers shall have dominion over sons. Do you not think our lord the King knows what is best for his heir?'

He took the child upon his knee, telling him of the love his father bore him and likening it to the love of God who will try hardest those He loves the most. As precious metal is smelted out of ore, he said, so our better qualities are brought forth only out of tribulation. But young Henry had seen the first fly which had awakened from its winter hibernation, and would not listen. He sprang down and danced about the chamber, smiting at it in its erratic passage with his cap, and Thomas finally gave up.

In spite of his undoubted charm, there was a certain shallowness in the child and he lacked the application necessary to succeed at his lessons. It was not so much that

61

he could not see, Thomas concluded, as that he would not. He worried over his responsibilities to the boy, remembering his heritage of an ungovernable temper. The distress of the last scene between the King and his son remained with him, and he chewed his lip as he recalled young Henry's defiant face after he had been dragged screaming from Thomas's skirts where he had taken refuge.

Afterwards, when Henry had expressed his bewilderment to him, he had been as much at a loss himself to account for the child's attitude. He had fallen back on platitudes, knowing the King's impatience with them as outworn, until Henry had begun to blame the Queen. Had he been right? Young Henry's remark had left a taint in Thomas's mouth he could in no way dispel.

And yet it seemed in the natural order that children should think their guardians opposed to them, never realising that the blow which seems aimed at themselves is in reality directed at Satan behind their shoulder. God, too, just and loving beyond any natural father, is resented when He thwarts the petty, human will.

It struck him forcibly – the similarity between young Henry and himself. He bore a grudge for his Heavenly Father as young Henry for the King; he had offered himself churlishly and with an ill grace, believing himself the sacrifice, and his sullen heart still chewed the bitter cud of deprivation. He stood appalled. 'Mother of God,' he whispered, 'help me now.'

And gradually, as he stood there, quietness stole over him. This human mind is my worst enemy, he thought, that plans and calculates and never will be still; it talks too loud for me to hear Thee. But then, You know, O Lord, for You were human too. Into the silence he had commanded a concept flowed and formed, wavered and settled – Godhead imprisoned by Its own choice in flesh, Purity shrouded in purulence, Eternity trapped in time, the uttermost of giving

given freely. . . . Something in him shrank away and tried
to hide its eyes but he caught at it and made it look upon
the face of anguish.

Humbled and shamed, he could not understand why God
should forgive him but he knew that it was so. By some
means, he had touched the hem of Christ's garment. He felt
his heart at peace then but that was because he had forgotten the King and his son and thought only of himself
and God.

May–June 1162
This day had begun as fair as every day in the preceding
week of scorching weather but about noon the sunlight had
taken on a brassy quality and everything hung limp and
gasping in the heat. A haze, first grey, then coppery, dulled
the sky.

Thomas the Chancellor found the King in the great hall
of Falaise Castle; it was crowded but the King drew him
aside and they went up upon the dais where they might talk
privately together.

'All's made ready, then, for embarkation?' Henry said,
tapping his leg with a cane he carried. He was dressed very
fine today in royal scarlet but there was a faint shine of
perspiration all over his face and his clothes looked as if
they had been flung on anyhow. Recently, his thinning hair
had been cropped very short for fear of baldness, and the
style was unflattering. Thomas noted the bags under his
eyes with a faint sense of shock. '*Tempora labuntur. . . .*' he
thought.

Henry was saying – 'I have not told you all, Tom.
There's another reason for your journey into England—'
He seemed to hesitate an instant as though searching for
words. Then he said, 'It's my will that you should be Archbishop of Canterbury.'

Thomas's eyes fell. It had come, then. No invitation, and

it appeared, no option. 'It is my will—' Yet he could refuse. Instead, he temporised.

'How religious and holy a man this is that you wish to appoint to that holy see over so famous and saintly a congregation of monks!' He recognised with horror the light, chaffing quality of his tone and knew that Henry would not take him seriously. He continued with a kind of hurried desperation: 'I fear that if God will permit it, you would turn against me, and the love that is between us would turn to hatred. You would demand things I could not agree to and jealous men would find plenty of opportunity to stir up trouble between us—' He had rehearsed these words too often, he realised, they were as empty of meaning as any cliche.

Henry smiled indulgently. 'Be not so foolish – come now, you do not mean that? This is a thing I have held in my heart for months—' He stopped and frowned, then his face lightened. 'It is not you talking, Tom,' he said. 'That's the honest fellow, my Chancellor and adviser, who must needs point out the snags to everything that I desire—'

There was a silence then while Thomas stood hangdog and Henry bit his thumb and watched him. 'No hurry for your answer,' he said genially at last. 'Think on it.'

When Thomas had gone, the King sent hurriedly for the Cardinal-Legate, Henry of Pisa. He, who had the task of watching events at Henry's court on behalf of Pope Alexander, would know all the good Christian reasons which would sway Thomas to acceptance, and he would do anything Henry asked in return for continued recognition of his master. The Anti-Pope, Victor, still threatened Alexander's security. Henry knew that all truly good men were reluctant to accept high office in the Church but the Cardinal would show Thomas where his duty lay. Once that was accomplished, his plan would go forward, he would have his insurance against a quarrel with the Church.

64

For that was what he feared; he sensed the growth of ecclesiastical power and knew that he must, somehow, curb it. He was the anointed king of all the English, clerical as well as lay, and all should acknowledge him their temporal lord. Doctrinal matters were no concern of his; on them men might appeal to the Pope as often as they pleased but the Church should not play politics within his kingdom. Tom would know how to differentiate. He did not give a second thought to his Chancellor's reaction to his announcement; he had dismissed the shallow pretexts as soon as they were uttered.

Thomas did not leave the castle; he went out of the hall and up the spiral stair of the keep to a platform by an arrow slit in the thick wall and stared out, leaning his forehead against the stone which was cool and clammy, even on such a stifling day as this. Intermittent gusts of wind blew in, ruffling his hair without cooling him. A strange, unreal light lay over the landscape behind Falaise. The tops of the crowding trees lashed suddenly and then fell quiet. Distant thunder prowled around the arches of the sky. He thought, 'Henry would contend even against God. But I will not. Until I know. . . .'

After a moment of breathless hush the rain began, first a few large splats and then an opaque sheet of shining grey so that all the runnels of the keep belched solid cylinders of water to the earth far below. Thunder rolled and reverberated overhead, then crashed continuously in mighty hammer blows as though Heaven itself had mounted an attack upon Falaise.

There was a tremendous crack directly overhead, a simultaneous dazzling flash and the rumble of falling masonry nearby. Thomas sprang back, the clangour of a thousand brazen-tongued bells echoing in his skull. Blinded by the lightning stroke, he moved uncertainly forward towards the sound of men's voices. The keep had been struck somewhere.

65

Still he could see nothing and he put his hands over his eyes, leaning on the wall. Then someone took his arm and he was hustled towards the stair while the storm raged on around them.

When it was over and the first fitful rays of sunshine brought back colour to a drenched and dripping world, Thomas knew he had his sign from God. As St Paul had been blinded that the eye of his soul might see, so had he. The wonder and the glory of it rose in him and filled him utterly.

Later, when the sun set in a bravery of golden light and towering purple clouds, he sat through a long and reasoned lecture from Henry of Pisa without hearing a word of it. 'I am to be Archbishop,' he thought, and 'God will guide me since it is His will' – and he pondered on great Augustine in whose footsteps he would follow. He, too, had cleaved to worldly things until he had put himself into God's hand – and God had taken that vile sinner and made of him a saint.

Gilbert Foliot was staying in the village of Stepney when the news was brought to him that Thomas the Chancellor had been elected by the Canterbury monks – 'though not without great travail of soul and conscience,' his informant, who was in the service of Richard de Luci, told him. (For it was the Justiciar whom the King had charged with the task of seeing that his beloved friend became Archbishop, and to that end, he, his brother Walter, Abbot of Battle, and three other bishops had travelled to Canterbury to coerce the monks to the King's will.)

'Persuade, persuade!' muttered Gilbert with some impatience; he refused point-blank to believe it possible to coerce a religious.

'Well, persuade, then, and enough difficulty they had; I was there and saw it all. My master, the Justiciar, after telling the monks that the King granted them full freedom of election provided they elected a man worthy of the office and equal to the burdens—'

'*Ut personam tanto oneri et honor eligatis,*' interjected Gilbert with a sneer.

'—went on to tell them that it behoved them to choose one under whose protection they might rejoice! For, he said, if the King and the Archbishop are linked in affection and friendship, the tranquillity of the Church is sure.'

Gilbert scowled. 'Cajolery, at least!'

His informant puffed with feigned indignation; he knew that the Bishop of Hereford liked to think his agents served him for loyalty to his principles, not silver. 'They were not gulled, you may believe me. They would have it in the open by pretending not to know to whom my master was referring. The older monks asked my master for advice on the King's wishes, saying everything depended upon that, and in the end the bishops were compelled to identify the King's candidate. Then they said that they were puzzled by his choice for the one he favours does not wear the habit of religion.'

'But they elected him. . . .'

'Many protested that such a worldly man should be permitted to lord it over them. But they were shouted down by others who said his virtues and graces shone bright enough for him to be the old Archbishop's choice.'

Gilbert jumped as if he had been stung. 'Did they say that? He is not even a priest!'

'Aye, some did, and others denied it. But it was all smoothed down and the bishops swore he was elected canonically and harmoniously.'

'Not unanimously?'

'Nay, that they could not say. They have appointed a day for the Prior and the monks to meet in London with all the bishops and abbots of the realm that the formalities of election may be completed.'

Gilbert nodded vigorously and rose to his feet. 'I thank you for bringing me this information. When we all meet in London – then we shall see. I shall assuredly raise my voice in dissent for this is not God's work afoot.' He laid his hand on the head of the great wolf hound lying by his chair and the dog flopped out a long, purplish tongue and turned its head to watch its master.

When Richard de Luci's man knelt to kiss the Bishop's ring, the dog made a low, grumbling noise deep in its throat and he saw its black lip wrinkle back. He sprang up rather too quickly and caught the faint smile that played on Gilbert's mouth, but when the Bishop told him where to find his Treasurer, his voice was as urbane as ever.

On Wednesday, the twenty-third day of May, a great company, learned and unlearned, gathered at Westminster Hall, so many that they overflowed into the streets and fields nearby. Thomas waited outside with a small coterie of his closest friends where he could watch the thronging crowds. The day was dry and warm, but grey and overcast with a still, humid air; people sat about and fanned themselves and all the time there was a constant coming and going from the Hall as those who tired of the arguments came out for food or fresh air, and those who were without forced their way in to listen.

Gilbert Foliot was as good as his word; he alone among the bishops made plain his opposition to the King's candidate. They all stared at him as the tenor of his speech became obvious, and he saw how the Canterbury monks whispered among themselves.

'Through many years the Chancellor has been a persecutor of the Church,' cried Gilbert, 'and has laid upon her burdens which she should not be asked to bear. Shall a son so despoil his mother?' He listed all the exactions which the Chancellor had demanded. 'These were shrewd blows, and we had no redress. But shall we choose such a one to be Primate of England?'

He was in fine, ringing voice today and he felt them wavering. He pushed hard at the advantage. 'Nor is it seemly that so important an election should be hurried through in the absence of the King. Let us agree to postpone the matter until the King be here!'

Bishop Hilary of Chichester glanced sideways at Henry of Pisa and raised his eyebrows. He had never forgotten his defeat in the case of Battle Abbey and this time he was numbered firmly and safely with the royal faction. When he stood up, he spoke calmly but severely as to a foolish child who has misunderstood the argument. 'The King has made his position entirely clear. The Chancellor is his chosen candidate.' He looked at the assembled faces, noting the doubtful expression worn by many. 'You are, of course, at liberty to advise him that you think he is mistook—'

An old abbot struggled to his feet. 'It has ever been customary for members of the regular clergy to be chosen as archbishops—'

Several more joined in, grumbling amongst themselves. Gilbert tried to speak again but the hubbub was growing in intensity, every man stating his own opinion and countering that of his neighbour. Through it all, the Abbot, who was evidently very deaf, harped on and on – 'since the days of Augustine' – 'secular status' – 'ever been the custom of this realm'.

Hilary banged violently on the board. He glared at the abbots in the sudden silence and informed them cuttingly that they were like unto the Pharisees who would grant goodness to none unless they were of the same cut as themselves.

They subsided at that but continued to murmur to one another at intervals as Gilbert spoke again. But he knew now it was useless; Hilary's remark about advising the King he was mistaken had seen to that. They were all sheep,

Gilbert thought contemptuously, forgetting that he, as a shepherd, should think kindly of the creatures.

He had run himself down anyway by the time the Cardinal-Legate and Bishop Henry of Winchester took a hand, and they made it as easy for him as they could to withdraw his objections. He gave a brief nod at last in token of agreement. 'I have discharged my conscience and am satisfied,' he told himself, but his face expressed anything but Christian submission.

They called Thomas into the hall to hear the outcome from the lips of Bishop Henry. He was the brother of King Stephen and an old man now, past sixty. The little hair he had around his tonsure was white as snow, but he held himself straight and there was that in his hard unflinching stare made men feel no surprise when they remembered the violent dealings of his youth. But there was no violence in him now, the priest had swallowed the man, and he looked kindly on Thomas as he said, 'By Almighty God's providence and our common consent, you are chosen Archbishop of the highest episcopal see in all England, for the glory of the Holy Trinity, for the governance of the Church and for the good of the people. In God's name, we now ask for your assent.'

Thomas's eyes fell upon young Henry who sat there wearing his new crown and a look of acute boredom. He wondered for an instant what the child made of all this, then turned to Bishop Henry with his answer. He had gone over it again and again but now the moment was upon him his throat was full so that his voice came out low and husky as he referred to his own unworthiness, but it strengthened a little when he spoke of the burdens he must bear and of the fact that he had not been released from his secular obligations.

Bishop Henry addressed the young King (for so he was although as yet uncrowned, having been accepted by the magnates soon after coming into England). 'The lord Chancellor, our Archbishop-elect,' he said, 'has now for a long time held the highest place in the household of the King your father, and in the whole realm, and has had the Kingdom in his charge, nor has anything been done in it during his time except by his authority. We ask, therefore, that he be handed over to the Church of God and to us, free and absolved of all services and connections to the Court, and from all suits, accusations and other charges, and that from this hour and henceforth he may be emancipated and unencumbered, freely able to perform the duties of God. For we know that the King your father has delegated his authority to you in this matter and that he will gladly ratify your decision.'

Young Henry jumped as if someone had poked him below eye level and ceased to fidget. 'Yea,' he said loudly, 'let it be so,' and he wriggled and screwed up his mouth lest he should laugh for he had been warned that he would be well beaten if he did.

Bishop Henry beckoned Thomas nearer. 'Sweet son, do not grieve,' he said in a lower tone. 'Hereafter, you will mend whatever you have broken. Remember how Paul opposed the Church of God and later upheld her most of all and glorified her at last with his blood.'

A little chill ran over Thomas at the words; he was silent because he thought it passing strange that the old Bishop should have cited Paul's example to him, who had done that once already for himself. He did not realise it then, but because of Bishop Henry's analogy, the promise of a martyr's crown became linked in his mind with the great precedent he had thought of during the storm at Falaise.

He roused himself and answered quietly, 'God's hidden will and yours seem alike in this matter. I assent, although in great fear.'

* * *

Afterwards, when he looked back upon that time, it seemed to Thomas that he had been a mere onlooker at the proceedings that shaped his destiny. The period between the election at Westminster and his consecration in Canterbury had a dreamlike quality without substance, his awareness of God so sharpened that events around him were reflections rather than reality. He knew, though, that the tide which carried him was the breath of God and he rode it as a child will ride his father's shoulder, safe, comfortable, secure.

He heard of the quarrel that arose over who should consecrate the new Archbishop without concern, thinking it all one to him who had the honour since the Bishop of London, whose prerogative it was, was dead. That was until he learnt that Archbishop Roger of York was claiming the privilege.

'Nay!' he said sharply to Herbert of Bosham who brought the news. 'Nay, that sits not well with me at all!'

Herbert's face brightened; he scented some old feud here and perhaps the makings of trouble. Polemic was the breath of life to him. He had watched and approved Thomas the Chancellor from a distance for years and had been overjoyed at his election, but since his appointment as Master in the study of Holy Writ to the Archbishop-elect, he had found it hard to recognise the same man in him. Now he heard the clash of swords in Thomas's voice. It cheered him.

Thomas heard it too, and looked up under his hand at the big fair Englishman who would advise him in the discharge of his archiepiscopal duties. But Herbert's face expressed only a pleasure that was almost conspiratorial as he said, 'Nay, that we cannot have – unless York will profess obedience to Canterbury.'

Thomas smiled faintly. That this was improbable to the point of absurdity both knew. Thomas recognised Herbert's instant approval of his rejection of Roger of York and thought it due to the rivalry between the two sees; Herbert saw deeper and knew kinship when he met it. He had not mistook his man after all. He would tell Alexander Llewellyn, that fiery Welshman who was Cross Bearer to the Archbishop, that here was a lord they could serve with pride. He exerted himself in the most artful manner possible to tell Thomas how Roger of York might best be put out of countenance.

Only William Fitzstephen, watching with a jealous eye, brooded darkly upon the influence so contentious and imperious a character might have upon his beloved master, and he said nothing.

So Archbishop Roger's impertinent claim was quashed by Herbert's simple stratagem and Thomas was satisfied when it was announced that the choice had fallen upon Henry of Winchester – not, he told himself, that he had been motivated by personal dislike of the man who had made his life miserable twenty years before, but that it would be a happier augury for his ministry that he should be consecrated by one whom he respected – and since that last scandal, he could no longer doubt that Roger was a paederast. But he was not going to allow that deplorable business to disturb him at this time, and mentally washing his hands of the Archbishop of York, he turned his thoughts firmly towards his forthcoming ordination by the worthy old Bishop of Rochester.

He was musing contentedly upon the agreeable outcome of it all as he rode a little apart from the others on the journey to Canterbury, and running over in his mind the curious dream he had had the previous night– so vivid a dream that it might almost be called a vision. An old and venerable man had stood beside him and had counted into his hand ten talents; in the dream he had thought it was Theobald but he knew now it was not. It was some saint of olden time, mayhap, but whoever it was, the meaning of the dream was very clear to him. It was a heavenly injunction to follow the parable and use his talents in the service of the Lord.

Beset by a sudden impulse, he put his horse forward to come alongside Herbert. 'I had a vision last night,' he said, and recounted to him the dream. Herbert nodded with the air of one who has had his own opinion confirmed but offered no comment; after a while Thomas glanced at his strong, handsome profile and said slowly, 'Hereafter, Herbert, I desire you to tell me candidly but in secret what others are saying of me – and if you see anything in me that you regard as a fault, feel free to tell me. I know that from now on people will say behind my back what they dare not to my face, and I would have one truthful friend who will not permit me to go wrong for want of warning. It is dangerous to those in power if men fear to tell them the truth. I have seen the effect it can have.' He was thinking of Henry and of how different he was now from the cheerful boy he had once known; how much of the change had been due to his sycophantic courtiers?

Herbert nodded again; the onus which the Archbishop-elect was placing on his shoulders did not worry him; he thought Thomas fortunate to have at his right hand a man such as himself, capable of interpreting the motives of others and ready, even zealous, in exhortation. And he adjudged Thomas a clever man for his instant recognition of his, Herbert's, true worth. He was well content as they jogged at an easy pace over the ancient stones of Watling Street, going gingerly where the paving was cracked and subsided, or taking to the verge where ladies' slipper and red clover hid among the grasses. Overhead, too high to see, he could hear larks singing in a racing wind which drove light clouds swiftly along before it, but below, where they were, was no more than a gentle breeze.

Thomas rode in silence after that but when they came near Canterbury and the groups of eager watchers thickened

74

into crowds, waving and welcoming their new Archbishop, Herbert saw him put his hand up to his cheek to wipe it. He felt his own eyes moisten. 'The common folk love him for that he's English like themselves,' he thought, 'and he'll not dissemble that his heart's touched by their greeting. He's a good man and humble. I must watch to see that none take advantage of him – that gentleness turn not to weakness.'

It was raining when Thomas rose before dawn on the Octave of Pentecost, the day set for his consecration. Yesterday he had been ordained; when today's sun set, he would be Archbishop of Canterbury and Primate of England. And still it seemed incredible.

But he was not nervous. Even though the high and mighty of the realm would be there to watch – all except Henry and a few of his chief officers who remained in Normandy – he had no real qualms. Young Henry would be there in his father's stead, Richard de Luci, John of Salisbury, William Fitzstephen, Herbert of Bosham – all the old familiar faces, praying for him, wishing him well. And the great magnates, and many bishops and abbots.

When he came in the midst of a great procession to Christ Church, the sun was out and the bells shouted their exultation to a sky of radiant blue. Waiting to enter, he saw the Great Tower reflected in a long puddle, perfect and entire; then the surface of the water trembled as a horse trod near and it shivered into golden shards.

Throughout the long ceremony he did not think of anything; he kept his mind empty of all but the thought of Christ crucified that the grace of God might flow into him unimpeded. From the corner of his eye he could see the eight steps leading up to the Patriarchal Chair, carved from a single block of stone. Before him was the altar, a massive beam above it carrying images of Christ, of St Dunstan and

75

St Alphege, all enamelled in brilliant colours, sanguine, blue, grass green, and seven chests of relics, shining with silver and opulent with gold. To the east of the altar were two wooden columns ornamented with plates of precious metal, and between them a gilded cross hung round with glittering crystals which danced and swayed, sending back sudden flashes of colour. He saw these things and did not see them.

When the age-old solemnity was over, he ascended to the Patriarchal Chair to speak to the eager, sweating, silent host crammed within the cathedral and to tell them that henceforth this day would be held a festival in England in honour of the Holy Trinity. They cheered him, then, knowing they had a true Archbishop for the naming of a new feast day indicates a man who will live the rituals of the Church, not merely conform to them.

The Solemn Mass began in the Chapel of the Blessed Trinity; Thomas's first Mass as Archbishop. He remained upon his throne, mitred and vested in cloth of gold, until the time should come for him to consecrate the holy elements.

'*Introibo ad altare Dei*,' quavered Henry of Winchester, and the deep, thrilling chanting of the monks echoed him with the assurance that God gave joy to their youth.

'*Confiteor Deo Omnipotenti*,' sang Bishop Henry in his cracked, old voice, and Thomas bowed his head and smote his breast – '*Mea culpa, mea culpa, mea maxima culpa*' – affirming the resolve he had made on his Ordination Day to be a new man henceforward. Above the transept the great organ pealed and the voices of the choirboys rang in the vault like the voices of archangels, aspiring ever higher, pure, blissful, epicene.

To the eyes of most of the onlookers Thomas was haloed in glory, no less distant and sumptuous than the gilded cherubim above the Altar of the Holy Cross. But a taste as bitter as gall lay on the tongue of Gilbert Foliot as he watched him descend the steps, and under cover of the rustle as the congregation fell to its knees, he muttered to his neighbour, 'The King has worked a miracle! Out of a secular man and a soldier, he has made an Archbishop.'

Archbishop Thomas was no longer aware of the congregation. '*Lavabo inter innocentes manus meas,*' he murmured. 'I will wash my hands among the innocent and I will encompass Thine altar, O Lord, that I may hear the voice of praise and tell of all Thy wondrous works. O Lord, I have loved the beauty of Thy house and the place where Thy glory dwelleth. Take not away my soul, O God, with the wicked nor my life with bloody men, in whose hands are iniquities; their right hand is filled with gifts. But as for me, I have walked in my innocence: redeem me and be merciful unto me. My foot hath stood in the right way; in the churches I will bless Thee, O Lord.'

Slow and deliberate his recital of the prayers, graceful his gestures as he moved, bowing, kissing the altar stone, so that Gilbert shuffled, watching him askance. 'Hypocrite!' he thought – and – 'This the exhibitionist who bled the Church to pay for his aspirations to knighthood! What are we come to?' At God, he directed a fierce, tormented plea but to what end he did not know, other than that he might witness no more such posturings.

The sacring bells tinkled, clear and sweet, heralding Christ's coming. Thomas bowed lower, caught fast by transcendental mystery, and whispered the sacred words that only He might hear. '*Hoc est enim Corpus Meum.*'

He knelt upon one knee, his eyes fixed upon That between his hands, infinite, omnipresent God. The silence was suffused with light, radiant, ineffable, an eternity of bliss compressed to a point, a flood of love so vast and all-encompassing that it might burst the heart. Tender and slow, he lifted high the white translucent Wafer that men

77

might see Him and adore.

Three times the great bell sang its sonorous message to the sunlit countryside – the message that God was brought to earth again to be sacrificed anew for men.

There were few in England that day who found such a thing incredible though not all of the faithful were happy thereby. Certainly Gilbert Foliot was not.

But far away in France Henry was content. He had heard Mass secure in the knowledge that his Chancellor was now his Archbishop also. Nothing could go wrong now, with Tom as ruler of the Church and their two minds as one.

He smiled to himself and Eleanor, watching him, saw that smile. She misinterpreted it. Since Princess Eleanor's birth, nine months ago, his visits to her chamber had been infrequent. That meant he had other women, or perhaps one other woman of whom she knew nothing. Rage filled her. 'Damn you!' she thought. 'Oh, damn you, damn you! If I could only find some way to make you suffer. . . .'

He saw her eye upon him and nodded to her. 'I'm well pleased with this day's work,' he said, and knew with sudden surprise that it went deeper than that. Something in him had healed, he was at ease.

He let himself think of Hikenai again. She had been part of his youth and that was over. He could not expect to know again that sweet and painful joy. . . . Nor did he wish to.

There was always Tom – Tom who would keep faith as no woman could. All the rest of his days lay before him, Tom at his side, Eleanor in the background (the exciting, mysterious shapes of unknown women beckoned on the borders of his consciousness) his sons growing to manhood. Everything had fallen to him, after all. Why should he not be content?

IV

August 1162

T HOMAS OF LONDON, Chancellor of England and Archbishop of Canterbury, smiled upon young Henry as the King's son served him at table. The boy was improving in manners and graces daily; he had remembered to bring Thomas's fennel water in a hanap that the guests might not be embarrassed at drinking wine while their host abstained. Neither did he need to be reminded to place only the smallest portion of the festal meats before his master who now dined chiefly upon bread. Thomas commended him with a nod before turning his attention once more to Alexander Llewellyn's reading from the Scriptures.

On the dais where he sat with his clerks to his right and a group of monks on his left, he was able to concentrate on the Crossbearer's fluent Latin, for the knights dined at a table far enough removed that they might not be bored by a language they did not understand and where their noisy conversation would not interrupt the more sober pleasures of the clerics.

But if you ignored the trappings of religion at the High Table and the long black cappa and white surplice he wore, there seemed little different in Thomas's hall. Dinner was served with the same splendour as before, the wines as fine, the food as rich and carefully prepared; only now, as was customary in the household of an Archbishop of Canterbury, the second sons of noble houses ran to and fro as pages. The changes that had come about were unseen; here, at any rate.

Yet the change in Thomas's life was very great. No longer did he rise early to hunt or to practise sword-play; now he rose in pre-dawn darkness to his Office and to the study of Holy Writ with Herbert of Bosham. Every day in the early morning he washed the filthy feet of thirteen of Christ's poor, fed them and sent them on their way with a present of four silver pennies each, asking only that they pray for him. So far he had managed to keep this charity secret but word had spread among the beggars; every day more presented themselves. When they began to fight for the privilege – as they would, Thomas knew – it would not be the same. It would degenerate into another meaningless ceremony with the recipients of his bounty carefully chosen by other men.... But as long as he could, he would do good by stealth.

Linked to the fear of his personal unworthiness for his high office was the fear of spiritual pride. It was this which made him refuse to say Mass daily, reserving that holy and transcendent rite for the greatest feasts. Only a very few of his closest associates knew of his use of the discipline on bare shoulders, and none but God of the hair shirt which was a constant irritation to his scourged back.

Even without the knowledge of these things, it seemed to men of goodwill that Thomas of London would be a true shepherd to his flock. He lived an orderly and regular life in the public eye, neglecting nothing that should be done. He dispensed justice with the utmost fairness, and moreover, he dispensed it free, refusing the gifts and fees which all lords accepted as a matter of course.

Deep in himself Thomas was happy but he would not

yet admit that part of that happiness was a great relief at being no more a member of the King's disorganised entourage, no longer dependent on his sudden whims and changes of mind. That feeling, though, had been at the back of his decision to resign the Chancellorship forthwith. Master Ernulf had left for Normandy a week ago bearing the Great Seal, and the Archbishop was his own man at last.

Alexander Llewellyn had finished his reading, and Thomas glanced along the table towards John of Salisbury and Lombard of Piacenza. These two, with his other old friend, John Belmeis, the Treasurer of York, had but today returned from Montpellier whither they had journeyed to fetch Thomas's pallium from the Pope, and he had much to tell them of his plans to recover some of Canterbury's alienated property. Always, when a see lay vacant more than a month or two, the tenants of its lands tried to insist that they held of the King, not the Church, and Canterbury had been no exception.

Thomas was not the man to suffer injustices quietly and he was hotter in pursuit of Church rights than ever he had been of the King's. He had had no difficulty in seizing back land from lesser men with the aid of his knights, but he was meeting stubborn resistance from the Earl of Clare who had refused point-blank to do him homage for Tonbridge. He would ask his friends' advice when dinner was over.

But when he did, John of Salisbury at least, seemed oddly dubious and finally reminded Thomas that the earls of Clare had held Tonbridge without homage since the reign of Stephen, and that Theobald had acquiesced by remaining silent.

Thomas was indignant. 'Right is right,' he said, 'and Theobald was an old man and ill for many years. Shall I sit by and see man rob God?'

'If you argue over Tonbridge, you must claim Rochester, Saltwood and Hythe as well, and I fear they are lost by default.'

'I shall claim them all,' said Thomas firmly. 'They are all the property of Canterbury. And that reminds me – I have appointed a young clerk named Laurence as Vicar of Eynsford, and William de Ros, lord of that place, has refused him entry. Not only refused him but violently ejected him! He, it seems, had presented his own clerk and insists he has the right of advowson.'

John pursed his lips and looked at Lombard who put his old, veined hand on Thomas's and asked him, smiling faintly, 'Is he not as good a man as your Laurence, then?'

'Why, as to that, I know not. He may be or he may not—'

'Discover that if you may. And if he be as good a man, leave well alone.'

'But if I do, William de Ros will have the annates – a whole year's revenue of Eynsford church!'

Lombard peered at Thomas through his cataract-veiled old eyes. 'Aye – silver!' he said. 'That's what the great lords squabble over. Shall an Archbishop quarrel over money, too, or shall he care for his flock?'

'That money is Canterbury's – and therefore God's, said Thomas obstinately.

'And does God care more for money than for the souls of Eynsford? Nay, if Eynsford's lord's clerk be a good and holy man, let be! Your Laurence can be found another place.'

Thomas frowned. This was not the kind of advice he had wanted. But of course, Lombard of Piacenza was an old man – such as he would always take the path of least resistance. . . .

'I shall bear your words in mind,' he said with a mendacity he described to himself as tact, and then he heard the latch rattle as Herbert of Bosham entered and they all fell to discussing the portion of Scripture Alexander had read earlier.

Thomas had his reasons for dismissing Lombard's words.

82

Once, long ago, fear had kept him silent when he should have spoken and he had betrayed his principles out of cowardice. Never again would he put opportunism before probity. For despite his past weakness, God had chosen him as Archbishop – not Lombard who was gentle, not John who was clever – but Thomas of London who had learnt the hard way to hold fast to truth and justice in the face of all odds. It was a charge not to be lightly undertaken and Thomas did not take it lightly.

What belonged to Canterbury belonged to God, and if he must outface the King himself, he would do it. But – that no accusation of over-zealousness might be levelled against him – he would wait awhile.

So he did not mention the matter again to John when they talked privately before retiring, confining himself to uncontroversial topics. John himself seemed ready enough to indulge in light hearted gossip about the Papal Court, amusing Thomas by pricking through the conceits and self-importance of many of the great men there, though of Pope Alexander he had only kind words to say. When he had told all his news, he said with sudden seriousness, 'And what of you, old friend? Are you happy?' He had his answer in Thomas's expression as he smiled at him.

'So Archbishop Theobald – God rest him – was right? But you must surely miss the company of the King – or have you found some other who can take his place?'

Thomas shook his head. 'None will ever take his place. But it was true what Prior Aschetinus told me – if you will but give freely to God, He will return an hundred fold. For me it has been all gain. I have never been happier.'

'And are the men you now find yourself among congenial to you? What of Alexander Llewellyn?'

Thomas grinned. 'Now he does remind me somewhat of the King! All froth and fury one moment and loving kindness the next – but that's the Welsh for you!'

83

'And Herbert of Bosham?'

'Herbert is a true friend,' said Thomas with sincerity. 'He has many fine qualities.'

'Well,' said John with a droll look, 'I would not disagree with that and neither would he! Though he will be the first to tell you that modesty outweighs all his other virtues!'

Thomas burst out laughing. 'When I know them better, I shall ask the others how you sum me up,' he said.

'Ah,' said John, 'will you? You will not get any satisfaction. I have never told them.'

Thomas pulled a face of mock disbelief.

'The calculation gives a different answer every time,' John said.

Master Ernulf had come up with the King at last in his pavilion on the banks of the Loire near Coucy. He had lost a great deal of time chasing Henry from one place to another – as usual the King never arrived where he was expected – and it was only at his much-publicised meeting place with King Louis and the Pope that Master Ernulf had finally run him to earth.

Henry was looking far from pleased. 'Well, by God's eyes!' he snapped. 'Why has the Chancellor returned the Great Seal to me? The Pope agreed that he should keep his office.'

'He feels – he feels the burden of two offices will not enable him to do justice to either.'

'*I* feel that he no longer cares to serve me. Tell him that.'

Master Ernulf looked at his feet.

'Well, get you gone! You have fulfilled your commission, at least.'

Henry turned away abruptly and Master Ernulf dared to sneak a long curious look at his back but it told him no more than that the King's waistline had thickened considerably since the last time he saw him. As he went past the door-keeper he reflected sourly that a messenger might gauge the palatability of the tidings he carried by the rewards offered – and here, apparently, he was not even to be fed. Well, if the King were truly as vexed as he appeared, perchance it were well not to linger. . . . He left the camp within the hour.

Left alone, Henry gave a great sniff and wiped his nose upon his sleeve. Under the petulance he was wounded to the quick by the Chancellor's resignation. What had he ever done to be treated so by Thomas? Had he not raised him from nothing to be the greatest in the land next to himself? Where was gratitude? Where now the deep fondness between them? He felt he had received a slap in the face.

And when he thought back, it was not only Thomas who had disappointed him thus. Eleanor too had treated him with contempt. Neither of them, it seemed, had as deep an affection for him as he had imagined. Only from Hikenai had he received love and compliance to the last, and God had taken her from him. Hallowed by death as she was, he would not remember her betrayal but it lurked beneath, adding to his hurt.

Over the next few days mortification deepened into smouldering wrathfulness which he found difficult to conceal from the Pope when he spoke kindly of England's new Archbishop. Alexander had fled from Rome to Montpellier as the Emperor, intent on placing his own candidate, the Anti-Pope Victor, on the Papal throne, advanced southward through Italy; now he was straining every nerve to enlist the support of both Louis and Henry, and to make a lasting peace between them.

Louis of France hung upon the Holy Father's words and treated him with deference but Henry appeared bored and inattentive so that the Pope soon saw it was England he must woo, were he to survive. And if he must, he would, for Alexander was a diplomat as well as a man of high courage and deep spiritual convictions. His care was the whole

Church, sinners along with saints, and heretics and back-sliders were as much his children as the good and faithful. He trod his difficult path with delicacy and precision, ever aware of the pitfalls on either side, judiciously balancing firmness on matters of principle with toleration of political necessities.

Now, as Louis knelt to kiss the Fisherman's Ring his shrewd dark eyes never left Henry's face, and after Henry in his turn had knelt before him, he raised him up and had him stand beside him, apart from all the others that were there. He spoke softly in his halting French, 'Does anything trouble you, my son?'

Henry was taken aback. He was not entirely at his ease; he suspected that this sophisticated Roman who was Christ's Vicar on earth considered him a rude barbarian and it made him tongue-tied. He was displeased on both counts. He began to mutter an excuse and then abruptly told the Pope of Thomas's resignation.

'Hmmm,' said Alexander, and then with a penetration that disconcerted Henry once again. 'You should not feel this is the *diffidatio* – his renunciation of fealty to you. As Archbishop, he is still one of your tenants-in-chief.'

'He excused himself by cause of overwork' – resentment suddenly spilled over – 'and still he holds many other prefer-ments! He is Archdeacon of Canterbury yet—'

Alexander's voice was soothing. 'Will you that I shall order his resignation of the Archdeaconry?'

Henry looked at him sharply. 'No need for that,' he said, 'in my kingdom! I will so order it.'

Alexander nodded without comment and turned once more to Louis. But when the kings had gone, he sat some while in thought and then called for a scribe with parch-ment and pens. He began to dictate a letter to his old friend, Jocelin de Bohun. Jocelin was Bishop of Salisbury in England.

Ysabel was late in starting for Sutinstocke, indeed Simon Rutele who was to escort her had been stamping up and down for a full half hour while she tried to comfort a tearful Cicely. But nothing could dim the tragedy the child had just witnessed, and with the evidence lying on the mounting block in the shape of a dozen pigeons with their necks pitifully wrung, she would have none of Ysabel's kindly urgings towards good sense.

'But you know we must eat – and wherefore do you think we keep the doves?' said Ysabel, at once puzzled and distressed.

Cicely wailed that she had asked old Jem what he was at when he put his hand in the dovecote – that she had begged to hold the dove between her hands. She held out her grimy little paws to Ysabel as if in supplication and burst into a fresh storm of weeping. 'He killed it,' she mourned, 'and put it in my hands all dead!'

Suddenly impatient, Ysabel patted the child's shoulder. 'Come now, you will like to eat the pigeon pasty,' she said briskly, 'and I have kept Simon waiting too long already. Run to your mother, there's a good girl.' But she turned her eyes quickly from the misery in the child's face; it struck too near the emptiness that was the reason for her errand.

This was the third time this year that she had gone to Sutinstocke to visit the anchorite in his cell and to petition his prayers that she might bear a son. She went with the baron's permission, even encouragement, for it was his silver that jingled in her purse. In a way, she dreaded these visits for she was more than a little afraid of the anchorite who had been walled in for many years and stank so strongly of holiness that she had to nerve herself to approach the opening through which he communicated with the outside world. She wondered fearfully what he would say this time. When he did give utterance, she could not always follow the thick, throaty speech, and anyway his observations were interspersed with so many astrological references that he might as well have been speaking a foreign tongue.

It was a perfect autumn day with a cool vagrant breeze and a promise of more wind to come in the long feathery mare's tails high in the pale blue sky. But Ysabel's spirits sank a little as they entered the silent, forbidding woods; among the green-stained trees was a smell of damp and mildew, and noisome fungi grew about the bases of their trunks. Here in the dusky hush, she thought of old tales, half-believed. As they came out, though, and approached Sutinstocke, the prospect brightened; a group of spreading elms had carpeted the ground with clear yellow and a few of its deep crimson leaves still clung to a small dogwood bush.

They saw the anchorite's boy sitting over a small crackling fire; he rose as he saw them coming, his sharp, sly face eager. What a life for a boy, thought Ysabel, the earlier reminder of the hapless sorrows of childhood still with her. To live here lonely, running errands for the holy man – few come this way. . . . She smiled at him with a rare sweetness, uncaring for once of the hideous gap in her mouth.

'To see the anchorite, lady?' he asked, extending a filthy palm. She dropped a penny in it and he ran before her to the cell built up against the side of Sutinstocke church. As she came forward to kneel by the opening, he backed away to where Simon waited.

She bowed her head as in the confessional and whispered, 'The lady of Sir Robert Fitzurse, that is barren, is come to crave your prayers that she may bear a child.' There was no reply and she peered into the gloom within. She saw a movement, and then a pair of eyes watching her, brown eyes ringed with the filmy blue of age. She untied her purse with fingers that trembled and withdrew the heavy, shining coins, mint-fresh from Bristol so that there was no fear of

88

their being clipped. They fell into the cup inside the cell with a sweet tinkle.

'The lady of Fitzure's of Williton?'

'Of Fitzurse's son. Baseborn son,' she said with difficulty.

The old eyes watched her, then became vacant. He muttered something under his breath and she strained to hear but could make nothing of it. He began to cough chokingly and she heard him spitting on the floor. When he spoke again, his voice was clearer. 'Robert Fitzurse shall have heirs,' he said. 'His heirs shall have Williton and more besides—' Her heart gave a great jump. He was prophesying, as she had heard he sometimes did when the Holy Spirit moved him. She lost the last of what he said in her excitement. When she finally raised her shining face, she saw him clearly in the shaft of sunlight that had penetrated the cell, clearly enough to see the lice thick in his matted beard, the sores on his face, and the hand which looked like the scaly, yellow claw of a dead chicken raised in benediction.

'Pray for me,' he said.

She felt that her face must show her awed incomprehension. It was not until she returned home that she began to wonder why he had gazed at her with such compassion.

January – February 1163

After being delayed more than a month by contrary winds, it was the last week in January before Henry and Eleanor finally sailed for England from Cherbourg. Throughout the autumn and early winter the King's curiosity had been whetted by the stories brought by a constant stream of messengers and tale-bearers from across the Channel; now his impatience to see Thomas was at fever pitch. 'Thomas the Archbishop was a different man from Thomas the Chancellor' was the recurring theme. Henry found that hard to credit.

Nonetheless, there was food for thought in many of the

tales that reached his ears. His new Archbishop had evidently been laying about him with a heavy hand, recouping the losses suffered by Canterbury during the vacancy. Well, he could hardly quarrel with that seeing he had granted permission for Thomas to do so; but it was beginning to appear that he was using the full weight of the Church's displeasure in matters that scarcely merited such means. Some of the men who had come to appeal to him had actually been frightened.

That did trouble Henry who had certainly not intended to set up a rival when he installed his greatest friend as Primate. Yet although he filed it away at the back of his mind on the debit side along with uncalled for resignation, he was not really worried. Thomas had said that men would try to stir up discord between them and undoubtedly he had enemies. Henry reserved judgment until they met again.

There were no worries in Thomas's heart as he waited in Southampton for the King to come ashore. It was a clear, cold day so that *Esnecca* was sighted in good time for the welcoming party to get down to the quay. Thomas stood between young Henry and Herbert of Bosham with the hood of his fur-lined cloak pulled up against the icy wind. The sea glittered and sparkled; far out white horses were racing so that all the little ships bobbed and dipped, coming one by one past the green cushion of the Isle of Wight and safe to land.

Thomas felt young Henry's hand slide confidently into his as the King appeared but it was to his mother and his brothers that the child ran the moment he saw them, leaving Thomas and Henry face to face. There was a fractional pause before Thomas fell on one knee and kissed Henry's outstretched hand so that Herbert, stepping back quickly, wondered if the formality were usual between them. Others, he saw, were watching their greeting with interest. But King and Archbishop kissed as the fondest of friends and walked together with linked arms, talking and laughing, interrupting each other often and behaving as those who have been unwillingly separated always do when reunited. Herbert could see the amity between them and gave a faint superior smile in the direction of those who had, as he knew, been hoping for something very different.

At dinner that night Herbert was able to get a long look at the Queen who was, according to some accounts, very beautiful and very free. He could see no evidence of that for she looked mostly at her dish, but he could not deny her beauty. He wondered why the King should look beyond her couch and shook his head sadly, though whether at the depravity or lack of taste he was unsure. He did not think about it very long anyway, for they began serving brawn which diverted his attention to the pleasures of the table; the fare of the monks at Canterbury was exceeding plain now.... He glanced along the board once and saw the Archbishop raise his hand in refusal; Herbert gave one more resigned shake of the head and then applied himself assiduously to the meal.

Henry listened to Thomas's recital of his actions in noncommital silence; it was plain that Thomas did not expect any comment nor feel the need to justify himself. Henry betook himself to bed earlier than usual in a thoughtful frame of mind.

The next day they set out for London, the King and Thomas riding side by side apart from the rest as they had always done, and if Henry found less to say than in the old days, Thomas talked volubly enough not to notice it. He was in the middle of a long dissertation on the *Decretum* of Master Gratian of Bologna which he had recommended Henry to read when he was interrupted.

'I have not received your resignation of the Archdeaconry of Canterbury,' the King said smoothly. 'Doubtless you have overlooked it.'

Taken aback, Thomas eyed him. Henry continued to gaze straight ahead, a small smile playing round his lips. There was a pause, then Thomas said doubtfully, 'If that be your wish. . . .'

'Oh yes,' answered Henry, 'as it must be yours also. Surely to be Archbishop is enough for any man. I would not overburden you.'

Thomas nodded. But somehow, after this ample proof of the King's lack of interest in Master Gratian's works, Thomas's flow of conversation languished, and as others rode nearer to join them, he left the King in their company and fell back a little, filled with a vague unease.

In spite of his expressed wish not to overburden the Archbishop, Henry apparently expected to enjoy his company as frequently as ever, and in the month that followed, Thomas found that Henry's calls upon his time were interfering more and more with his ecclesiastical duties. Worse still were the inroads made into the period he had set aside for his private devotions. Several times the King was kept waiting or even refused, and although he passed off his complaints as jest, Thomas sensed beneath the levity a hidden current of meaning.

He wished fervently that the Queen and the royal children would return from Marlborough – or that Henry would find a new confidant whose time was his own. Once, laughing and only half in earnest, he suggested as much, pointing out that he would not be in so ambivalent a position but for the King's wish and reminding him of his own attempts to dissuade him. The oblique look Henry gave him and the silence which followed bothered him a little until he decided that any regrets the King might have were probably due to natural jealousy. He had always been used to coming first, and it was his nature to take exception to any thwarting of his personal desires.

Thomas decided to humour him until the Queen's return but now, oddly, Henry lessened his demands and news that he was surrounding himself with a new coterie gradually filtered through to the Archbishop's household. It was John of Salisbury who first mentioned it, lightly enough but with a note in his voice that Thomas knew, so that he raised his head immediately from *Policraticus* which they had been reading together.

'There is no reason why the King should not seek new friends,' he said, quick to answer and rather defensive as he laid his finger on his place.

'No, of course not. It is just that their influence may not be quite what we would wish.'

Thomas sighed. He knew that John and the King mutually distrusted one another. 'You cannot expect him to find congenial companions among the grey-beards. And since I have so little time for him now— Anyway,' Thomas threw a faintly surprised look at John, 'what are you worrying about? If there are few saints among the courtiers, there are few men of really evil repute, either. Who is it whose influence you do not like?'

'Roger, Earl of Clare,' said John, 'William de Ros of Eynsford—' He listed more than half a dozen names. Every one of them had been dispossessed or was at present engaged in litigation with the See of Canterbury.

March – April 1163

Determined to make a start on his cherished reforms, Henry called a Council in London early in March. He knew that he must appear to uphold the established order and justify any changes as a revival of old English laws, but he would manage that somehow. Some sort of change in the level of taxation was necessary for the national revenue was declining alarmingly. Most of this regular income was raised by the sheriffs by whatever means they might choose and

93

Henry had long suspected that much of the money they collected never reached his Treasury. The sum they paid yearly into the Exchequer was fixed on their appointment and some had held office since Stephen's reign; their farm (as the amount due from them was known) was far too low for the present financial conditions. Harvests had been good and trade was increasing. Their king intended to have his share of this new prosperity. To that end he ordered the Archbishop of York and Reginald de St Valéry to begin an overhaul of the nation's finances.

At the same time he set in motion an inquiry into the feudal tenure of land. William the Bastard's records were now out of date and Henry wished to know exactly how many knights were owed to him for service. Without that knowledge he could not be sure that his barons were not evading large sums in scutage, and the payment of shield money in lieu of personal service was becoming accepted by an increasing number. The system suited Henry too, because it enabled him to hire mercenaries who, knowing there was no chance of ransom should they be captured, fought like madmen. And he would need mercenaries when he marched against the Welsh in the summer.

The last matter under discussion was the filling of the vacant See of London. Henry half expected some opposition from Thomas to his own choice of Gilbert Foliot, but the Archbishop had acquiesced immediately so it only remained to get the Pope's consent to the translation of the Bishop from one see to another. Henry foresaw no difficulties from that quarter.

He was in cheerful mood, therefore, at the feast for the conclusion of the Council and watched a group of young people near by with an indulgent eye as they ran, screaming and laughing, in some game. Among them was a very pretty girl with long loose hair the colour of dead beech leaves; she shrieked and giggled louder than the rest, flinging back her hair with swift, impatient gestures. He thought, That's for some man's benefit – and wondered idly who he might be. Then as she turned he caught the quick look she shot in his direction, and leaned forward to look closer. But she, seeing she had got his interest, now kept her back towards him so that he could not see her face.

'Who's yon maid?' he asked Reginald de St Valéry who sat at his left hand. 'The one in the blue gown.'

'Her? – that's the Earl of Clare's young sister.'

'Is she married?'

'No. . . . I think not. Roger'll not part with her except to his advantage. I believe the man she should have married died—'

But Henry was not listening; he had turned his head to follow the progress of the blue bliaut about the hall. Now the young ones had formed themselves into a ring; she was on the right. Fractionally she turned, and seeing him looking her way, prattled animatedly to the lad beside her. Reginald put his hand up to his cheek on Henry's side and pursed his full, pale lips as though to hide a smile.

Others had noticed her behaviour too. Gilbert Foliot, on Reginald's other side, eyed her bleakly and muttered under his breath but Reginald ignored it, still secretly watching the King. Eleanor, seated next to the Archbishop, appeared to see nothing; the faint, amused smile on her lips did not alter but she kept her eyelids lowered.

Henry whispered to Reginald, 'Present her to me – and,' he added hastily, 'to the Queen.'

When the game ended and the young people drifted across the hall, Reginald beckoned Roger de Clare to approach. He excused himself to the others and came with swift, cat-like tread; a broad, square-faced man with a marked gap between his two front teeth, obviously a good deal older than his beautiful sister. Reginald whispered to him in the silence that had fallen on the High Table, and

95

Roger looked quickly at the King and made a little bow.

Eleanor continued to smile as the earl's sister was brought forward; long practice enabled her to hide her inward perturbation at Henry's obvious interest. When she looked more closely, her worry died. Nay, he would not be caught by her, she decided. I know the type. A born coquette, and like them all, basically cold. . . . She turned her face away, thinking, That will soon blow over.

Roger de Clare was saying to Henry, '– my sister, Annora.' Henry gazed at the top of her bare head as she knelt before him. Her hair shone as if it were polished, falling like a curtain past the rosy cheek; her eyebrows were fine and thin and her lips full and red, made for kissing. But when she looked up suddenly he was taken by surprise at the startling colour of her deep-set, narrow eyes – intense greenish-blue, the like of which he had never seen. He held her hand, staring, and she allowed her lashes to flutter down before she gave him a side-long glance that made him catch his breath. Then she was presented to the Queen who hardly looked at her, and finally withdrew while some others of the young folk were brought up in their turn.

For the rest of the evening Henry never took his eyes off her, and he kept Roger de Clare behind his chair, asking him many questions concerning his Honour and where his lands were situated. No open arrangements were made but by the end of the evening it was plain to the interested observers that the King would shortly visit Roger's manor of Tonbridge when his mother and his sister were in residence.

Roger was having difficulty in repressing his grin of delight and triumph at this fortunate turn of events. He had a particular desire just now to be in the King's good graces, firstly because that upstart new Archbishop was pressing for the return of Tonbridge to Canterbury, and secondly because he was associated with Robert de Montfort in his quarrel with the Constable, Henry of Essex, of whom the King was very fond. If the King were enamoured of his sister, he would not stand to lose whatever happened. Again he urged the King to visit Tonbridge before departing for Windsor.

The Queen was retiring from the hall with her ladies; she stopped at the door and made a slight obeisance in the King's direction. He nodded to her, faintly smiling, and then turned back to Roger. His eyes were very bright. 'Aye,' he said, 'I'll come – I can spare three days.' He laughed and touched Roger's hand. 'To meet your lady mother, eh? I shall look forward to it – and now, it is time for bed. Give you good night, my lords.' He sprang up and Roger saw him mutter a swift word to the Gentleman of the Wardrobe before he left by the same door the Queen had used.

Roger stroked his chin, his eyes narrowed a little, then he sat down by Reginald de St Valéry. 'Is that not the way to the Queen's apartments?' he asked.

Reginald fixed him with a sardonic eye. 'Aye,' he answered, 'but methinks there'll be three in that bed to-night!'

Henry's mind was not occupied exclusively with Annora de Clare after the Great Council broke up but the thought of her remained at the back of his mind; it kept his mood sweeter than it might otherwise have been.

At this time a continuous stream of reports was reaching him concerning sentences inflicted by ecclesiastical courts – sentences that he saw as perversions of justice, for the Church, while insisting that only she had the right to try her own, had no punitive powers other than defrocking. In his own royal courts laymen guilty of violence would be mutilated or imprisoned if they were lucky enough to escape with their lives. Such glaring inequality between subjects could not be allowed to go on but Henry could not see how to right matters without coming into direct conflict with the hierarchy and, he feared, with Thomas. The niggling worry

97

that the Archbishop no longer saw eye to eye with him could not be shaken off.

Outwardly he gave all his attention to affairs of state, discussing with Thomas the arrangements for the expedition against that troublesome Welsh prince, Rhys ap Gruffyd. Henry could not shrug off a faint regret for the old days when Thomas would have accompanied him – had he perhaps traded gold for dross? But he looked in vain for any sign that Thomas felt the same. It left him with an inescapable feeling of rejection.

His heart lightened, though, when he set out for Tonbridge with the Earl of Clare and a handful of his intimates, and his good cheer was in no way diminished by Roger's apparently idle comment that the castle they were bound for was a bone of contention at the moment between the Archbishop and himself. Indeed, the remark made no impression on Henry at all, although several of his companions glanced at one another with meaning. He was wondering if de Clare's sister could possibly be as beautiful as he remembered.

That night, after his gentlemen had helped him to bed, he knew that it was true, and staring up at the painted cloth tacked on the rafters rehearsed in his mind every look she had given him, every touch of her small white hand. Her eyes were like flowers, set deep and hidden in her lashes. And full of promises. . . . He grinned as he remembered her mother's confident demeanour and the deep, harsh, self-assured tones with which she had greeted him – the voice of an experienced whore, he told himself. There would be no difficulties from her. Nor from de Clare either if he had interpreted their conversation aright.

Common sense informed him that de Clare would expect a *quid pro quo* for so valuable a property as his sister. He ran over in his mind Roger's seemingly light grumbling about the rapacity of the Archbishop to be sure he was

98

correct about the implication, and having satisfied himself, allowed his thoughts to dwell once more on his conversation with Annora. Oddly enough, though, when he thought about it he could not remember anything she had said.

They hawked next morning over the flat fields and along the streams; the ladies accompanied them but some way off so that their smaller birds should not upset the King's great gerfalcon. Both groups had fine sport until huge dark ragged clouds began to cover the sky, and soon a sleety shower drenched them. It passed as swiftly as it came, the light brightening with fantastic speed so that all the gaunt leafless bushes were spangled with round, glittering drops, then a breath of wind sent them rattling down about the company's ears as they turned for home.

The soaking and the cutting short of one of his chief pleasures had not put the King out of humour, however, for a little smile still played about his lips at intervals; seeing it, Cornwall came up alongside him and embarked on one of the interminable, pointless stories he found amusing. The King listened in an absent way but after a time he crooked his finger at de Clare, and presenting his shoulder to his uncle, began to talk to him about his sister. De Clare did not say much but Henry was quite satisfied with their inconclusive conversation. He had the impression that Roger understood him very well.

All at once, he checked his horse. 'Pretty!' he said appreciatively, nodding towards the blackthorn whose dark, dripping boughs were pearled with tiny, greenish-white buds. Roger granted it was with an air of faint surprise and eyed him curiously, but Henry's face remained rapt and withdrawn as he gazed at this first sign of spring.

Roger thought with amazement, can he be truly smitten with her? He marvelled as any brother would at the blindness of those who will lose their hearts to his sister.

99

Henry did not suspect that he had lost his heart a second time; he only knew that his desire was urgent and that he would have no peace of mind until it was slaked. Somehow, though, when he recalled the languishing glances of those shining, blue-green eyes, he could not think he would have too long to wait. He came out of that pleasant reverie abruptly as de Clare began to talk about his friend, Robert de Montfort, and his accusations of treason against the Constable.

'I hope he will not openly accuse him,' said Henry restively. 'For my part, I think him innocent.' He hesitated momentarily, then went on, 'However, I am prepared to believe his accusers are acting in good faith.' But he was thinking, It's plain de Clare will make whatever capital he can out of this. And he has the delicacy of approach of a wild boar. . . .

When they were back in the castle, warm and dry, Henry closeted himself with a clerk to sign some documents a messenger had brought. The door lay open to the hall and he went through the parchments quickly, jabbing with the quill and spattering ink on the board, lifting his head from the task at the footsteps of every passer-by as though he watched for some one. When he heard the sound of light, female voices, he stopped with the pen poised, then dropped it, leaving a black streak across the parchment, and went swiftly to the door. Annora was passing with a group of the castle maidens.

She waited for him with an air at once diffident and bold, saying nothing until he bent his head to salute her. As he did so, she parted her lips to speak and the kiss of greeting, awkwardly delivered, landed at the corner of her open mouth. He heard her catch her breath and pulled her hard against him, kissing her with a passion that drove every other thought from his mind. She yielded immediately so that the soft weight of her body almost unbalanced him, and suddenly mindful of the time and place, he raised his head and looked about. The damsels were gone and the clerk's back eloquently turned on them as he riffled through the documents.

He whispered, 'Where may we be alone?'

'Come to my bower before dinner; I will dismiss my ladies early. You have – you have spoken with my lord, my brother?'

He thought with a wild and dizzying joy, She is as eager as I – and felt the hot blood burning in his face. 'Yes,' he said, 'we understand each other – as you and I do.'

She traced his lips with her finger. 'No more now,' she said, and with a wicked downward look at his tight chausses, 'You are the finest figure of a man that ever I did see. But take care none other notice it!' And she skipped aside from his playful slap at her backside, leaving him to rearrange both his dress and his features before he went in to the clerk again.

By the time Henry reached Windsor at the end of the month few were ignorant of the fact that the King was in love again, and the kindness of his temper told them it was love fulfilled. Eleanor affected to notice nothing but she felt that if she loosed the iron hand of control upon her feelings, she would do murder. That he should have fallen under the spell of that silly chit! It was worse than his affair with the English whore – at least, she had never been obliged to acknowledge her in public. If Henry should force Annora de Clare into the Court, she would have difficulty in keeping her nails from that soft, smooth face.

Fortunately he did not. Annora remained in Tonbridge; the only de Clare who came to Windsor was her brother Roger, and it was not long before everyone knew that he was one of the chief participants in the latest stage of the feud between Robert de Montfort and the Constable. Their quarrel was an old one, begun over property to which both laid claim, but it had progressed far beyond that and now de Montfort's antagonism would be satisfied with no less than his enemy's ruin. Having set himself to encompass it, he had lit on the one chink in the Constable's armour – his dropping of the Royal Standard before Basingwerk six years before.

Henry, who had heard of his plans from de Clare, tried to avert the issue by keeping them apart. If de Montfort got the chance to accuse the Constable point-blank of treachery in his presence, the only course open to him would be a public trial. And he would not have that if he could help it.

But that petty quarrel was the last thing in Henry's mind at this time; he did not even notice that both men were present when he met his greater lords to inform them of the dispositions of the troops in the forthcoming campaign. The meeting was nearly over when de Montfort stood up and shouted his challenge before them all: that the last time they fought in Wales Henry of Essex had cried out that the King was slain, that he had flung down the Royal Standard and had fled from the field of battle.

There was a moment's horrified hush before bedlam broke out, then Henry roared them all to silence. But he knew it was too late, the genuine fury and indignation of the Constable demanded redress. He could do nothing to help him now. And he wondered fretfully if the Constable had in fact been guilty of momentary cowardice. De Clare was adding his accusations to de Montfort's. He had been there. He had seen it all. He had retrieved the Standard.

But when the King looked at Henry of Essex trembling with rage, the veins corded on his stringy neck, he dismissed the thought. He preferred to believe his story: that he had dropped the Standard because of a blow on the arm, and that another blow on the helmet had so dazed him that he had lost all sense of direction.

Afterwards it was with a worried face that Henry drew him on one side, pointing out that he was de Montfort's senior by many years and that his age might tell against him in the ordeal of trial by battle.

The old man's face was proud and cold. 'Would you have me refuse such a challenge? Accept such a slur upon my honour? Never! Death would be preferable.' But his face relaxed when he saw Henry's genuine concern. 'I know you believe in me, my lord King. *You* know that I have always served you faithfully, but outsiders do not. They will hear only an unanswered accusation and it is the nature of men to believe the worst of anyone. I shall have to kill my accuser to prove my innocence.'

'And supposing *he* kills *you*?'

Shock was plain on the Constable's face. He replied with thinly veiled reproof. 'God will protect the right.'

'Aye....' said Henry, 'Aye,' and under his breath, 'Perhaps.'

The contest was to take place on a small island in the Thames. The marquees and equipment were rowed over on the previous day; fortunately the weather seemed to be set fair but in early April it could change within the hour. Henry looked at the sky with apprehension; he would not give much for the Constable's chances against a younger opponent in a driving rain-storm. But the heavens smiled and the temperature was perfect for fighting, not so cold that hands would grow numb in mailed gauntlets and not so warm that sweat might blind the contestants.

It began at the fourth hour after dawn. Henry sat with his lords in a stand that carpenters had erected for the occasion; only men were present for this was no joust bedecked with fluttering pennants and ladies' favours but a trial on which a man's life depended. And it was likely to be a bloody business.

103

The King watched gloomily at first but Henry of Essex, for all his age, was a skilled fighter, and Henry's spirits rose as he saw him weaving and feinting around de Montfort's lance. They fought for more than an hour until the horses were lathered and steaming and their trappings spattered with blood – their own or the horses', it was hard to tell.

By now the stretch of turf was churned into mud by the hoofs; it lay slippery and shining in the sunlight between the two antagonists as they pulled on the reins at opposite ends of the field, preparatory to turning. They had discarded the lances and were using their great broadswords, hewing and jabbing at the other's head and shoulders – the watchers gasped as the Constable's weapon clanged on de Montfort's helmet, making it ring like a bell. He sank across his horse's neck as Henry of Essex thundered past once more, then rose in the stirrups, swinging the whistling blade in a great arc. It skated down the Constable's mailed arm and struck his horse's neck. The horse's forelegs collapsed slowly, depositing the Constable on the ground but he regained his feet quite easily and faced de Montfort's charge with the point of sword.

De Montfort wheeled past and came at him from behind, baulking again as the Constable's sword narrowly missed the legs of his horse. But now he saw that the left arm of Henry of Essex hung useless at his side while blood dripped from the mailed glove. The King saw it too, and the tigerish smile on de Montfort's face. He half rose in his seat.

Henry of Essex seemed to stagger, then de Montfort's bulk was between him and the King, and there was a scream. It was the sound Henry heard without a tremor in the hunt but now he jumped and closed his eyes. When he opened them the Constable lay huddled on the ground and the oozy mud beside his throat was no longer black but crimson.

After they had left the island and the body of Henry of Essex had been delivered to the monks of Reading, Henry rode away, silent and abstracted. In this, as in so many things of late, he doubted God's intervention. He had believed the Constable's denials and he still believed them, whatever the outcome of the trial. A good and honest man had been disgraced – to what purpose? Trial by battle (or fire, or water) was a sham, a counterfeit of justice. . . . And if God did not intervene so that truth might be known, what then?

Well, if God would not vindicate the just, Henry Fitz-Empress must find the means to do so. Something perhaps along the lines of the Church's method of compurgation whereby twelve or more men who knew the accused well swore to his incapability of committing such a crime. . . . He would reflect upon it; it would not do as it stood for it was too easy for the rich and powerful to hire oath-helpers, and the Church's belief that God would strike down a perjurer fell into the same trap as trial by ordeal.

He straightened his shoulders and stared ahead as certainty grew in him that God cared nothing for justice, and his eye fell on a tower of black cloud that reared threateningly from the western horizon into the pale sky. The sun caught the rim of it blindingly for an instant, edging it with shining gold. Even as he watched, it moved, passing in front of the snowy heaps of cumulus, dulling and dispersing until it was no more than a grey sheet to the south. He gazed upward for a long time after that; the random movement of the clouds in the eternal sky echoed something in his mood so that when he came back to earth again he was faintly surprised to find it all the same. A little way off his companions laughed and chatted as if nothing had happened, as though the Constable, who such a little time ago had been warm and breathing, were not now stiffening in death.

Reginald of Cornwall rode beside him. 'The supply lines will be all right this time?' he asked, and Henry realised he was speaking of the campaign to come.

'I made the dispositions clear, did I not?' he replied rather shortly.

'Oh, yes,' said Cornwall. 'It will be all right this time then?'

Henry breathed hard. 'If you follow orders, nothing will go wrong.'

Cornwall nodded sagely to himself. 'Obey orders – aye. . . .' He started to ask another question but Henry jabbed his heel into the horse's side and went off, leaving him to wonder what had made the King so irritable.

Left with the rest of the ladies in the castle at Windsor that same bright April day, Eleanor was bored. She had never liked the undiluted company of her own sex; with a few notable exceptions she found other women shallow and self-centred and quite unable to think of anything beyond their own immediate concerns. Today, still smarting under the recently acquired knowledge that she had yet another rival, she was in no humour for feminine gossip with its emphasis on the misbehaviour of men and the attendant half-contemptuous pity for their unfortunate wives. Yet she could not escape it.

They were all at it, gabbling away nineteen to the dozen, tearing reputations to shreds and then patching them together haphazard with a few poisonously kindly words, while she sat with her eyes on the pages of the book open on her knee, reading the same lines over and over, unable to shut out the chattering magpie voices.

'My darling babe who, I am sure, is the strongest and handsomest child anyone could wish to see! The wet nurse swears she never saw so large a babe at three months old. He resembles my father—'

'A pity your husband has so many other children to be provided for. I cannot think what lands he can grant to your children.'

106

'Oh, do not worry about that! My children, however many God may grant me, will not be landless. Already my husband is quarrelling with his elder sons.'

Eleanor raised her eyes slowly to watch the two ladies and saw the younger move nearer the other to murmur in her ear. But her whisper was sibilant enough to overhear.

'I will not say I did not drop a word in season to help the quarrel on! But I must care for my own.'

Eleanor set her teeth together and turned the page.

'When he is in my bed, he must listen, perforce. It is no bad thing to have an elderly husband. He is grateful to me as a young one would not be!'

Eleanor reflected bitterly on the ingratitude of youthful husbands.

'—if the babe was born at Christmas? Surely you did not conceive in Lent?'

There was the faintest pause before: 'He was born a month too soon.'

The older lady's voice dripped sweetness. 'And such a great child at birth! '

Oh, what a nonsense it all is, thought Eleanor. What husband – Henry included – ever took notice of the Church's ban on intimacies in the Holy Season! And yet they will torment each other with such pinpricks!

She stood up and the hum of conversation hushed. 'I shall visit the royal children in their apartments,' she announced. 'Mabille will accompany me.'

Conscious of their bright, blank eyes upon her – like a flock of carrion crows, she thought – her mood was suddenly savage. She knew she would not be two steps beyond the door before they were discussing Henry's latest affairs with tolerant amusement and her own situation with hypocritical sympathy. The thought galled her.

The children were playing with a ball on the strip of greensward by the private door to their apartments, the sweet spring sunshine having lured the women out of doors. Now that the wind had risen chilly, they would have preferred to retire within again but Richard and the two Geoffreys, heated from their game and revelling in freedom, would not be coerced; they tossed the ball and ran to and fro, always one jump ahead of the floundering, flustered women, while Matilda standing beside the wet-nurse who held the baby, watched them with disapproval. So the Queen and Mabille found them.

Eleanor hushed the wet-nurse who would have called a warning and put one hand on Matilda's shoulder. The little girl moved close against her skirts, gazing up at her mother, but Eleanor's eyes were fixed on Richard and she pushed the child aside as she stepped forward. Only the nurse saw Matilda's face and put out a hand, then finding it ignored, withdrew it.

But once they were within doors Matilda had a few moments of her mother's attention as together they encouraged the baby's first staggering steps; it was not long, though, before Mabille had taken the Queen's place and Eleanor had gone the length of the room to read to the boys. For in spite of herself, she had come to accept the elder Geoffrey (who was, she had been disgusted to discover, exactly the same age as Matilda) and, while making it clear to the nurses and tutors that he was in no sense the equal of her own children, had found herself unable to make such overt distinctions. She treated him, in fact, with the same kindly indifference as she treated all her children except Richard, and she was helped in this by his striking likeness to them. Pretty soon, her own Geoffrey, who at four would rather tumble with the baby than listen to verses, moved back to the others and his half-brother followed him, leaving her alone with Richard.

The fact was that had it not been for Richard, Eleanor would scarcely have bothered to visit the nurseries. She was not fond of young children once they had passed the endearing baby stage, but Richard's precocity fascinated her. He soaked up information, and every day gave fresh evidence that he was possessed of intelligence beyond the ordinary. Eleanor did not know the extent of his knowledge for his acuity was allied to a most unchildlike reticence and he had listened silently to many a conversation whose participants had no more considered his presence than that of the dogs. He was not yet six and had picked up enough to know that the mother he adored had been mischievously dealt with in some way by his father, and by judicious remarks he had learned that it did not displease her to hear him spoken of slightingly. She would say, 'Richard, speak of your elders with respect,' and then squeeze his hand and give him the smile she reserved for him alone. So he knew he might despise his father even though he was the king. Besides, he remembered his brother Henry's tales of the many beatings he had received through the royal agency once he had been withdrawn from their mother's protection. Already he had resolved that his father should not gain that power over him.

His mother had just finished the tale of a pure and chivalrous knight who had loved a Queen. Richard rested his head against her knee. 'When I am a man I shall be such a knight,' he informed her solemnly, 'and the Queen that I shall love is you.'

He saw the corner of her mouth dimple. 'When you are a man I shall be an old woman. I hope you will find a fair princess to love and marry.'

'I had rather marry you.'

'But I am married already to your father.'

'I would be kinder to you than he is.'

He saw her smile die. 'Yes,' she said, 'I expect you would. And indeed I hope that you will be a gentler lord than he has been to me. . . . Avoid the sin of greed, Richard, for that

is his chief fault. Greedy for lands, for wealth, for women—'
She stopped abruptly, appalled at the quick, knowing look
he gave her, and turned her head away.

After a moment he took her hand and squeezed it. 'I shall
be your knight, mama, when I am grown. And I will avenge
you.'

She shook her head but she did not rebuke him; instead
she laid the hand he was still holding against his cheek.
Then she began to read again.

The King and the Archbishop had attended the Palm
Sunday procession of the Canterbury monks together; now
as the April evening deepened into dusk, they sat alone in a
private chamber in the Archbishop's palace with a dish of
walnuts on the table in front of them.

The King ate the nuts quickly and hungrily, one after the
other, without a pause. He had cracked the first one in his
teeth but the taste of the salt in which they had been stored
made him grimace and he broke the rest between his big
chapped hands, dropping the brittle shells into the rushes at
his feet. While he chewed, he speculated aloud on Gilbert
Foliot's attitude to Thomas, now that he was Bishop-elect
of London.

Thomas watched him with a loving, faintly indulgent
smile which reflected his feelings, for since he had left the
King's service the affection he felt for him had returned
with all its former strength.

After a time Henry sat back and sucked his teeth. He did
not look at Thomas and said with apparent casualness. 'He
was fiercely opposed to your elevation if you remember,
Tom.'

'Well, I can scarcely blame him for that,' answered
Thomas, still smiling. 'I shared many of his doubts.'

Henry's eyes flickered up at him sharply. 'But you
managed to overcome your reservations.'

Thomas nodded. He wondered what Henry was getting at. Surely he was not trying to stir up resentment in him against Gilbert? He felt none; he respected his brother bishop for his honesty and for his unswerving devotion to the Church's interests. He was quite certain of Gilbert's loyalty to the Archbishop, no matter what he thought of the holder of that office. So he shied away from the subject and began to talk about the forthcoming campaign in Wales.

Henry let him, only muttering, 'I would I had the Constable still with me when we meet the Welsh.' Then he said more loudly, 'He is recovering of his wounds – the Constable, I mean. Did you know that, Tom?'

Thomas stared. 'We heard he was dead,' he said on a note of deep surprise.

'Aye – left for dead. But the monks found he was not dead when they took him; they tended him well.' Henry leaned forward and took another nut, swore when he found it bad and threw it in the fire. 'It makes but little difference – he was declared outlaw when he was vanquished and his estates confiscated. So now he will join the monks at Reading. His life is over just the same.'

'But he has been given time to repent and make restitution to God,' said Thomas gently. 'That is a great mercy.'

Henry's head jerked up. 'Repent! Restitution! For what?'

'He was found guilty of treason, was he not?'

'He fought in single combat,' said Henry in a clipped voice, 'against an opponent younger and stronger than he. He lost. Does that prove his guilt in your eyes?'

'God protects the just,' said Thomas, innocently repeating the Constable's own words.

'Oh yes, oh, yes,' returned Henry in a heavy, sneering tone. 'Just as He—' He stopped short. He had been about to say, 'Just as He protects the victims of those rapacious clerks we hear so much about.' But he had realised in time that this was a remark he could not make to an archbishop.

The issue of the clerks and the over-light sentences of the ecclesiastical courts would be raised soon anyway – that was one thing, but his own private doubts he would keep to himself. He had no wish to bring down a hornet's nest about his ears and the look of consternation on Thomas's face was warning enough.

He forced himself to smile. 'You are right, of course, Tom. I am allowing my love for the Constable to cloud my judgment.'

'God's judgment is always best. We must bear in mind that our own judgments are limited by our human minds—' Thomas leaned forward, unable to repress the impulse to lecture Henry upon the necessity for trust in God. But he had not spoken more than a few sentences when the bell for Compline began to ring so that he excused himself with a hasty apology and a promise to pray for the Constable.

Henry did not offer to accompany him to the Cathedral. He waved his hand with what Thomas thought was his usual impatience with theological disquisitions and returned to the walnuts.

V

May 1163

THE KING'S EXPEDITION into Wales was quickly over; apparently the Welsh were in no mood for battle or they had exhausted their energies fighting among themselves. At any rate, they offered no resistance to his advancing troops and after Owain and Rhys were run finally to earth, Henry retired satisfied, with hostages against the Welsh princes' promise to appear and do him homage in England later in the year.

He was now impatient to see Annora again, and leaving her brother in undisputed possession of his Cardigan castles once more, he turned his face for England. Leaving his army to travel at its slow pace, he posted on with a handful of his trusted henchmen, stopping only when he must for a snatched meal or a few hours' sleep. Behind him, strung out over many miles, came his lords and barons cursing his impatience and the breakneck speed he set, their own saddle sores and the lack of provision in castle or hunting lodge where he had been.

'God's blood,' groaned old Cornwall as he hobbled stiff-legged into the hall at Clarendon, 'why do we not lay the reins on our horses' necks and amble? Wherefore this haste? Is he even human?'

My lord of Leicester smiled wryly. 'Do you not remember the words of Peter of Blois quoting King Solomon? "There are four things a man cannot know: the path of an eagle in the sky, the path of a ship in the sea, the path of a serpent on the ground and the path of a man in his youth." He added a fifth: the path of the King in England.' He gave a sudden laugh, looking across the narrow, raftered hall. 'Well, we have found him at last – and others, besides!' He had heard the light voices of women.

'Ah . . .' said Cornwall and sniffed, rubbing his nose with the back of his hand. '*That* was the reason for the haste.' He peered uncertainly. 'Not the Queen's ladies, are they?'

'No-o,' said Leicester. His long face was faintly disapproving. 'I see de Clare's mother among them – talking to the King.'

He followed Cornwall as he began to push his way forward but they were not halfway through the press when the talk hushed and heads turned. They turned too, and saw Annora de Clare approaching from the other direction. Leicester felt Cornwall jab him sharply in the ribs and his eyes went momentarily back to the King, but he looked away quickly; Henry wore the look of a man who sees before him the opening gates of Paradise.

And Henry did not care who saw it. He had marvelled himself at the eagerness which sent him rushing to Annora's side when he had for so long believed that those sweet transports had ended with his youth. Now, past thirty as he was, he was glorying in his attachment like a green boy, floundering helplessly deeper into love with every day that passed. Three days they had been here together and he knew that he would never tire of her – this was as unlike those swift lusts which a hurried hour could slake and another wipe from memory entirely as was wine to water.

Now he watched her coming towards him. She was dressed in some rich stuff the colour of the sea with her bronze hair loose about her shoulders in the manner of virgins. Full lips deliciously pouted, heavy lashes shadowing her downcast eyes, she knelt submissively before him.

Cornwall moved restively, staring, and muttered something under his breath; and Leicester remembered that his youngest daughter was just the age of this girl. He also remembered how often the wives and daughters of the magnates were unaccountably absent when the King was in the vicinity. His face lengthened even further.

Henry, quite disabled by his new-found joy, was waiting for Annora's dazzling upward glance, nor could his awareness that she used the same trick on every man destroy its heart-lurching effect on him. Putting both hands on her shoulders, he kissed the moist uplifted mouth and felt her tongue touch his lips. He trembled and tightened his grip on her, hearing the laughter gurgle in her throat. 'Later . . .' she breathed against his cheek.

'Do that again,' he whispered in her ear, 'and I will throw you down and take you here before them all!'

She pulled away, flashing a glance at the onlookers, her eyes shining and brilliantly blue. 'Oh fie, sire! You have me blushing clear down to my bosom! Where may a maid find protection from such a one as you?'

'Who, by the rood, would dare to offer it?' muttered Cornwall.

Leicester looked sour. 'Born harlots need no protection,' he returned, 'And all the wit God gave her, He put between her legs!'

Cornwall snorted softly. 'She uses it to good effect!'

'Aye, and her brother will reap the benefit. But I'd not buy a castle – nor yet a kingdom – with the honour of my womenfolk.'

'But does he realise what de Clare's about? He's fair besotted with her, that's plain.'

'Oh, yes!' said Leicester with a depth of displeasure that

made Cornwall stare. 'Oh yes, he knows that. What he has forgotten is that Tonbridge is not his to bestow. It belongs to Canterbury and the Archbishop!'

June 1163

Gilbert Foliot had consented to his translation to London with mixed feelings, for the warm glow of pleasure he had felt at the flattering comments of the King and the Pope on his suitability for the position had been immediately dissipated by the equally complimentary remarks in a letter from the Archbishop urging his acceptance. He had told himself again and again that he should have expected so adept a humbug to know the uses of blandishment but it did little to ease his sense of outrage. Nor had it helped that the Archbishop had presided over his enthronement in St Paul's Cathedral.

Now, having transacted the day's business, he indulged himself with a few moments' unaccustomed idleness as he awaited the coming of the lord Archbishop of York. He was alone but for the great wolf hound stretched out near the hearth. A small fire had been lit there in the visitor's honour, for the June day was chill with sudden fluctuations in the light as the heavy clouds thickened and parted; when the sun came through at intervals it laid elongated patterns of the tall round-headed windows across the floor and paled the flames to near invisibility. Gilbert sat some way off across the big room in the Bishop's chair with his large, bony hands resting relaxed on the arms; he was cold there but he did not give that any consideration.

After a bit he went across to one of the boxes on the table, sorted through the papers within and took out the offending letter. He stood there perusing it again; when he came to the last sentence which read, 'Thus not only sincere affection but proximity of place unite us both in the same good work, to give one another mutual assistance in ministering to the necessities of God's Church', he clicked his tongue against his teeth in disgust and muttered under his breath, 'Mutual assistance, indeed!' The hound twitched and raised its head, eyeing its master, then lowered it to its forepaws and dozed again.

Gilbert sat down and continued his cogitations. He was the King's confessor now, and perforce admitted to an intimacy that having nothing of the personal, yet told him a great deal of the inner workings of the King's mind. Names were but rarely mentioned but he could not miss allusions to one who had been beloved and was now all too often a source of bitter irritation, and the awareness that he must forget this private knowledge made it the more impossible to suppress. He could not help but know the King regretted making his Chancellor Archbishop.

That enlightenment had helped to strengthen his refusal to profess obedience to Thomas of London. For why should he? Had he not taken the oath of canonical obedience once already to an Archbishop of Canterbury in the person of old Theobald when he first became Bishop of Hereford? What need to repeat it on his translation to another see? Besides, there was always the faint chance that the Pope would raise London to archaepiscopal status. . . . But another part of his mind that he rarely acknowledged and believed he ignored told him something else: that it would not be difficult to encourage the King in his disillusionment with his erstwhile friend.

Thomas was back in England now, doubtless flushed with the success of his triumphal progress across Normandy from the Papal Court at Tours. There had been no monkeys on the horses' backs this time but little else had been lacking, he'd be bound. How the man loved to flaunt himself! A word or two on his presumption dropped lightly in the King's ear might make him see this impostor in his true colours – certainly it's no more than duty to warn him how the rest of the world views such self-aggrandizement in a subject, something whispered to him darkly, while the surface of his mind speculated on the impression England's new Archbishop had created on the Pope. It was strange indeed how few men saw through outward dazzle – witness the plaudits of the common folk when he went among them.

But – Gilbert comforted himself – Roger of York was one who did, and he had been at the Archbishop's elbow throughout the Council of Tours. From him he would learn of all that had passed. He felt a tickle at the back of his nose just then, and knew with ill-humour that while Thomas of London had been regaling himself in the sunny south, he had caught another of his colds.

So that when the Archbishop of York was shown in a few moments later, he was met by a stare that was hard and ready to be angry – not with him, as he at once realised, but with the way things were now when knaves who lacked breeding were up and righteous men down. But it would have taken more than cold looks from Gilbert Foliot to dent Roger's satisfaction at this moment. He swept in on a wave of scent, imperious, plumply pleased with himself – and far too clean, thought Gilbert whose disapproval of pandering to the flesh extended to the cleansing of it more often than was strictly necessary.

After the dog had been dragged out bodily by its scruff and the proprieties observed between them, Gilbert said abruptly, 'Well?'

'A most successful Council,' puffed York. 'Aye, most successful.'

Gilbert cocked an eyebrow.

'The greatest honour was shown to the representatives of the English Church – seventeen cardinals were present yet I and Canterbury were seated either side of the Pope.'

'He to the right?'

But Roger waved that small prick aside, being in haste to

118

lay before Gilbert the story of the delicious snub administered to the object of their detestation by the Father of the Church.

'Since so many people – townspeople and Churchmen alike – poured out of the gates of Tours to look upon the man who was converted overnight by a miracle of God, only two cardinals were left in attendance on the Pope. And when the Pope himself came out into the great hall to greet him – he followed by this crowd acclaiming him – you may imagine his preening. He prostrates himself thus at Alexander's feet' – Roger flung up his arms and brought them down in a sweeping bow – 'and the Pope gazes down at him and says, small and cold, "Go and rest, brother, for rest is necessary after labour." '

Gilbert allowed the faintest smile to lurk for a second at the corners of his mouth as Roger laughed long and wheezily.

'He *was* acclaimed, then?'

Roger shrugged. 'When is he not?' He began to tell Gilbert of the excommunication of the new anti-pope and about the condemnation of the damnable Catharist heresy which had arisen in Toulouse.

Gilbert interrupted him. 'The anniversary of his consecration fell while you were there. Was no mention made of his uncanonical election?'

York hitched his chair a little nearer. 'I cannot swear to this but there was a strong rumour to the effect that, not having received it honestly, he secretly resigned the Archbishopric into the Pope's hands.'

Gilbert's voice was sharp. 'And then?'

'That the Pope reimposed upon him the burden of pastoral office.'

Gilbert shook his head disgustedly. 'I do not believe it.'

'What? You do not think—'

'I do not believe the rumour. Would such a man risk losing all that he has won? No, you may depend upon it he would not.' He looked narrowly at Roger. 'Did he not ask for the primacy of England?'

York blew out his cheeks and swirled the dregs around the bottom of his winecup. 'He obtained confirmation of the privileges of Canterbury, if that is what you mean.'

'The Church in England is in perilous state with such a one to rule over her. His greed is as unendurable as his pride. Money flows through his hands like water. But if the Pope has seen through him—' Gilbert clamped his mouth together and looked deep into Roger's piggy, little eyes. 'We must take care for the Church if he will not,' he said on a note of barely hidden meaning.

Thomas had taken great pains to avoid the Archbishop of York throughout the Council and on the journey home to England so that he was quite unaware of Roger's visit to Gilbert Foliot. Indeed, he would have been astonished to learn that there was any relationship whatsoever between the unprincipled enemy of his younger days and the austere and upright Bishop of London.

In Thomas's eyes, at least, the two men stood at extreme ends of the scale. It was impossible for him to feel any respect for Roger whose thrusting ambition for ecclesiastical honour was unredeemed by the least trace of spiritual feeling, and whose suspect private life tainted even the magnificent buildings he raised to God's glory, but Foliot, he thought, was a different matter.

Thomas desired Gilbert's friendship for a variety of reasons. Here, he felt, was a man after his own heart, a high Gregorian who like himself believed in the supremacy of the Church and things spiritual, tenacious of principle and respected by all. The support of such a man might be invaluable to him. Thomas also had a very human desire to prove to this paragon that his assessment of his Archbishop's character had been a mistaken one, and towards that end, had considered writing to acquaint him with the Pope's wholehearted endorsement of his election. It was only after much heart-searching that he decided the risk of appearing vainglorious was too great – no man should be his own apologist. So he hugged to himself the glorious knowledge that he was as great a success as Archbishop as he had been as Chancellor, and wondered faintly at his earlier dread of high ecclesiastical office.

It had been Pope Alexander's attitude towards him which had finally confirmed his growing confidence in God's favour and blessing – that and the delirious acclamation of the multitude who had flocked to see him. Yet his first meeting with the Pope had had more than an element of discomfort. Forced forward as he had been by the noisy, excited crowd almost into the Holy Father's arms, his composure had deserted him at the crucial moment of first impression so that he had simply stared for a tell-tale second or two at the unexpected sight of that small, white-clad figure.

Flanked only by two cardinals whose expressions of extreme distaste were surely not caused only by the strong smell of bodies, the Pope had taken one pace backward and coolly extended his hand. Thomas's cheeks still burned in retrospect at his double-edged words of greeting. But starting off on the wrong foot as he had done had come to matter not at all.

During their first private conversation the Pope had quickly seen his mistake in thinking Thomas imagined his fame and popularity qualified him to set down Christ's Vicar on earth, and had said as much; it set the style of their relationship and from then on each had opened his heart to the other in matters of feeling, if not of policy. They were, it appeared, in temperamental accord. If Alexander had felt some surprise at finding this variously reported prodigy so entirely of his own mind, he did not allow

Thomas to see it; instead he listened to his opinions with obvious pleasure and commended him several times on his spiritual insight.

But Thomas, always ready to generalise and to air long-cherished beliefs, kept his own counsel about his future course of action, not so much from secretiveness as from a certainty that he, being English, could find his way through an English maze more easily than a stranger. And a few days later when Canon VII was discussed, it seemed to him that he had been right not to worry the Pope with Canterbury's internal affairs, for there it was in black and white – the confirmation he needed in his disputes with lay lords over Church property. To find one's instinctive attitude amply justified by law is always sweet. Thomas gave the matter no more thought; he received the kiss of peace from the Pope and departed from Tours secure in the knowledge that the thunderbolt of excommunication was his to use against the defiant barons if they continued to disobey him.

But when he returned home, he discovered other, more immediate matters claiming his attention. Henry, at first as eager as ever to see him after a protracted absence, seemed curiously distrait in his company, and manifestly uninterested in travels that did not concern his personal business. Sometimes the old intimacy would reassert itself, as when Henry had begun to expound eagerly on the success of his Welsh campaign, only to go quiet and leave the story in mid-air for no reason that Thomas could see. It was true that he had interrupted several times when something the King said reminded him of a particularly interesting point the Pope had raised, but it was unlike Henry to take offence at interjections. On thinking it over, Thomas decided that the reason for this sudden coolness had its roots in the new love affair the King was engaged in. That was a subject better left ignored, he felt. Gilbert Foliot, as Henry's confessor, must concern himself with that. At least, he thought, this one is Christian – and then did not know whether he should be pleased or angry that it was so.

Whatever was on Henry's mind, he did not mention it and left almost at once for Woodstock with the assurance that the Archbishop would meet him there early in July when the Council would open. Henry had taken to holding these Councils at more frequent intervals since Thomas had become Archbishop; he had no regular Chancellor now and found that on the whole he preferred it so. He could hear the advice of his chief barons at first hand and it surprised him at first to discover just how secular their outlook was. Thomas, he began to feel, had been at times a disingenuous go-between. In fact, it was now becoming obvious that Thomas had more faults than he had realised – and faults which were dangerous in a Chancellor were more so in an Archbishop.

Henry was sagacious enough to see that the haughtiness his barons complained of was Thomas's growing assurance in his sphere, but it troubled him when he remembered his Chancellor's diplomatic and politic behaviour. It seemed to betoken a designing time-server who had hidden his true colours until he felt himself unassailable. Henry buried his suspicions as well as he could but it was not easy in the face of his lords' continual grumbling about the Archbishop; and that business of the criminous clerks which must come to a head before long. He knew there would be trouble with the Archbishop over that.

But at the moment his mind was more occupied with financial matters. His treasury was still alarmingly low; the overhaul of the national revenue begun a few months ago had not so far produced any significant result. It was the more embittering that it was the loss of Canterbury's revenues to Thomas that had so diminished his resources. He arrived at Woodstock in a glum and fretful state of mind which a heavy summer cold did nothing to improve.

July came in hot and sultry with all the oppressiveness of thunder weather. It was airless in the Great Hall at Woodstock (which was a misnomer; it was, in fact, a very small hall), even though the doors stood open. The Archbishop and the King arrived together rather late. That was Thomas's fault; he had been complaining to the King at length about the refusal of certain persons – to wit, Roger, Archbishop of York and Clarembald, Abbot of St Augustine's, Canterbury – to profess obedience to him, and Henry was very restive in consequence, mostly because he had forced Clarembald on the unwilling monks and he thought Thomas was striking at him in oblique fashion because of it. After sneezing several times, he said, 'We shall see to it – we shall see to it, all in good time.'

He said this, loudly and irritably, just as they entered the hall so that a good many heads turned their way. Among them was Roger de Clare's; he turned back quickly but not before Thomas had seen on his face a look that was both pleased and calculating.

Thomas felt annoyance rise in him at that look and he determined there and then to summon Roger before his episcopal court to answer for his contumacy in the matter of Tonbridge. He glared across at him and Roger, the King's back being turned, faced him with cool insolence, then leaned towards his neighbour and whispered something out of the corner of his mouth. A smothered titter ran through the group.

Thomas took his seat, his cheeks uncommonly warm. How ready were these nobles to seize hopefully on anything that might betoken a rift between the King and himself! He fumed silently for a while, considering how best to deal with back biters; it was more difficult now than in the old days when he and Henry had been inseparable.

He was vaguely conscious that Richard de Luci was

124

speaking of monetary matters – something about a payment of two shillings per hide of land for the fisc – and roused himself to listen. Gradually he became aware that it was the customary gift known as sheriff's aid which was under discussion. Apparently Henry was demanding that the aid be paid directly into his Treasury. Thomas heard the speech out with growing exasperation. Whose idea it was he did not know, but it was a foolish one. Had he still been advising him, he would never have allowed the King to make such a grave tactical error.

If the sheriffs – who had a hard enough task in all conscience – were deprived of their aid, they would certainly reimburse themselves by cheating the Treasury or by illegally exacting more than their due from the taxpayers. Either way, Henry was placing great temptation in the way of the very men he relied on for honest and efficient fiscal dealings.

He shook his head at Henry. 'Nay, nay, my lord,' he said, 'that will not do! We shall not give it to you as revenue but if the sheriffs and officials of the shires serve us worthily and defend our vassals, we will not withhold the aid from them.'

Henry's head came up with a jerk, his colour rising visibly. 'By God's eyes,' he snapped, 'it will so be given, and inscribed in the King's roll! Nor shall you contradict me when no one is trying to impose any burden on you!'

Thomas straightened in his seat and his eyes widened slightly, their pallid frosty blue very brilliant against the unrelieved black of the Augustinian cappa he wore. He answered slowly and deliberately. 'By the reverence of those eyes on which you have sworn, my lord King, it will not so be given from my land, and not a penny from any land under the jurisdiction of the Church.'

They faced each other for a moment. Henry looked away first. He saw the expressions on the faces nearest him, embarrassed, stricken or eager, according as each man had viewed the scene, and his eye roamed further, to that bench where sat his vassals of note. He saw the malicious amusement in the dark eyes of Rhys ap Gruffyd, the careful unconcern of Owain Gwynned and Malcolm of Scotland. The corner of his mouth twitched once or twice. An uncertain murmur of conversation began and ceased abruptly as he raised his hand to it. Then Richard de Luci began to deal with the rest of the financial business and the tension slackened and died away.

Henry had rarely been so angry and remained silent. That Thomas should speak so to a king before his assembled nobility! He sat and bit his nails until the quicks filled up with blood, quite unable to give his mind to anything else. Halfway through the afternoon he heard the rain begin to mutter on the roof but the promise of coolness did nothing to alleviate his impotent wrath. He was just beginning to realise that by making him Archbishop he had forfeited his power over Thomas. He could not relieve him of that position, no matter how troublesome his behaviour. Only through some matter affecting the clergy could he touch him at all.

Well, there was one ready to hand and he had temporised over it long enough. *He* had not wished to upset the delicate balance between the claims of Church and State, but Thomas apparently had no such care. Since his arbitrary interference in secular affairs had effectively ruined Henry's plans to increase his revenue (for a sufficient number of the barons had agreed with him to get the measure outvoted), he would find that his king could do as much in ecclesiastical matters. And he would see that the fines imposed on lawbreaking clerks should cover his losses.

It was raining furiously now and the day's business was nearly over. Henry leaned across and whispered at some length into de Luci's ear. 'A report?' said de Luci. 'On all the capital crimes committed since the beginning of your grace's reign?' His eyes were veiled but there was understanding in his face. He shot the barest hint of a glance towards the Archbishop, hardly moving his lips as he spoke again. 'Paying particular atention to the crimes of the clergy? It shall be prepared this very night, my lord King.'

In the last of the twilight, sweet and fresh after the rain, Reynold Fitzurse, Will de Tracy and Hugh de Morville sat on the bench outside a small tavern on the road to Oxford; it was the best they could do for lodgings because, as usual where the King was, all the good accommodation had gone. Summoned to Woodstock unexpectedly in their capacity as barons, they thought themselves lucky to do as well as this, even though they were sleeping three in a bed.

They were discussing the Archbishop's extraordinary behaviour – at least, Reynold and Will were discussing it; Hugh merely listened with his habitual sweet smile of malice, only now and then interjecting a barbed comment which seemed aimed more at their conjectures than at the object of their criticism. He glanced up lazily from toying with his mug as a slight, broken-nosed young man came out of the tavern door, his eyebrows lifting in surprise. 'Well, le Bret,' he said, 'and are you, too, tasting the delights of this hostelry? For myself, I swear I've slept in pleasanter pigsties when following the King.'

Le Bret nodded to him and looked round quickly; when his eye fell on Reynold he stopped and punched him familiarly on the arm. 'Ho, Reynold!' he said. 'I did not know you were here. How are you, you old whoreson?'

Reynold assured him he was in the rudest health and asked politely after his sister. She had recently taken le Bret's brother as her second husband; it was at their wedding that the two had met. But neither of them was much interested in Reynold's elder sister and they soon ceased to talk of family matters; when Will started to speak again of the Archbishop's brush with the King, le Bret attacked the

Primate with a venom that took them all aback.

'Will you disparage our liege?' said Hugh in a tone that made le Bret eye him suspiciously; their paths had not crossed much because le Bret was a man of the King's youngest brother, William, who came rarely into England. But trifling and inconsiderable as many thought that prince, he had evidently aroused love and loyalty in Richard le Bret for it was on his master's account that he was angry with the Archbishop.

'A truer man never lived,' he told them. 'Aye, the best of all Count Geoffrey's sons. Not rapacious like King Henry nor quarrelsome like his other brother Geoffrey – well, God rest him, but so he was. Perhaps if my lord William had been more like him, he'd have got more – the King's not one to give anything away unless his hand's forced. But here he thought he'd be able to provide for him without being out of pocket himself—'

How? Reynold and Will asked him.

'Why, by marrying the Countess of Warenne to my lord – you remember Earl Warenne died on the way back from Toulouse?'

They nodded, remembering too the rich lands of King Stephen's younger son; his widow was a prize for any man.

'And that whoreson Archbishop has forbidden the match on grounds of affinity – because my lord's her first husband's second cousin. It leaves my lord landless as he's always been.'

They muttered indignantly over such deprivation.

'That's not what cuts him deepest, though—' The agitation on le Bret's face was genuine. 'The fact is he's been sweet on her from the first time he saw her. She's a fair woman, I'll own it. And all was going as merry as a marriage bell until that fellow interfered.'

Reynold pulled his lower lip. 'A dispensation—' he began; but le Bret cut him off impatiently, saying that his lord was for Rouen and the Empress, his mother; and he should follow him so soon as the Council was over. 'I'll wait awhile,' he told them, 'for this Archbishop may overreach himself – he's turned mighty arrogant of late. If he upsets the King again—'

'If I were king,' said Will dreamily, 'nor archbishop nor pope should gainsay me. What use to wear a crown except to have your will?'

'Then you'd not be king but tyrant,' objected le Bret, and that set him off again on the tyranny of Churchmen and of the Archbishop in particular. He was still railing when the bats began their darting, noiseless flight and it grew too dark to see.

Yesterday's rain had done nothing to moderate the heat; as the sun rose higher in the cloudless sky, the air, charged with moisture, hung still and heavy like tepid water. In Woodstock Great Hall the barons sweated, mopped their brows and cursed, fanned themselves and vented inexplicable irritations on neighbours who pressed too close. A crowd stood round the door, grateful for the least breath of air, then pushed and fought to reach their seats as the Archbishop arrived.

The King came soon after but my lord of Leicester was not the only one to notice that his greeting of the Archbishop was perfunctory and that the usual whispered asides between them were conspicuously lacking. Henry sat hunched in an ominous and watchful silence, reminding Leicester uncomfortably of a cat at a mousehole.

The long hot hours dragged on as one tedious matter after another was debated. The contagion of unease had touched everyone so that the hall was very quiet when de Luci finally announced that they had come to the last item of the day's business. The King accepted the parchments from him, ran his eye over them and remarked curtly that he noted more than one hundred murders had been committed by clerks in England since the beginning of his reign. In view of the number and gravity of the crimes, he would look into juridical procedure. A ripple of interest ran round the hall. Abruptly Henry asked de Luci to enumerate some of the offences.

Thomas did not look up but he listened carefully, wondering where all this was tending. Surely Henry would never try conclusions with the Church? The Gregorian theory of universal papal surveillance had been gradually accepted over the last thirty years and in its wake a great tide of religious zeal had swept Europe; even the schism had not stilled it. Was it possible that Henry did not realise how men's attitudes had changed since the dark days of Anselm and King William Rufus? It was one more pointer to the fact that the quality of the advice he was now receiving was dubious in the extreme. However, Thomas was sure he would be able to make him see his error once he had explained the position clearly.

'Philip de Brois, a former canon of Bedford, tried in the Bishop of Lincoln's court for the murder of a knight, and cleared by compurgation—' read Richard de Luci from his list, then stopped with a glance of apology at the King as the Archbishop was heard to murmur that it was surely pointless to rehearse the numbers of those subsequently found innocent.

'Hear the rest of the story before you comment!' said Henry coldly, and nodded at de Luci to go on.

'Having reason to doubt the justice of this verdict, the Sheriff of Bedford, Simon Fitzpeter, arraigned the said Philip before his own court. He responded by beating the sheriff's messenger half to death and heaping abuse on the sheriff himself. The sheriff has reported to the King this offence to his royal dignity.'

'Well?' snapped Henry, staring at Thomas. 'Do you approve such behaviour in the priesthood? A man of violence masquerades beneath his cloth! He should be punished, both for homicide and for the abuse of a royal official!'

Startled by the vehemence of Henry's attack, Thomas tried to temporise. 'Certainly, my lord King, he must be punished for his insolence to your sheriff but the question of homicide does not arise. He was tried and adjudged guilt-less—'

'Tried by one of your bishops. We all know the Church sweeps her scandals beneath her skirts. Simon Fitzpeter *knew* he was guilty; that was why he reopened the case.'

Thomas saw the tell-tale signs of undisciplined fury appearing in Henry's face, the distorted mouth and glaring eyes, the throbbing temples and the patch of high colour on each cheekbone. He thought with sudden shock, This is aimed at me personally.

He answered with a calm he was far from feeling: 'It is impossible that he be tried again on the same charge, just as it is impossible that he be tried in any but an ecclesiastical court. However, I will myself have him arrested and will try him in my own court.'

When he had finished speaking there was a stunned silence. He looked quickly at Henry who sat as though turned to stone; all the colour had left his face. 'I will see to it instantly, my lord King,' Thomas said in as firm a voice as he could summon.

He would have been very glad at that moment to get himself out of the hall unobserved, yet by the time his retinue had gathered together their inks and quills and parchments, he managed his obeisance with all his usual stately courtesy. He was also apparently quite unruffled by the King's failure to acknowledge it.

But beneath his surface composure Thomas was filled with the uncomprehending disbelief of a man felled unexpectedly by a mortal blow. That Henry, to whom he had wished nothing but good— He mounted his horse and spurred blindly forward, intent only upon escape.

When he finally became aware of him, Thomas realised that Herbert had been declaiming for some time on the King's iniquitous behaviour, and so denunciatory was his tone that it could not be allowed to pass. 'Lay it not all at the King's door, Herbert,' he said, 'others are at fault here, too.'

'Nay,' returned Herbert roundly, 'I will not allow that any blame is yours.'

A little line appeared between Thomas's brows. 'I? – you mistake me. I meant the King's new friends and advisers. Roger de Clare in particular. He sees me as his enemy over the affair of Tonbridge castle and he is set on turning the King against me.'

'If you had excommunicated him when I advised it—'

Thomas shook his head.

'Why not? What use to wait? Attack is always the best means of defence; you, as a soldier, know that. Cut them off, root and branch, all those great lords. You have the right. They are defying you – defying Holy Church! Were I archbishop—'

Thomas smiled thinly. 'Perhaps that is why you are not.'

He returned to his own thoughts as Herbert fell into a sulking silence but now they were, if anything, more uncomfortable than before. For he knew it was not gentleness that had kept him from smiting de Clare; it was the knowledge that Henry was enamoured of de Clare's sister.

He left for Canterbury without attempting to see Henry, Herbert's words still working in his mind. A series of heavy thunder showers delayed the journey so that it was made up of short sharp dashes for cover with the heavy wagons rolling and pitching perilously behind them, and a leisurely ambling through suddenly sun-drenched dripping villages where people ran out to cheer and cry upon their Archbishop for the sacrament of Confirmation. The cavalcade halted on a number of occasions that Thomas might administer the rite. He never objected to being delayed thus, especially for the young, remembering how the Lord had always had the children brought forward. And it was while he was delivering the ritual slap to the cheek that he thought of a reprisal which should serve as warning to Roger de Clare. He would excommunicate that lesser magnate, William de Ros, who had had the temerity to lay hands on one of his servants. De Ros was not so close to the King that his action would look like a sideways blow at Henry, but Roger would see the writing on the wall.

With bell, book and candle, he uttered the fulminations against William de Ros the day after reaching Canterbury and sent out the letter conveying the sentence to the victim immediately. Herbert, passionately partisan, was quite unable to sit on such exciting tidings and spent his spare time recounting the story of the Archbishop's firmness in the face of the royal wrath and its resounding sequel to all who would listen; nor could Thomas make him see that there was no connection between the two events.

Perhaps Henry, too, thought there was, for a week later a letter from him arrived, ordering Thomas to absolve William at once. And while Thomas was still mulling over its decidedly peremptory contents, John of Salisbury who had been away on official business was announced.

One look at John's face showed something was very wrong. He faced Thomas without ceremony. 'What have you done?' he said.

Thomas frowned very slightly. He had noticed before that his friends were sometimes inclined to presume overmuch. 'I have excommunicated William de Ros,' he answered distantly, 'which he has well deserved.' He waved his visitor to a chair. 'Sit down, John. You look hot and tired from travel.'

John sat down and wiped his forehead with his hand. 'Yes,' he said, 'but I must speak now. Herbert said you had stood out against the King on a matter pertaining to finance – state finance. And he said that because the King was angered against you, he attacked the Church courts.'

'That was not the reason. De Clare and his sister have been working against me, dripping poison into the King's ear—'

'Over Tonbridge castle?'

'Of course.'

'I warned you not to push those claims too far. And now you have excommunicated one of his men. Why?'

'Why!' exclaimed Thomas, 'Why! You know that William de Ros forcibly expelled my priest Laurence!'

'That was nearly a year ago.'

Thomas turned round and walked to the window. He was breathing hard. 'Those barons need to be taught a lesson.'

John said with an unwonted sharpness, 'It seems to me that I still hear the voice of Herbert of Bosham rather than that of Thomas of London.'

Thomas kept his back turned, and knowing he was angry, John softened somewhat. 'Even I am well enough acquainted with the King to know that such an action will infuriate him. How much better should you know it. William de Ros is one of his tenants-in-chief.'

Thomas froze. How could he have forgotten that the King's permission was necessary for the excommunication of a tenant-in-chief? Bad as that law was, it had stood for a hundred years and Henry's inflexibility on the question of royal prerogative was well known. He was suddenly fearfully conscious that he had made a mistake and that John had known it instantly whereas he. . . .

He set to work to justify himself, and began to think he was succeeding until he saw that John did not look at him but kept his eyes lowered as if in distress. He remembered then how his friend had always been able to prick through his arguments in the old days. He sighed and abruptly told him of Henry's message. It was almost a relief to hear John put forward all the sound and prudent reasons for complying with the King's demand, for truth to tell, he was more apprehensive than he would have cared to admit. Henry's letter had taken him by surprise, as much by its tone as its content.

If he must outface the King, said John, let it be for good reason and not for something that could be construed as personal spite. Thomas opened his mouth to speak at that and John told him some of the tales which had been reported to him. 'Do not offend the King needlessly,' John finished. 'Hold to his friendship, then if there is a clash of interests, you may bolt it out in private. I am sure that he will be as good and gracious to his friend the Archbishop, as ever he was to his friend the Chancellor.'

When John had gone Thomas went off alone to his bedchamber which was the only place he was not likely to be interrupted. The pallet had been taken off the boards and flung across the sill to air; he could smell the sun-warmed straw mingled with the scents of summer on the air that breathed gently through the unshuttered window. The room was very bare; it contained only a press for his clothes, a plank bed and a prie-dieu in the corner. He knelt down as though to pray, then suddenly stood up again. He had come here, as he thought, to ask God to show him what to do but now he found that he had already decided to write Henry a conciliatory letter, begging an interview.

John was undoubtedly right; it would be positively danger-ous to take liberties with the King at this time. Nor, he thought with a slight flush rising on his cheekbones at the memory of John's biting comment, would he take quite so much note in future of Herbert's counsel. He was, perhaps,

135

a little too aggressive.

Thomas's miscalculation was even greater than he imagined. His efforts to recover Church property had further offended those great magnates who had not liked the elevation of a parvenu to the highest seat of ecclesiastical power. There was not another bishop in the land who was not connected by blood to the noble houses, and many of them to two or three, for the descendants of the Bastard's followers had inter-married until all the great families of England were linked by bonds of kinship. Quarrel among themselves as they might, they would close ranks against an outsider – and the ranks were closing now against that pretentious upstart, Thomas of London, who had been so foolish as to imagine himself their peer.

Henry, still smarting under the Archbishop's refusal to pay him the sheriff's aid, declined to meet him anywhere. Nor would he answer his letter but swore that he would communicate with him only by messenger until William was absolved.

Why? he shouted at de Clare in default of the offender – why should he be deprived of the company and advice of one of his tenants-in-chief because of the arbitrary action of the Archbishop? (For William had been obliged to retire from court lest the contagion of his excommunication touch the King.) Why? How had he dared? – and much more in the same vein while de Clare by carefully slanted remarks added further fuel to his fury.

When he had run down at last and sat in a silence broken only by his heavy breathing, de Clare said, 'I am ordered to present myself before the Archbishop's court to answer Canterbury's suit against me for the castle of Tonbridge.'

Henry's face grew even darker. 'He will deprive me of everything, it seems. Did not your predecessors hold it of mine? And now he thinks to placate me by a harsh sentence on Philip de Brois!'

De Clare's eyebrows went up.

'Can you believe this? – the Archbishop's court stripped him of his possessions and his income, and sentenced him to a public flogging!' Henry laughed shortly. 'Would they have done so much, do you fancy, had it not been for my intervention? When it was reported to me I told them, "Now you will swear to me that you have judged a just judgment and not spared the man because he is a clerk!"'

'An insult to your officer should have been tried in your court.'

Henry did not answer that so that de Clare wondered how far he was prepared to push this dispute over clerks. Instead the King muttered something about the tight grasp of the Church on worldly goods and his own poverty. Obviously Canterbury's claim to Tonbridge was rankling.

De Clare considered for a moment, then he said softly, 'The Archbishop's knights do not lack insolence, either. They were very free with their threats when they came to Tonbridge.'

'I suspected something of the sort when the Archbishop complained of their reception.'

De Clare decided that a little embroidery of the facts could do no harm. 'It was something overheard by one of my men that caused the trouble.' He stopped artfully as one who realises he is saying too much.

'Yes?' said Henry.

'I – er – cannot remember exactly—'

Henry eyed him. 'Why do you not wish to tell me?' His voice sharpened. 'Come, now, you cannot leave it there. Something said by one of the Archbishop's knights? Which one?'

'That I do not know but I will tell you the story. This knight was overheard to say that if de Clare hoped to keep

Tonbridge by pimping for his sister, the Archbishop bids him think again.'

Henry gave a start, overturning the winecup at his elbow. 'What,' he said, 'What!' His mouth worked soundlessly for a moment, then he began to cough. 'God's splendour!' was all he managed to get out between the crowing, whooping gasps. The paroxysm seemed to last a long time; Roger watched him with some anxiety, thinking that a summer cough like that was sure to last the season out.

Henry looked up at last with bloodshot, streaming eyes and before him de Clare shifted uneasily in his seat. Had he perhaps gone too far? Then he reminded himself that the famous rage was not directed at himself and put on his most candid expression. 'I had not meant to tell you,' he said.

The King looked beyond him. 'It's well you did.' After a while he said, 'Did you believe that observation came from the Archbishop himself?' De Clare half shrugged and made a noncommital movement of the head.

'He takes too much upon himself,' Henry muttered, 'but he shall see who's master in this kingdom.' And then more loudly, 'You did not let that fellow go scot-free?'

'Nay, he has a little memento to show for his impertinence.' Roger laughed, the wide gap between his front teeth very obvious. 'My men told him to show the Archbishop de Clare's reply!'

He did not quite catch what Henry said except that it sounded something like 'Plantagenet's reply'.

While not being altogether sure whether the Archbishop were truly the author of the offensive remark, Henry was unable to put it completely out of his mind. It sounded sufficiently like the old Thomas to arouse all his former scepticism about overnight conversions to holiness. He remembered that acid tongue of old, and the censoriousness regarding women. Yet he was equally suspicious of Roger

138

de Clare.

One thing was certain; Thomas needed to be taught a lesson. He must be vanquished in this battle over criminous clerks.

Grimly Henry began to consider his position. Undoubtedly the churchmen would follow Thomas's lead; so might some of the younger barons whose memories extended back no further than the anarchy when Church courts were the only law. They would not recall the firm hold his grandfather had kept on the clergy, refusing them even the right to visit the Pope without his consent.

So he would have it! He would not risk an Archbishop working against him as Theobald had worked against Stephen. They were *his* bishops, *his* subjects before they were the Pope's. It was Stephen's weakness which had brought about his situation; if he had dealt justice with a strong hand, the Church could not have encroached on his prerogatives.

It occurred to him suddenly that a number of the abbots and bishops might not be entirely wholehearted in support of Thomas – he had not been accepted by them without reluctance. Clarembald, Abbot of St Augustine's, and Gilbert Foliot were refusing still to profess their obedience; Chichester and York were old enemies of his.

But would their personal feelings outweigh their loyalty to the Church? He remembered then how Roger of York had outfaced him on a question of Church immunity over that blackmailing Dean of Scarborough years ago, and swore under his breath. So had the Treasurer of York, John Belmeis of Canterbury – and he was Thomas's friend. No, he feared they would stick together against a threat to the Church's power, however much it went against the grain to back Thomas of London. He must think of some way to alienate them from him.

He cast back and forth and could think of nothing. Well,

it might be that the Archbishop's assumptions of infallibility would do it for him. . . . In the meantime, two sees were vacant, those of Poitiers and Worcester. He would separate one friend from the Archbishop, at least, by giving Poitiers to John Belmeis. That reminded him of that other John – John of Salisbury – who was, he was convinced, the malign influence which had caused this change in Thomas. No honours for him – banishment should be his portion if he did not watch his step. Worcester he would grant to his cousin and boyhood friend, Roger, brother of the Earl of Gloucester. And be damned to any objections by the Chapters or the Pope.

Henry received Thomas's letter informing him of the absolution of William de Ros with a satisfaction he took care to hide lest it be reported to him. He flung it down before the messenger, saying shortly, 'I owe him no thanks for this now.'

He was hearing Mass next day when he realised the letter had contained no apology for Thomas's flat refusal to accept royal jurisdiction over clerks. Could it be that Thomas truly believed himself in the right? He knew that in this matter he was right and Thomas wrong. Why could Tom not see it? How had things gone so wrong between them? The fault was not his, he was certain, but the wall between their two minds was now so high that his old friend seemed a stranger. And always he came back to the hard fact that Thomas could not see what was self-evident.

I will have justice, Henry vowed. Murderers and rapists shall not walk unchecked in my kingdom and laugh in their sleeves at the soft fools who imagine that to be unfrocked is the worst ill that can befall a clerk. They shall feel the weight of royal punishment. He brooded for a while on Thomas's well known sentiments on mercy and atonement, shrugging his shoulders over such naivety concerning men of the kind they were dealing with. Tom had always prated much of the need for time to repent, blinding himself to the fact that most evil-doers wish only to continue doing evil.

That's what is wrong with the hierarchy, thought Henry with sudden shock. They see men always in relation to God while the secular arm sees men in relation to one another. The better men among the clergy have such care for the souls of the wicked that they forget the bodies of their victims. Well, he would not – and strangely, because he saw himself ranged on the side of the innocent, his anger began to turn towards the Church. He bent so indignant a glare on the officiating priest that the poor man visibly faltered in exhorting the congregation to behold the Lamb of God. Henry noticed nothing; his thoughts ran on. . . . In a harsh and wicked world, talk of mercy was so much moonshine – and anyway, the Church, confident of God's compassion, should be happy to send repentant sinners to a Judgment which cannot be mistaken. Though if God forgave – his mind hesitated a moment at his daring – where would justice be?

Mercy and justice are incompatible. He hesitated, only for a moment, at the tremendous truth. He did not know he had built another course on the wall of misunderstanding between himself and Thomas, nor would he really have cared. Justice was coming to mean much more than love.

Every day brought news of some fresh outrage committed by members of the clergy – a murder in Salisbury, the theft of a silver chalice from a London church, an accusation of rape and murder against a clerk in the diocese of Worcester. Henry's determination to punish the offenders grew in proportion to his indignation on behalf of the victims.

Three weeks previously Thomas had consecrated the King's cousin Roger Bishop of Worcester. Here – with this last case – Henry saw his chance. Roger would know whom to obey. He commanded trial in the royal court. When, a day or two later, he heard that the Archbishop had forestalled him by ordering his new suffragan to put the accused in the episcopal gaol, his threats against his relative frightened the onlookers almost into a panic.

But Roger of Worcester had the martial blood of old Robert of Gloucester in his veins and he stood firm in obedience to his metropolitan. For the moment, there was nothing Henry could do. That only hardened his determination to bring Thomas low.

VI

September 1163

By THE EARLY AFTERNOON the Queen had tired of hawking, and despite the entreaties of the young knights, would return to the castle and less strenuous pastimes. She affected not to hear them, merely turning her dazzling smile in their direction; their protests died away and the inevitable shoving and manoeuvring to gain the place nearest her began. She laughed to herself as she pulled round the horse's head, they were so young in their eagerness to be brought to her notice. But the ardour in those beardless faces pleased her nonetheless.

Shadows raced over the wide sweep of downland that rolled away northwards, an ocean of yellowed grass, strewn with great grey boulders. To the north, in the direction of Marlborough, low hills broke the skyline where the forest ended on an escarpment above the town. A strong, whipping wind had brought colour to her cheeks and a sparkle to her eyes; Henry Fitzgerold, her Chamberlain, coming up behind, was struck with her glowing look. He took his right hand from the reins and waved dismissively behind him. He had reasons to speak with the Queen privately.

When they had sufficiently outdistanced the rest of the party they slowed the horses to walking pace and rode quietly side by side, the Queen listening with interest to all that the Chamberlain of her household had to tell of the deepening rift between the King and the Archbishop. Tale bearers had wasted no time in bringing word of the public quarrel to Eleanor and she had been equally swift in ordering Henry Fitzgerold to garner all he could of the rumour and hearsay that was circulating in the King's court.

She glanced at him now, a man with big bones and little flesh, cadaverous and gloomy looking. But for all his melancholy appearance, he had an unexpected dry wit that pleased Eleanor and besides, he was her devoted slave.

She laughed. 'It's over then, at last – the great love affair!' She saw his eyelids flicker and instantly regretted the unfortunate turn of phrase. It must remind him of her husband's shaming pursuit of other women. She held her head higher and kept her gaze unflinchingly upon him. 'So strong an attachment between men from such disparate backgrounds—' She shrugged. 'It could not last. Doubtless ambition drove the Chancellor to pretend a deeper affection than he truly felt. But now—' She stopped there because she saw the hungry worship in his face and knew he was still thinking of the King's latest affair. He had undoubtedly heard more while he was gleaning other gossip on her behalf; but he would not repeat that to her, the subject was unmentionable between them.

All she knew of it she got from Mabille whose husband served the King, and there were times when she wished she had no such source. But here in Wiltshire it was not forced upon her notice and she was gradually surrounding herself with kindred spirits. She had her friends, her children, her admirers; her own court in miniature for numbers of young knights were attracted by its reputation for light-hearted frivolity. And if they (and Henry, for she knew he had his ears as she had hers) took the surface froth for the whole content, Eleanor was prepared to let them.

She never forgot her own inheritance. The knowledge that the lords of Aquitaine would welcome her return, would rise as one against her husband if she gave the word, had been an anchor to her in the darkest days. She was no helpless, slighted wife without redress should he think to divorce her. . . . And even if he did not try to cast her off, she was determined to go home eventually, and to take Richard with her. But all that lay buried in her mind, hardly recognised as yet.

For the time being, life was pleasant enough at Marlborough. She had invented a most diverting new game, the Courts of Love, in which questions concerning the code of courtesy were posed by the knights and deliberated upon and decided by the ladies. Devised in the first place as a mockery of Henry's mania about his own royal courts, she had been amazed at its success; now scarcely a day passed without the charade being played out. Knights and ladies both seemed to take it all so seriously, and its influence on the young men was already plain. Their deference to womankind was approaching that of the troubadours of her youth. And for herself, she liked to sit back and listen; it was so easy to read between the lines of question and answer. They did not appear to realise how much they gave away about themselves.

There were one or two frequent visitors who said as little as she did herself – notably that tall, dark knight whose beauty had so impressed itself upon her the first time she saw him. She knew his name now. It was Hugh de Morville. He came often, sometimes alone but usually with an equally silent companion. She had not taken any account of him though, after noting that he lacked both wit and good looks. She had wondered why they came at all, seeing they took no interest in any of the ladies until it occurred to her they might be spies. She had decided to try to uncover their object.

145

When she saw them in the hall that night, their eyes fixed unwaveringly on her as always, she smiled to herself. I cannot complain of their taste, she thought, though with so many younger ladies present. . . . A young knight called Bertrand had just asked a very complicated question which had to do with a choice between allegiance to his lord or to the lady of his heart.

Eleanor raised her hand. 'Before we decide, let us have the judgments of some of the other knights to see what they have learnt from us.' She leaned forward, fixing de Morville with her eyes. 'Seigneur?' she said.

De Morville swept his slow, insolent glance around. He is quite extraordinarily handsome, she thought. How unfair for such looks to be wasted on a man! Yet nothing about him stirred her heart, his beauty was a thing to marvel at rather than desire.

'I should have no hesitation in obeying my lady's wishes in such a case,' he said.

'Oh – oh! How do you square that with your feudal oath?' they all cried.

The breaking of an oath, he informed them solemnly, cannot enter into it. We swear our homage by life, limb and earthly honour – none of these are affected for our lives and limbs are at the disposal of our lord still, and earthly honour must give place to spiritual honour at all times. It is spiritual honour we give our lady, as Heaven is the seat of love.

Eleanor blinked. She was finding it hard to hold de Morville's gaze. He is talking nonsense, she thought.

'Who is your lord, seigneur?' she asked as if in idle curiosity.

'Archbishop Thomas of Canterbury.'

'Oh!' they shouted, 'Now we see where spiritual honour comes in!' And the crowd dissolved in laughter.

'The ladies will withdraw to give their judgment,' Eleanor said.

She was no wiser than before as to his reasons for coming

146

but now she did not think he was one of Henry's spies. And
his reply had recalled the Archbishop to her mind – and the
things Henry Fitzgerold had said were being repeated of
him. The man must be mad – or drunk with his newly
acquired power. Well, she had never liked him, had always
thought that pale, candid gaze denoted guile. But then,
Henry had always a talent for loving the wrong people. His
troubles were of his own making.

The twisted smile that marred the sweet curve of her lips
was not a pleasant thing to see. Any hint that he might reap
what he had sowed pleased her now. When the ladies asked
her for her verdict she was not sure what they were talking
about.

October 1163

As the King rose to speak, the low murmurings among the
bishops and magnates died away; they straightened in their
seats and turned their faces from lesser men to give him
their full attention. A few of the temporal lords glanced at
the Archbishop of York to see what would be his reaction
when his sovereign's anger was unleashed against him for
refusing to accept Canterbury's supremacy, but they looked
quickly back at the King in surprise when they heard his
opening words and his use of the royal plural.

'We have been silent awhile,' he announced, 'and meekly
listened how you bishops are willing to dispose yourselves
towards our royal rights and rule here in England. Now
while we have watched your doings we have been searching
our mind as to what kind of fault you might happen to have
found in us that we must needs be less worthy than other
kings who have been before us. We desire at this time to
turn our speech chiefly towards those men of forfeited lives
whom you name clerks, but we call much worse than lay-folk
in that they have the foolhardiness to push themselves into
the ordinations of Holy Church, turning her dignity into

147

mockery. They may rather be called doers of the works of the devil than consecrated clerks.

'Now you, the bishops, maintain that it is written in your canons that such dishonourable doings should be protected. You think that none besides yourselves are able to understand the laws of the Emperor or of the Church—'

Thomas dropped his eyes and compressed his lips as the tenor of Henry's speech sank in. So this Council, which had purported to deal with Canterbury's claim to primacy in England, had been called here at Westminster with a very different object: to press home the King's claims to jurisdiction over ecclesiastics. Henry had tricked him into coming here and it was plain that he intended to force the issue.

He looked up and met Henry's eyes as he drew to a close: '—demand of you, the bishops, by the honour and obedience you owe the Crown, that you deliver all such clerks as you let wrongfully slip away from our power into our hand for rightful punishment.' Henry gave him a long level stare as he added, 'And as to this matter, we desire to have clear answers from you!'

Thomas smiled as well as he was able. 'We shall consult together, my lord King,' he answered, and watched by the lay lords who were muttering and whispering to one another, the bishops withdrew to one side of the hall. There they all began to talk at once except Roger of York and Hilary of Chichester who put their heads together a little apart from the rest, and Gilbert Foliot who sat alone, drumming his fingers on his knees and looking at no one.

Henry of Winchester stepped forward, and laying his hand on Thomas's arm, said, 'We shall be faithful to your judgment, my lord Archbishop.' He threw a challenging look at the others as he spoke and old William of Norwich nodded tremulously, 'Aye, where you lead, we will follow.'

'It must be the desire of all of us to heed the King's will in all things,' said Thomas quickly; he had seen the apprehensive looks of the Bishops of Lincoln and Chester. Now, as Walter of Rochester, brother of the late Archbishop Theobald, drew closer to his elbow, he added, 'Save only when it sets itself up thwartingly against the will of God and the laws of Holy Church.' And he hurried on to tell them that the ancient decrees of the Fathers thus ordained: 'If clerks shall be taken in such unseemly deeds as manslaughter, theft or robbery, they shall for a beginning be suspended from all offices and then be excommunicated and degraded from all orders.' And he added that as long as he could uphold it, the law of the Church should not fall.

Hilary of Chichester, with an air of impartiality that sat ill on a bishop when the Church's laws were threatened, pointed out that the crimes of clerks were the more reprehensible by reason of their orders and should therefore be punished more harshly than the crimes of laymen.

Thomas gave him a look expressive of the contempt he felt. 'No,' he said, 'We cannot hand over the clergy to the King for further punishment. *Nec enim Deus judicat bis in idipsum* – God judges not twice for the same offence. And would it not be scandalous that the hands consecrated to God, to fashion the image of the Saviour of the world, should be tied behind the back, and the head anointed with the sacred chrism should have a rope about its neck on a shameful gallows?'

Only Gilbert Foliot brought nothing to the discussion but continued to tap his knee impatiently; however, when the others finally accepted the Archbishop's suggestion that they might promise whatever the King wished providing the rules of their Order were not infringed, he nodded shortly and followed them back into the body of the hall.

Thomas faced the King with confidence. 'The customs of Holy Church,' he stated, 'are set forth in the canons and decrees of the Fathers.' He saw Henry's mouth tighten and rushed on, determined to get in his preamble. 'It is not fitting for you, my lord King, to demand nor for us to consent to any innovations. We who stand now in the place of the Fathers ought humbly to obey the old laws.'

'That is all I am asking of you – that you obey the old laws of my predecessors. In their days there were holier and better Archbishops than you who never raised any controversy about obeying them!'

'Whatever was done by former kings against the Church's laws, and whatever practices were observed out of fear of your predecessors ought not to be called customs, but abuses,' Thomas returned sharply. 'Holy Writ teaches us that such practices ought to be abolished. You say the bishops of that time kept silence but that example does not give us leave to assent to anything that is done against God or the Church or our Order.' He suddenly became aware that his tongue was running away with him and finished hastily. 'However, you will always find us obedient in everything we can possibly consent to, saving our Order.'

Henry, who had been holding himself in with the greatest effort, suddenly hammered on the table. 'Will you give me an answer?' he shouted.

'I have told you that we will do whatever you wish, providing it is not contrary to the rules of our order.'

'By God's eyes,' screamed Henry, 'let me hear no more of your order! You shall obey me.' He had sprung to his feet, face crimson and eyes distended, but Thomas refused to look at him; he carefully arranged his gown and seated himself as one who has no more to say. But he felt his hand jerk as Henry continued to bellow imprecations at him, and hoped that no one had noticed the involuntary movement.

The King turned his attention to the bishops, demanding of each one separately that he give his assent to observe the customs of the realm. Thomas was thankful that he began with Henry of Winchester, that man of steel, who replied firmly that they would do so, saving their order only. As the obnoxious phrase was repeated by one after another down the line, Henry's jaw knotted; when he came to the Bishop of Chichester he barked the question at him in such a way that Hilary, perhaps remembering the last time he had tried to outface the King, visibly faltered and substituted *bona fide* for *salvo ordine meo*.

Convinced at this that Hilary was trying to trick him in some way, Henry began to scream and swear like a madman. He rounded on Thomas again, and hurling abuse at him, demanded that he swear without any reservation to observe the customs of the kingdom. Thomas drew a deep breath. Henry was shifting his ground here from a specific issue to a much more general one, and one that contained many hidden dangers.

Thomas knew his history and he remembered how the first Henry had left bishoprics vacant indefinitely that he might appropriate the revenues, and how Stephen had made the Chapter of London pay him £500 for the privilege of electing their own bishop. It could mean handing over the Church to the King. That he would never risk.

When he spoke his voice was grave and steady. 'My lord King, we have already sworn fealty to **you** by life, limb and earthly honour. We cannot promise to **observe** them in any other way.'

Henry's mouth moved and he made an inarticulate sound that was almost lost in the clatter of his booted feet as he sprang up. Abruptly he stormed out of the hall, leaving them all in a hush that was absolute for a few seconds. When the hall was emptied of the lay lords who followed him swiftly, the bishops turned with one accord upon Hilary, angrily blaming him for altering their agreed-upon formula and thus bringing down the wrath of the King on them all.

Yet when they emerged into the quietness of an autumn

afternoon almost as warm as summer, Thomas knew only a curious feeling of calm and release. The long awaited storm had broken and had passed and he had weathered it without disgrace. No dread of what the future might hold could yet compete with his sense of an inner victory. He had nailed his colours to the mast and with that he was for the moment content. He even smiled as he saw a child nearby picking the last flowers from a clump of tall ragged daisies that grew in the angle of the wall. As he raised his hand in blessing, he caught sight of Gilbert and Hilary, the one tall and spare, the other short and rotund, standing side by side watching him narrowly. But there was nothing of satisfaction on their faces.

And Thomas was jolted out of his euphoric mood abruptly when he came back from Prime next morning to find a royal messenger awaiting him. He listened in silence to the words coldly delivered in the King's name, removing young Henry from his care and dispossessing him of the manors of Eye and Berkhamstead which he had held since his Chancellorship.

After a pause he said carefully, 'Where is the lord King now?'

'He is returning to London,' was the lofty answer, 'and as I heard when I rode here several bishops follow him.'

'I thank you,' was all Thomas said.

But although he tried to return to his prayers when the herald had gone, he could not keep his mind on them. I know they have gone to him only out of fear, he thought, and smiled twistedly when he recalled the King's penchant for arson where bishops' property was concerned. Of course they are afraid that he will destroy their goods in his rage. I cannot really blame them. But if they all desert me. . . .

Outside, the wind was blowing. He shivered suddenly. It had turned much colder. Some of that coldness seemed to have settled round his heart.

Henry was hungry after a long day's hunting and none too
pleased when the Bishop of Lisieux was announced just as
he was beginning his meal, but the pride he took in his
availability to petitioners at all times prevented him from
postponing the interview. However, his manner made it
obvious that it would be useless to address him on a subject
of any importance until he was fed and rested, or so Arnulf
of Lisieux, being no fool, conceived.

He was grateful enough at being invited to sup with the
King in private and decided to confine his conversation to
gossip while they ate. But it was difficult to think of gossip
which did not concern the matter he had come about and
after several false starts which received no answers he fell
silent.

Henry ate voraciously, cramming his mouth to capacity,
with what the Bishop (who was not overly dainty himself)
felt was a complete disregard for the feelings of others. His
eyes fastened on a dribble of gravy on the King's chin which
embarrassed him further, particularly as Henry turned towards him, saying sharply, 'Well, are you another come to
parrot *salvo ordine meo* at me?'

Arnulf, who a few months before had been loudly ad-
vocating the cause of ecclesiastical supremacy, had the
grace to colour slightly but he covered it by the promptness
and vehemence of his answer. 'No, my lord King, I have
no desire to shelter criminals from justice nor to deprive
you of your rightful jurisdiction over subjects. I am come to
place my services and advice at your disposal, should you
wish for them.'

Henry leaned back, watching him with narrowed eyes.
'Advice? What advice can you, who have been in Normandy and out of touch with my affairs, give me?'

Arnulf spoke hurriedly. 'I have been acquainted with the

Archbishop of Canterbury for many years and I think I know his weaknesses. He is obstinate and quite unable to believe he may be mistaken—'

Henry gave a snort. '*I* know he frequently mistakes his own will for that of Providence!'

'—yet he finds it difficult to sustain his will without the support of others. He needs the approval of his peers. And this being so, he is likely to weaken if he is isolated.'

There was no doubt now of Henry's interest. 'Go on,' he said.

Arnulf fumbled for a moment. 'If you had considered imposing any penalties on the English bishops for disobeying you—'

Henry nodded slowly. 'Yes, I see. Better to win them to my side with fair words.' He nodded again and smiled rather twistedly. He was thinking that he liked Arnulf of Lisieux rather less than he had done before and that was very little. All the same, his tone was very cordial as he invited the Bishop's advice on how to set about the task.

Yet when Arnulf had gone, Henry found himself torn. Public insult still rankled but now that his rage had cooled sufficiently he could see that harassing Thomas was not the way to gain his ends. And angry with him as he was, enough of the old fondness remained to make him resent other people's abuse of the Archbishop. The Bishop of Lisieux – his lip curled – would trim his sails to any wind. No, he would not follow *his* counsel. Better by far to bring Tom himself round with fair words. . . .

It was more than three months since he had seen him alone – there lay the root of the trouble perhaps. They were growing apart, each sovereign in his own sphere and unaware of the other's difficulties; each beset by advisers who would be only too pleased to see an open rupture between them.

Surely when they were face to face he would be able to

make Tom see that all men must live under the same law. He would explain that clemency might have its place – indeed, he had already proved his tolerance by taking no steps to punish Thomas himself for his illegal excommunication of William de Ros. He had overlooked his usurpation of royal authority, too, in banishing Philip de Brois.

Henry began to feel rather more cheerful. Persuasion was the answer. He would order the Archbishop to meet him in Northampton for a private interview at the end of the month. Doubtless Thomas would be as relieved as he at the prospect of restored amity between them.

But when the time came Thomas apparently saw no need to placate him with any appearance of eagerness. He approached the designated meeting place in such dignified state that Henry hastily sent word to him to wait outside the city which was full to overflowing. The King would come to him.

Not to be outdone, he put on his finest clothes and ordered his finest charger harnessed. It irritated him as shows of grandeur always did but he firmly repressed his annoyance. He had no intention of losing his temper this time; he would be as amiable as anyone could wish if it would get him his own way.

When he saw the Archbishop waiting at the side of the meadow, so quiet and composed that Henry knew he must be nervous, a great rush of affection suddenly overwhelmed him. There sat the man who had won his boyish heart at their first meeting, who had served him diligently and well for so many years as Chancellor. . . . Nothing could finally separate them. Under the clerical panoply was still the same Thomas.

Joyfully he spurred the horse forward; Thomas did the same. Almost too late, Henry saw the rolling eye and lowered head of Thomas's mount and pulled wildly on the reins; a gallop full-tilt at each other meant only one thing to trained chargers. Thomas realised what was happening at the same instant; yelling a warning he passed within a yard of the King. Henry began to laugh and was chuckling still when he had changed to a more docile mount and come up to face Thomas again. 'Well,' he said cheerfully, 'even our horses are at odds, it seems.'

Thomas smiled ruefully. 'And without reason.'

'No more have you reason to quarrel with me,' said Henry quickly. 'What reason can there be for *us* to quarrel?'

'Malicious tongues?' queried Thomas softly.

'A few maybe,' Henry acknowledged, 'though you should give me the credit of being able to recognise malice when I hear it. Tom' – he wheeled his horse a little nearer – 'Tom, why do you oppose me?' Before Thomas could answer he rushed on. 'Did I not raise you from poverty and lowliness to the pinnacle of honour and rank? And even that seemed little enough to me until I made you father of the kingdom, putting you even above myself. How is it, then, that all these proofs of my affection which everyone else remembers can be forgotten by you? For it seems to me that you are not merely ungrateful but oppose me wherever you can.'

He had seen Thomas stiffening as he spoke but he was still unprepared for his answer.

'Far be it from me, my lord. I have not forgotten those favours which God deigned to confer on me through you; nor will I act against your wishes in anything that accords with the will of God. You are indeed my lord, but He is my lord and yours. It would do neither of us any good if I were to obey your will and ignore His, for on the fearful day of judgment we shall both be judged. As St Peter says, we ought to obey God rather than men.'

There was a moment's silence, then Henry said curtly, 'I don't want a sermon from the son of one of my villeins.'

156

'It is quite true that I am not *atavis edite regibus*,' returned Thomas, 'but neither was St Peter on whom the Lord conferred the keys of the kingdom of heaven and dominion over the Church!'

Henry's eye flickered as he recognised the quotation from Horace. Thomas, it seemed, was trying to impress him with his learning. So the thrust about his origins had gone home.

'*He* died for his Lord,' he said.

'I am prepared to die for my Lord when the time comes.'

Henry had had enough of debater's points. 'I think you rely too much on the ladder you have mounted by,' he said drily.

'I rely on God; cursed is the man who relies on man. Nonetheless, I am still ready to serve your good pleasure, saving my order. But you really ought to have consulted me whom you have always found a faithful adviser rather than those who hate me although I have never harmed them. They have stirred up this bad feeling between us. You cannot deny that I was loyal to you always when I was Chancellor. How much more should you believe in my loyalty now that I am a priest!'

Henry sighed impatiently. There were those three hated words again – 'saving my order'. What could be wrong with Thomas? One might almost think that he suspected his King of nefarious designs against the Church. And it certainly sounded as if he were jealous of Henry's present advisers, yet of his own will he had opted out of that position. He said as much.

Thomas did not answer him. By turns Henry pleaded and insisted that he omit that infuriating phrase. Finally, seeing that Thomas was obdurate, he wheeled his horse as though to ride away but hesitated for one last look at the man who had been the David to his Jonathan. Thomas had not expected that backward glance and his face was showing the struggle his words had masked.

'Please!' said Henry. 'I beg it of you.'

He saw Thomas's jaw set. 'I cannot,' he said harshly.

Henry jabbed his spur into the horse with such force that it gave a startled whinny and leapt forward. Thomas went slowly back to his waiting entourage.

December 1163

The short December afternoon was waning when the Abbot of l'Aumône and the Count of Vendôme arrived at the Archbishop's house on the manor of Harrow. By the time the last horse had been stabled, the windows were already showing the flickering yellowish gleam of candlelight.

Thomas came into the hall to greet them. The worries of the last few weeks had left their mark on him; he looked pale and tired. But there was genuine pleasure in the smile with which he met his old tutor, Robert of Melun, as well as some surprise. Robert was now Bishop-elect of Hereford; he had not expected him on this mission. They talked for a time of old friends and days long past, the Abbot and the Count listening smilingly the while and adding their quota of reminiscence as mutual acquaintances were mentioned.

It was not until after supper that the real reason for the visit became apparent when the Abbot delivered to Thomas the letters he had brought from the Pope at Sens. Thomas took them with anxious care, glancing down at them from time to time while the Abbot was speaking, twisting them in his hands, the very picture of one who dares not, yet longs to look.

When the Abbot had finished, he turned away to break the seals, grateful for the low murmur of conversation between the others. These messengers from the Holy Father were, after all, men of very different standing from Hilary of Chichester who had come to mediate between the King and himself a few weeks ago.

Thomas had wondered then why Henry had chosen to send so slippery a character as advocate, until he had learned with some thankfulness that only three of his bishops had withdrawn their support from him. Of those three Hilary was the least objectionable emissary. Henry would have realised the impossibility of sending Roger de Pont l'Evêque of York, and Gilbert Foliot, the third name, was too unbending in his attitudes to act as mediator in anything.

The fact that Foliot had deserted him had come as a shock to Thomas. And yet – was it such a shock? Gilbert had taken no part in the discussion that had followed the breach with the King; he had remained silent and non-committal throughout. And he was Henry's confessor. Thomas had reserved those facts for later reflection, and had listened to Hilary's arguments on the King's behalf with as much patience as he could muster.

But bitterness had grown in him at what he thought of as Foliot's defection and when Hilary pointed out that the King had the power to do as he pleased, with or without the bishops' consent, Thomas had taken him to task in no uncertain manner, accusing him and those others of bartering the Church's liberties for the King's favour. 'Never will you have me as accomplice in such horrible presumption,' he finished hotly.

Hilary, who had kept his temper, smiled a faint superior smile. 'What is this dreadful evil that only you can see?' he enquired. 'The King merely asks us for respect and honour. He has promised that if we concede to him, he will never demand anything of us contrary to our order. Where is the evil in obeying and honouring the King?'

'There is nothing wrong in honouring the King, so we do not dishonour God. But you may be sure the King will make *you* keep *your* promises while you have no way to make him keep his.'

And that was still true, he reflected, as he skimmed swiftly through the Pope's letter. Henry was notorious for broken vows. He would promise anything to get his way and then conveniently forget it. . . . Working his way through the ponderous Latin phrases before his eyes, he became aware that the Pope was not prepared to back him.

He read the letter again, more slowly this time. It reminded him how the schism, instigated by the Emperor, had confused the Church, warned him lest the weakness which beset the Church's head spread to the limbs. It counselled pliancy and restraint. For a moment, the rock on ·which the Church was built changed to shifting sand as he remembered the Pope dared not antagonise Henry. He rolled the parchment abruptly, and not bothering to open the Cardinal's letters, turned back to the visitors. Their faces told him they had known the tenor of the contents.

He eyed them a moment but if they felt his look rebuked them they did not show it, merely smiling and nodding to him pleasantly as though they had nothing to do with the Judas kiss he had just received. And in the face of their kind and gentle words he found he could not hold to his aggrieved attitude; in part because of the reluctant respect he must feel for the Abbot of l'Aumône who for years had been Prior under Bernard of Clairvaux and still carried with him a little of the charisma of that great man; and in part because something in him longed to escape this terrifying duty of defying the King. If even the Pope would not stand with him. . . . Who was he to imagine that his conscience could sieve out truth more finely than theirs?

Weakening, he heard their counsel, nor did he notice that their arguments were the same as those of Hilary whom he had rebuffed and sent away unsatisfied. The Abbot was saying: 'For the lord King has told me personally that he will never introduce any novel customs, nor require you to do anything contrary to your order—' Thomas sank his chin upon his hand and listened but another part of his mind was remarking the stubble on the Abbot's tonsure and a curious mole he had at the side of his neck. He collected his wandering thoughts with an effort.

'So if you will but withdraw the qualification from your promise,' the Count murmured persuasively, 'peace and goodwill will be restored. Our lord the King feels his royal dignity has been affronted,' and he threw out his hands, palm up, and smiled a little ruefully as a man of mature years is entitled to do at the prideful follies of youth.

Thomas eyed him doubtfully. If he dared only believe it. . . . Perhaps Robert of Melun saw the irresolution in his look for he chimed in, speaking as an old friend who has only his former pupil's good at heart. 'What can be gained by angering the King? He knows well the power you wield as Archbishop. Did he not place it in your hands, secure in the knowledge that you would work together for the good of Church and state? But if you allow his sense of injury to grow, the old trust between you may be lost for ever.'

Slowly Thomas nodded. His own sense of injury at the Pope's refusal to stand by him opened his eyes to that truth. Had Henry felt as he now did? 'I am moved to think again on the matter,' he said at last, 'but give me time.'

'The King's patience is not inexhaustible,' began the Count of Vendôme but the Abbot shook his head at him. 'Prayer,' he pronounced. 'Prayer is the answer. God will guide the man who seeks the way with humble heart.'

Thomas thought, if you gave that advice to Henry, I'd be surprised. He was instantly ashamed, and his instinctive wish to make amends inclined him nearer to the Abbot's case. Yes, I will ask God to guide me, he told himself, as unaware that his mind was more than half made up already as of the reasons for it.

In the background, Herbert of Bosham listened to the deputation's reassurances of the King's favour with a faint, knowing smile and tried to catch his master's eye. It mattered not at all that he was unsuccessful; he knew the Archbishop would no more be impressed by honied words than by threats. And the silence which met his gentle probing after the visitors had retired served only to reinforce his view.

Herbert met William Fitzstephen next morning as he was hurrying through the hall after Chapter Mass. 'Come, come!' he said impatiently. 'Why are you dallying here?' He paused to stare at William's clothing. 'Why are you dressed to ride?'

'Has no one told you we ride to Woodstock? I thought the Archbishop—'

'To Woodstock? To the King?'

'Why, yes. Now the decision is made, the sooner, the better. Nor will he wait for the weather.' William waved his hand despairingly towards the open doors beyond which the slanting rain beat a tattoo on the paved court.

'Ah yes,' said Herbert. His hand had tightened on the book he held. His eye wandered past William to the door of the Archbishop's chamber. 'I had forgot,' he said.

William looked at him dubiously. 'I thought you might not agree that submission was the wisest course.'

'It is somewhat different when one knows all the reasons,' answered Herbert loftily. 'But I have no time for gossip now.' He walked away, still trying to doubt what he had heard, and saw the Archbishop come out of his room, harnessed for a journey. He knew then that it was true, and in a rage of misery and disappointment, turned away his head.

Thomas called to him. 'Herbert! Good friend, I have been looking for you. Do not think ill of me for this. I must see the King.'

'I had expected you to die before you would submit.'

'Those are high words to use of a difference of opinion.'

'A difference of opinion is not what you called it before.'

Thomas bit his lip.

'Well, you will do what you must,' said Herbert. He added with great magnanimity and not a little difficulty, 'I shall pray for you.'

The rest of the party bound for Woodstock began to gather then. Herbert bade them all Godspeed but he did not stay to watch them ride away.

Thomas found it easier than he had imagined to make his submission. He told the King he would be obedient in all things and observe the customs of the kingdom in good faith. That was the very phrase that had so enraged Henry when Hilary had used it at Westminster, but he let it pass now without a murmur. Since Hilary had gone over to him, he no doubt found it an acceptable compromise.

But Thomas looked in vain for any sign of the King's returning favour. He was not asked to share his dish, nor even to sit beside him except when it was necessary for them to speak together, and even then the King was cool and formal. No mention was made of returning young Henry to his care or of the restoration to him of the castle of Berkhamstead; indeed it soon became plain that the Court was to spend Christmas there. It began to seem he had humbled himself to no purpose.

It was on his last evening in Woodstock that the King informed him that he was not entirely satisfied. 'For,' he said with that glinting, sidelong look that Thomas had often seen him use on other men when he intended to even some old score, 'you cannot deny it was a public slight you offered me. And you will feel it fair, I am sure, to make a public retraction. Then let you summon the ecclesiastical dignitaries while I send for the barons to a Great Council to be held at Clarendon in four weeks' time, so that in the presence and hearing of all, your speech may be repeated for my honour.'

Yes, thought Thomas, that was Henry. A public apology for a public offence, an eye for an eye and a tooth for a tooth. Well, he had humbled himself here before de Luci, de Mandeville, Reginald de St Valery and William Cade, all of whom disliked him; to do so before the rest made no difference. And then, when Henry's royal pride was salved, perhaps they could make a fresh start. . . .

VII

January 1164

Iт was a drab January day on which the Great Council
opened, and so dark that candles were burning on the High
Table behind which the King sat with his eldest son at his
feet. But the body of the hall where the lesser barons and
knights thronged was almost lost in murky dusk.

The Archbishop of Canterbury was at the King's right
hand and the Archbishop of York to his left with the rest of
the bishops in due order of precedence. Only two sees
were left unrepresented on this most important occasion;
Bath and Wells because its incumbent was sick, and Durham
whose wealthy, aristocratic bishop took no account of events
so far from his northern fastness.

Seven great earls, as well as the two Justiciars, were there,
all come to watch the Archbishop's retrieval of the gauntlet
he had flung at the King's feet. Thomas glanced at them,
seeking out friends and enemies. He had reason to do so.
He had no intention of taking the oath of submission they
were all expecting.

Ever since Christmas he had been bitterly regretting his
over-hasty promise to the Pope's emissaries, and the speed
with which they had hustled him before the King. He knew
Henry as the Pope would never do – knew his trickery, his
evasions, his use of intimidation and threats – and though

the Pope might be deceived as to his intentions, Thomas, who had forgotten none of the confidences he had heard when he was Chancellor, was not. Henry meant to rule the Church – and Thomas meant to stop him.

The decision to go back on his promise had not come easily. He did not think he had been influenced by Herbert's morose and disapproving silence but he had to own that life was pleasanter after; he had been getting a little tired of the texts Herbert chose for him to study, all dealing with the horrible fates of God's betrayers. . . .

He felt the King's son move and touch his knee, and smiled absently down at him. 'When shall I come back to you?' whispered the boy. Thomas felt a pang. When, indeed? He answered with another question. 'Surely you like better to have your own household?'

'I like it well – but best to be with you.'

The King put out an ungentle hand, and without looking at Thomas, turned the child's head towards himself. Thomas saw the boy scowl and looked hastily away.

Men were still pushing for seats on the lower benches; the proceedings would not begin until all were settled. He felt another qualm at what must come and eyed the earls again. Ferrars was there and Salisbury, Arundel and Chester, de Clare and de Mandeville, Cornwall, Leicester and de Luci. Of them all, only Cornwall and Leicester would not look at him; they were the only two who did not share the sense of gleeful anticipation which was general in the hall.

At a sign from the King, Richard de Luci hammered on the table for quiet. When the last coughs and shuffles had died away, the King leaned forward and began to speak. 'You have all heard,' he announced, 'that my lord of Canterbury has vowed to me in private that he will obey me. I have brought you together here that you may hear that promise from his own lips.' His face was faintly flushed and his eyes shining as he turned to the Archbishop; it made him look like the boy Thomas had first known so that he hesitated for a fatal moment, feeling his resolution waver. Henry's eyes narrowed and hardened at once; he made a peremptory gesture with his hand towards the audience. Thomas stood up, taking his time. He would not be hurried.

But somehow, now, at the crucial moment, the words he had carefully chosen deserted him. Inwardly aghast at what he was about to do, he evaded the issue, losing himself in wordy locutions until the earls began to fidget and a low murmuring arose from the ranks of onlookers down in the hall.

'Now watch the King!' Hugh de Morville muttered into the ear of Reynold Fitzurse. 'You shall soon enough see a right royal Angevin rage if I am not mistaken.' And they both grinned when the King started to shout and shake his finger under the Archbishop's nose.

'If you will not promise me here most solemnly,' they heard, 'what you have already promised me in private – to observe the dignities and customs of the kingdom – then I swear to you that my hand is ready on my sword!'

After that the noise in the hall grew so great, what with the yelling of the King's men and the crying of others for silence, that they could not hear any more of the King's threats. But the behaviour of the bishops was indication enough for they had clustered together as far away from King and Archbishop as they could, casting terrified glances at the King's knights who, infected with his anger, were shaking their fists and making lewd gestures in their direction.

'They look like a flock of sheep ready for slaughter,' said Hugh, but Reynold did not hear that either; he was too busy shouting 'Réaux! Réaux!' and other war-cries in concert with the rest. Hugh moved over by Will de Tracy who seeing the stubborn shaking of the Archbishop's head, was standing rooted with the look of a man who is undecided whether to fight or flee. He jumped when Hugh touched him. Then he said, 'What will come of this? Has he run

167

mad to go against the King in this way? I'll not share in his treason!'

Hugh laughed softly; he seemed lit by an inner excitement that was different in some way from that of the others. 'Madness?' he said. 'Of course it's madness but he'll call it by some other fine high-sounding name. And some will see it his way.'

'Not me,' said Will. 'Not after this. I'll make my peace with the King.'

Hugh turned his head and looked at him, and Will shifted his shoulders uncertainly. Surely Hugh did not mean to stand by the Archbishop? But he was a law unto himself and he could see further through a haystack than most men across an open field. Will felt a sudden doubt.

He watched the bishops file away led by the Archbishop. The King began to shout at the earls then and stamp up and down, and after a while, his uncle, the Earl of Cornwall, and the Earl of Leicester, one of the justiciars, rose up and followed them.

'Those two are friends of the Archbishop,' murmured Hugh in his ear. 'If he heed any, they may bring him to his senses.'

Will heard the disappointment in his tone this time. He scents blood, he thought, and will not miss the kill. That's why he'll never leave him. Not even for fear of the King.

In the small room to which they had withdrawn, the clergy had separated into two groups. Eleven bishops sat at one end silently watching the tableau at the other where William of Norwich and Jocelin of Salisbury continued to plead with Thomas as they had done for the better part of the day.

In characteristic fashion Henry had concentrated his ire upon these two who had offended him in the past; he was threatening both with death or mutilation. They knelt before the Archbishop now in a state of abject terror while Leicester and Cornwall beseeched him to take pity on them and obey the King.

Thomas's face was pale as ashes. 'I cannot,' he cried. 'You do not know what you are asking.'

Leicester looked grim. 'My lord Archbishop, you know we are your friends. Yet the King is in such a passion that we—'

Cornwall broke in abruptly. 'Unless you grant the King full satisfaction he will force us to commit a dreadful crime with our own hands. For God's sake, Archbishop, do not put us in such a position. What can we do?'

Thomas stared at him blankly, then closed his eyes. 'It would not be so unheard of if it should befall us to die for the laws of the Church,' he replied in a scarcely audible whisper. 'A host of saints have taught us that by word or example. The Lord's will be done.'

Old William of Norwich started to whimper softly. Leicester threw up his hands in desperation, then whirled round to face the door as the latch rattled. But it was only Richard of Hastings, Master of the Templars, and Tostes de St Omer, one of his knights, come to add their pleas to those of the rest.

'God's wounds!' cried Thomas, very loud, when they began their persuasions, but then he apologised and listened quietly to their arguments which were exactly the same as those the Abbot of l'Aumône had used a month earlier. They assured him that once he had publicly satisfied the King, he would never hear mention of the customs again. 'This we faithfully promise you,' they concluded, 'and may our souls be condemned to eternal damnation if henceforth the King demands of you anything contrary to your order.'

Thomas sat with drooping shoulders for a moment, staring into the tear-stained face of the old bishop who still clung to his legs. Then he straightened his back. 'So be it,' he said wearily, 'I am persuaded by your promise. I will submit to the King.'

There was an astonished silence. Leicester looked quickly

at the two Templars and saw they were as taken aback as he. He cleared his throat and turned away his eyes from the sight of William of Norwich busily wiping his nose on the hem of his gown. 'Are you ready then?' he asked, 'It would be – ah – advisable not to keep the King waiting any longer than we must.'

A hush fell over the hall as Thomas led his bishops back to their seats. When he stood up before them all to make his recantation his breath came too short for him to continue but after a pause he began again more strongly. 'My lord King, if the dispute between us had concerned my personal rights, I would have yielded to you at once. But where the laws of the Church are in question, you should not be surprised at my punctiliousness for I must account to God for my stewardship. Now, trusting in your clemency, I consent to your demand. I declare that I will observe the customs of the kingdom in good faith.'

Henry's mouth twisted as he tried to hide his triumph but it rang in his voice for all to hear. 'You have all heard what the Archbishop has conceded to me. All that remains is for him to command the bishops to the same.'

'They will satisfy your honour as I have done,' answered Thomas. He was calmer now, and felt himself beginning to relax. Relief was creeping into his mind – relief that the Templars' promise had freed him from the need to dare the King's wrath. He had never wished to quarrel with him and if it were true that this submission was merely a sop to the royal pride and no threat to the Church's interests, he was content. He sighed a little, wondering where the old intimacy between the King and himself had gone.

It was Jocelin of Salisbury's turn to take the oath but instead of kneeling meekly like the rest of them, he half-turned to the Archbishop. 'What shall I do, my lord?' he asked. 'Is it truly your will that I make this promise?'

Henry glared from him to Thomas. 'Well, speak,' he bellowed. 'Or have you still reservations?'

For a second, Thomas's tongue would not obey him, then he said sharply to Jocelin, 'Grant to my lord King the same courtesy as have we all!' To Henry he said nothing for he could not; the way he had looked at him still had him by the throat. But he thought distressfully and with a sinking heart of the love he had always taken for granted. Could it be dead? He knew then how much he had depended on it even when they were at odds.

His heart beat quieted as the rest of the bishops made their promises without interruption, and he stood up as soon as they were finished, waiting for the King to dismiss the Council. The afternoon was dying and he was eager to get away. But Henry made no move to rise. He addressed his barons.

'With your own eyes you have seen the Archbishop and the bishops vow to keep the customs and the laws of my realm. Now, lest any dispute arise later on this matter, let the oldest and wisest of the nobles retire, and with my clerks, recall these customs of my grandfather, King Henry. Let them be written down and brought to me.'

Thomas stood in stricken silence. So the Templars' promise had meant nothing – though perhaps they had not known of the King's intention. It was possible that they had been duped as he had been. And yet he dared not look at them in case their faces showed their foreknowledge; that would be more than he could bear. William Fitzstephen was pulling on his arm and he sat down blindly. Afterwards he had no memory of leaving the hall.

But he felt easier that night when he realised he would have a breathing-space; it would take time to prepare such a document. Many of those old customs were English, handed down since time out of mind and inherited by the Normans when they came here. Richard de Luci and Jocelin de Balliol were to discharge the task and something of the contents was sure to leak out before he was faced with it. Oh God, he thought desperately, let it not contain what it

171

will be impossible to agree to. Does Henry wish to crush me utterly? I was right to fear such a rupture between us from the beginning. But how has it happened? – and thinking back over all his actions since he became Archbishop, he could not see how he could have acted differently.

When his man, Roger, came in, full of concern at his wan looks, and ordered him a special posset of eggs beaten up with wine and soft ewes' milk cheese, he asked for Herbert. He had not even finished the cup when Herbert arrived which made him think that he had been expecting the summons. Surprisingly enough, there were no recriminations for his *volte-face*; something had softened Herbert. It did not occur to Thomas that it might be his own appearance.

And Herbert was easy to talk to. There was no doubt where his loyalties lay. His indignation far outdistanced Thomas's. To hear him talk you might think he would lay hand to sword himself and seek out the King to avenge his Archbishop. Thomas spent the remainder of the evening soothing him and pointing out that they had not yet seen the customs in writing – and that such fierce talk was not seemly in a clerk.

'He means to degrade you, though,' said Herbert. 'I saw his expression when he spoke to you. He will have you brought low if he can. But stand you fast! – God is at your shoulder as Satan is at his!'

Thomas shook his head but his heart failed again as he remembered too the look the King had bent on him.

Next morning they were just finishing their bread and ale in the dark January dawn when the King's herald arrived to summon the ecclesiastical lords to another meeting. Thomas's and Herbert's eyes met.

Yet when they entered the hall from a day even more gloomy than the previous one, they could not miss the pile of documents in front of Richard de Luci and Jocelin de Balliol, and the careful way they avoided the eyes of the bishops. My own man, thought Thomas furiously of de

172

Luci, who did me homage when I was Chancellor and never has renounced his fealty. All was planned in advance, done in advance. Anger rose in him like a tidal wave, reddening his cheeks and thinning his lips to a hard line.

But by the time the Council opened he was in command of himself, sitting shoulders hunched as the documents were read aloud. What he heard made it plain that Henry was determined to have his own way. It went far beyond anything he had feared. The Church was to be made answerable to the King and civil law to have precedence over canon law.

Henry's glittering eye roved about the hall as though seeking dissident expressions, yet his mouth was complacent. He is so sure he has me taken in his trap, thought Thomas, so sure of himself and his power. Presently as his mind grew cooler, he recalled the menacing attitudes of the knights on the previous day. I will speak softly, he decided, I will procrastinate. But seal his documents? No, I will not, come what may.

Henry was saying: 'You have allowed that these customs belong to me. Therefore, lest any question ever arise about them, we will that the Archbishop affix his seal to them.' The little smile that played about his lips was too much for Thomas.

'Never,' he snapped. 'Never, by Almighty God, will my seal be affixed to them while life is in this earthly vessel.'

A low buzzing rose from the hall. Henry stared incredulous, his mouth working. Then he turned to Richard and Jocelin.

Thomas sat down and looked at his hands. He was surprised at how they shook. He lifted his head and his eyes fell on Hugh de Morville, towering above the shorter men. Hugh smiled at him but Thomas looked away and kept his eyes firmly from that quarter thereafter. That smile, which from another of his knights might have warmed him, bothered him more than all the threatening glares of the

173

King's men.

Again the King asked him to seal the customs and again he refused. Finally a copy of the document was brought to Thomas and another given to Roger of York. Roger sat fingering it with downbent head, pretending to read, but the movements of his lids as he peered about under his eyelashes showed that he was watching for others' reactions.

All the while the noise from the hall swelled louder as the knights and barons down there argued over the Archbishop's unexpected refusal, and some yelling broke out as one of the flaring wall cressets sputtered and spat sparks onto the men near it. Thomas thought – If one among them draws his sword. . . .

He picked up his copy. 'I accept this,' he said clearly, 'not as consenting to it or approving of it, but as a warning to the Church so that by it we may know what is planned against us. Now that we are aware of the traps and petty snares laid for us, we shall be, God willing, more cautious.'

Henry heard these words with something near to disbelief. He had, as he thought, leaned over backwards to be fair to the Church in the written Constitutions. He was quite unable to credit a refusal of them. And it was plain that the rest of the bishops – even those three whom he had thought won over – were in agreement with Thomas. Henry was not often at a loss but for the moment he was completely baffled. He would never understand the scrupulousness that cannot bend under stress of circumstances. Now only the derisory yelling of his men made him aware that the Archbishop was leaving and taking his copy of the Constitutions with him. He spun round on the Archbishop of York.

'What do you think he means to do with that?' he enquired sharply. 'Does he think he has evidence of ill-faith on my part?' But he got no answer from Roger or from any of the bishops; something hung in the air and it enraged Henry. 'Well, by God,' he shouted, 'if I cannot move you to see what is justice, we shall see if I can move the Pope!' He sprang up and noticed young Henry, still huddled at his feet. The boy was crying bitterly. 'What's wrong with you, little missy?' he snapped. The boy stuck out his lip and turned his head away. Henry grabbed him by the shoulder and pulled him up. 'Now you see what your dear foster-father is truly like! Is it he for whom you weep? Well may you do so – you will not see him more, I promise you. He shall pay his debts to me, and with interest.'

The bishops kept their eyes down. They knew that Henry's threats were aimed, not at the Archbishop this time, but at his heir. And seeing the child's tears, they knew the reason why.

Thomas would wait for nothing when he got out of the hall; although it was past the ninth hour and rain hung in the air, he must set out at once for Winchester. The common people lined the road to see him go, crying upon their Archbishop to bless them, but he took no notice and their calling died away at last into a glum muttering. Herbert and Alexander Llewellyn, coming behind, heard their gabble – of sin and the synagogue of Satan, of storms and showings, and of the flight of the shepherd from the flock.

By the time they had been on the road an hour, a thin creeping drizzle had set in and darkness was falling. Spirits were low and conversation languished; men pulled forward their hoods and thrust freezing hands into armpits, allowing the horses to plod through the mire unguided. Thomas rode solitary with bowed head.

Alexander suddenly spoke more loudly than he had meant out of his train of thought. 'What strength indeed has he who has betrayed both conscience and honour?' Herbert leaned across and nudged his arm sharply as the Archbishop turned back his head towards them. But Thomas had overheard and he spoke stiffly. 'Of whom do you speak, Alexander?'

There was a little pause and then: 'Of you, my lord

Archbishop,' answered Alexander stoutly. 'Yesterday you betrayed conscience and good fame, and left to posterity an example odious to God and contrary to righteousness. You stretched out your hands to keep customs of impiety and united yourself with Satan's ministers. Because of it, those evil customs are written down to the destruction of the Church's freedom. And now, seeing it too late, the shepherd flees and the sheep are scattered before the wolf.'

'*Miserere mei Domine*,' whispered Thomas, and such a groan burst from him that Herbert and Alexander brought up their horses either side of him in sudden consternation. They stared anxiously as he rode with tight-shut eyes and shot each other uneasy glances when they saw tears squeeze through the lids. When he lifted his head, though, they were a pace or two behind, exchanging angry whispers. 'I meant it when I said I would never seal that document,' Thomas said in a little while, without looking back at them.

'The verbal promise was the sin and that you have not retracted,' returned Alexander, ignoring the fierce glare Herbert gave him.

They saw his head go down. 'Yes,' he whispered, 'I know that to be true. I repent it bitterly. I am unworthy to approach as a priest Him whose Church I have so vilely bartered.' His voice dropped still lower so that they had to strain their ears. 'I shall not celebrate Mass again until I am absolved by the lord Pope. Leave me now to my grief.'

Before Herbert opened the door of Thomas's chamber that night in Winchester, he heard his light footstep as he paced up and down. He had the walk of a man half his age; hands behind back and head poked forward, following his nose as his knights said of him. He rapped on the door and heard the pacing stop. But Thomas seemed glad to see him.

Herbert had just endured an hour of Alexander's complaints about the Archbishop – that he consulted no one's wishes but his own, that he was as changeable as water, and that he, Alexander, was beginning to have grave doubts

176

concerning his judgment. All this had caused Herbert (who had been entertaining similar thoughts himself) to take up the cudgels on the Archbishop's behalf. So now he had come to hear his side of it.

When it came down to it, though, he found to his surprise that he had no stomach for demanding explanations of Thomas in this mood. Instead, they went through the document together.

The first clause dealt with advowsons and ordered that the right of presentation to benefices should be decided in the King's court. 'That is a direct stroke at me over the matter of William de Ros and his desire to have his own clerk at Eynsford,' said Thomas wearily, 'It seems that this whole business is aimed at me personally – I cannot help but feel that if another man had been Archbishop, none of it would have come about. All the guilt is mine. I should never have allowed the King to make me Archbishop. I feared this from the beginning—'

'Tsk, tsk!' said Herbert under his breath as he read on, so that Thomas fell silent, not knowing whether Herbert's disapproval was aimed at what he was perusing or at his own self-absorption. Herbert glanced up when he stopped speaking. 'God chose you for the task,' he said briskly 'We have joined battle with Satan now and we must plan our campaign. That is your task, my lord, and the breast beating must not take precedence. Do not take Alexander Llewellyn's words too much to heart. Like all Welshmen, he's too self-opinionated.'

But even Herbert did not guess how deeply the rebuke had cut Thomas; he could not forget it and Alexander's later half-apologetic likening of him to David and to Peter, who had also fallen from grace, brought him no comfort. He was determined not to say Mass again until the Pope himself had absolved him, and from that stand nothing would move him.

Once back in Canterbury, he brooded long over the constitutions of the document he had brought away from Clarendon and each further reading of it told him more clearly that he could never accept its provisions. There seemed no way out.

He bent over the document again, winced and straightened up. A familiar pain had returned as it always did when he was deeply worried. He massaged his back gingerly, nervous lest it make the irritation of the hair shirt worse. Depression was settling on him like the fall of dusk. Was he in the right at all? It was a terrible thing to defy his sovereign lord. He became aware of a gentle tapping on the door and raised his head in sudden irritation. He had given orders that he was not to be disturbed. 'Who's there?' he called.

'A visitor, my lord – Master John of Salisbury.'

John! Depression vanished instantly. He had not seen John for weeks since he had retired to Salisbury with his brother out of reach of the King's wrath. What had brought him back to Canterbury so suddenly?

John came in on the servant's heels and the first look at his woebegone countenance gave Thomas a hollow, empty feeling. 'What is it, old friend?' he asked anxiously as he led him to a chair.

'It has happened – what we always feared. The King has banished me from England.'

Thomas's shoulders sagged. Another thing for which to blame himself. Did John blame him, too? But apparently not for John was already explaining that he feared his books were the cause of his troubles. 'In them I stated my views so clearly that the King cannot help but know I shall never agree to abide by these Constitutions of Clarendon. And it seems to me that he will rid himself of everyone who does not agree with him.'

Thomas said, 'He will not find it so easy to be rid of me.' He stared down at the documents on the table. 'There they are. Will you look at them?'

'Yes, of course. But first – I come as a suppliant, or rather,

178

as a beggar. The King has sequestrated my revenues; he says he will hand them over to those bishops best able to deal with them. For all I know, they may go straight into his Treasury, but either way I am penniless. Can you help me?'

Thomas felt the heat of his indignation rise in his cheeks. The magnanimity Henry prided himself on did not extend to those for whom he felt personal dislike and here was proof of an almost childish spite. 'You may have ten marks at once,' he said, 'and more if you will give me time.'

John heaved a sigh of relief and relaxed. 'I would not have worried you at such a time had I been able to get money elsewhere.'

'Where will you go? To the Pope?' It ocurred to Thomas as he spoke that it would be no bad thing to have so able an advocate at the Papal Court.

'To King Louis first, I think.' John saw no need at this juncture to tell Thomas of his lack of confidence in the Pope. Had his old friend Adrian the Englishman been living still, it would have been a different story – but from all he had heard, Alexander was forever blaming his predecessor on account of his partiality for his native land. 'Louis is a true son of the Church – you need have no fear that he will take the King's part against you.' He held out his hand for the parchments. 'Let me see them. All I have heard is rumour; the facts may not be so bad.'

'I think it could hardly be worse. To tell you truth, John, I am at my wits' end. Now I am not even sure that I am in the right.'

There was a silence while John read the documents. When he had finished he looked up at Thomas. 'There can be no question of your sealing these,' he said. 'Absolutely no question. This is an issue on which you must stand firm.'

'I have made a great many mistakes—'

'Well, they are in the past.' John spoke lightly but Thomas heard something different from his usual tone, a curious gentleness that alarmed him. If John did not intend to take him to task in his usual manner, something was wrong – something more than his punishment by Henry. He tried to match the lightness of John's tone. 'One mistake too many, perhaps?'

John examined his fingers with great care. 'It is always a mistake to confront a King, to be too unyielding. One should know when to bend. But it is too late now and at least you will have the backing of the bishops in this matter of the Constitutions. Once the King sees that you are all of one mind and that you decline to be browbeaten, he will let the matter slide. That is his way. He will try to come at it from another angle – one on which you may be able to accommodate him. Try to do so. And now, I have not much time for I have a great many arrangements to make. I must arrange for the transport of my library.'

'All of it?' said Thomas in amazement.

'Certainly. My books are among my most treasured possessions.'

Shaking his head, Thomas rang for his Treasurer. The fact that John intended to take his library of thirty volumes with him had brought home the reality of a long parting.

After they had taken an affectionate farewell of each other, he sat down feeling more lonely than before. With John gone and John Belmeis in Poitiers, who was left to trust? Herbert whose truculence was a byword, Alexander Llewellyn with his wounding tongue and William Fitz-stephen whose love and loyalty would always cloud his judgment. . . . All the others he had called friends were waverers or openly hostile.

But still he had the greatest Friend of all. God was with him and would remain with him so long as he trod the path of righteousness and repentance. And that was really all that mattered.

His eye, running vaguely down the parchment in front of him, suddenly settled on the seventh clause which forbade the excommunication of a tenant-in-chief without the King's knowledge. Thomas put his finger on the place and his chin upon his hand. Without the King's consent was what it meant. That old law had got him into trouble once already and Henry's determination to retain it proved that he intended to deprive the Church of her rightful powers. What he was demanding was the authority to decide who should be admitted to the Sacraments. That was too grievous to be borne.

He went back to the third clause which was the one that had first made him refuse to ratify the Constitutions. It dealt with jurisdiction over criminous clerks, repetitiously insisting that the state had the right to punish them. The further he read, the plainer it became to him that John was right and compromise on this issue was impossible. Yet where before he had been depressed, now, because uncertainty had gone, his spirits began to rise.

He had taken the first step on a path there was no retracing and the sense of destiny was strong. What dangers that way held he knew not, neither did he care. He knew now it was the road God meant him to walk.

When Gilbert Foliot returned from his audience with the King, he found a number of the bishops waiting for him. They were in as great a taking as chickens when the cook's boy is among them with his chopper, swarming around him with questions as he came in. At his silence, their eyes grew round and anxious.

He saw that Henry of Winchester was not there, nor Nigel of Ely, warriors both; the ones who waited here trembling were the old and the timorous. Then he saw Bartholomew of Exeter, and Robert of Melun who now ruled his old see of Hereford, and had to concede reluctantly that there were others like himself who would not be coerced by fear but would make their decisions according to the facts.

Presently, when the hubbub had died, he allowed them

to draw from him the story of his interview with the King. 'He is shocked,' he told them, 'as are we all at the Archbishop's behaviour for that he perjured his sworn word.' He stopped as Bartholomew lifted his hand but continued when he saw it fall again. 'Aye, shocked and pained at such behaviour in the leader of the Church who should show the way by example. So he will send to the Pope to ask him to ratify the acceptance of England's ancient customs.'

Bartholomew's eyebrows went up. 'You expect the Pope to ratify them?'

'He will not!' the others cried, and 'No, never!' but Gilbert waved his hand imperiously and went on.

'Ask yourselves,' he said with passion, 'who is the prime cause of all this trouble. How did it arise? Through the arrogance of our Archbishop who, unlike his predecessor, Theobald of lamented memory, knows nothing of patience, or of firmness in the face of adversity. He, who started with every advantage, has cast all away in the interest of his stiff-necked pride.' He saw one or two mouths begin to open and raised his voice. 'Is it not true to say that many of us agreed with the King about the punishment of criminous clerks? The matter would have been easy to resolve with goodwill on both sides. But because the Archbishop would not give way, the King had no recourse but to appeal to the old customs – and see what that has brought in its train. Even then it might have passed off easily if he had submitted at once. But no, he must persist in his intransigence until the King was forced to put the customs into writing. Then we all saw many things to which we could not in conscience assent.'

Bartholomew of Exeter, a big bulky man a little past his middle years, spoke up then. 'Like all men who come to God late in life, he is somewhat overconscientious. But he will learn when it is permissible to yield a little.'

'And while he learns, we – and the Church' – Gilbert added hastily, 'will suffer. Before Christmas at Woodstock he promised the King he would observe the ancient customs of the realm. We do not know why he made that promise, any more than we know why he later refused to repeat it in public at Clarendon. We were left completely in the dark. Still, we were in agreement with his refusal, as you must all remember. And what father was ever better supported by his sons?

'Yet he did not even consult us when he capitulated once more to the King; he parted from our company and counsel, deliberating and deciding alone. Were we the ones who failed in the face of the nobles' threats? No, indeed! – for surely it was not Henry of Winchester, nor Nigel of Ely, nor Robert of Lincoln, nor Hilary of Chichester, nor Walter of Rochester, nor Bartholomew of Exeter, nor Richard of Chester, nor Roger of Worcester, nor Robert of Hereford, nor Gilbert of London!' He cried the names like a paean, like a roll-call of the saints.

'All these stood firm. It was the general of our army who deserted, the captain of our camp who fled. Were we not thunderstruck when he acquiesced to the King's demands and obliged us to bind ourselves by a pledge of obedience? And having forced us to this course, he changed his mind again! Now are we forsworn also, do we follow him. Patience and care must be our watchword in these evil days, else we shall bring a hornet's nest about our ears. Let the King send to the Pope; the onus will then be on him and we shall have a respite.'

He looked around at them. No one seemed prepared to argue with his summing up of the situation. 'So,' he said briskly, 'the King has informed me that he will ask that the Archbishop of York be made Legate. Arnulf of Lisieux and Richard of Ilchester are the chosen emissaries.'

They accepted that in silence too, though a few eloquent looks were exchanged. Having said all he wished to say to them, Gilbert turned away, beckoning York to follow him. When they had gone a glum silence reigned apart from a little whispering here and there as clerks and servants were summoned preparatory to departure.

Bartholomew of Exeter looked sideways at Robert of Melun who had been consecrated Bishop of Hereford four weeks earlier by Thomas. 'Some distortions were evident in his recapitulation, I fancy,' he murmured. 'Did you notice the omission of Norwich and Salisbury from his list of stalwarts? And one does not have far to look for a reason for his dislike of the Archbishop.' When Robert made no answer he added, 'I do not know Canterbury well but he strikes me as an honest man.'

Robert nodded shortly. He was not going to be drawn on the subject of Thomas's character (which he might be expected to know, having been his teacher years ago). His disillusion with both King and Archbishop was too overwhelming for him to be able to think of anything beyond the fact that neither man's word could be trusted. So he turned with relief to Roger of Worcester, another pupil of his (and high born and spiritual to boot), when he saw him approaching. But Bartholomew addressed Roger before he could and he was obliged to stand listening to their pleasantries whilst his servant helped him on with his heavy cloak.

Roger said in answer to a question of Bartholomew's, 'The Bishop of London's oration told us as much about himself as about our lord the Archbishop, did you not think? Yet his advice was good.' He smiled at Robert. 'We are all three new to the episcopate although you both have the advantage of me in years and wisdom. But if you really want my opinion I will tell you that my trust is in the Archbishop — of Canterbury, I mean.' The implication that he was less than overjoyed at the choice of York as Legate did not pass unnoticed by the other two.

Bartholomew nodded vigorously as if in satisfaction. He liked this young man's open face and shining eye. There was a faint look of the King about him which was not surprising seeing they were cousins, but he was finer featured, slenderer and darker in colouring. 'Instinct does not often lead one astray,' he said.

'Hrrmp!' said Robert. As a scholar and an intellectual, he despised and distrusted those emotions loosely described as instinctive. 'Better to judge men by their deeds.'

But he said it to the air because the other two were half-way across the room with their heads as close together as if they had known each other for years. 'Well, like calls to like, I suppose,' he muttered, meaning no compliment to either, but he felt a jealous qualm, knowing that of all his brother bishops young Roger was the one whose respect he would most deeply prize. He wished that he had had the chance to explain to him why it was that he inclined to Foliot's view of the situation but he was not yet very clear in his own mind about the underlying reason. He only knew that he had just discovered that Thomas of London was a very dangerous man.

January – February 1164

For some time past Sir Richard Fitzurse had been hearing rumours that all was not well between the King and the Archbishop. He got them from his tenants or from visiting knights mostly, though Robert sometimes returned from the shire court at Taunton with a tale to tell. The baron did not place much credence in the stories; gossip grew in the telling, he thought, and he would certainly hear from Reynold if half of what they said was true. Anyway, he had lost interest in the doings of the great. His world was small now, tied as he was by infirmity to his own holdings.

In that small world, his personal concerns loomed large. Last summer Lady Maud's condition had improved sufficiently for her to come below again, and all had gone peacefully enough until she had demanded the household keys from Ysabel. That the baron would not allow and she had sat silent and brooding in the corner for a week or more until some trifling mischance had upset her. He had known when she began shouting that he should lock her away again but, because the one thing he longed for was freedom from her oppressive presence, he had put it off. And regretted it.

He would never forget how he had felt when he returned to the hall, hurrying because of the fearful stink that filled it. Robert was there, and several of the menservants; they had her already under restraint but too late for three of a litter of newborn pups which she had thrown into the heart of the fire. They had had to restrain him, too, for a little while.

So she was back in the tower chamber, and with her absence, the whole household breathed freely once more. Ysabel sang about her duties again and Cicely came to pay her respects each morning and remain to chatter as she had always done before. She heard about the pups from the servants and wept against his knee with the abandon of childhood while he had patted her head, unable to offer any comfort for the helpless anger that still filled him.

The baron had missed this hour while Maud was among them but had thought it wise to keep Cicely out of sight. She was now ten years old and the once fair hair had darkened but this only made her likeness to himself the more striking. Maud could not have helped but see it and be reminded of what she thought of as her wrongs. But before the rest of the world he was prepared to acknowledge – nay, to flaunt her – for his love and pride in her were enormous. Indeed, he was indulgent towards her to a degree that shocked Ysabel who knew what happened to children who never felt the rod, and kept discipline as firmly as she could.

She knew more of Cicely's misdemeanours than anyone but she was not sure enough of her own position to carry tales to the baron, even in the child's own interest, and so Cicely went her way, her bad habits ignored or only lightly punished. And she had many. She would steal into the dairy when she got the chance to lap cream from the pans, and on one memorable occasion she consumed the whole contents of a crock of butter and had not even the grace to be sick of it after. That did come to the baron's ears through Cook, and he was very angry but only because he, like all Normans, found the English habit of eating raw butter disgusting. He thought it fit only for cooking. And even then he had not beaten her, only explained quite gently that she must not do as villeins did.

'As though,' said Ysabel, moved for once to bitterness, 'half her blood were not villein! She is growing very sly, with all this spoiling.' This was in the autumn when Ysabel had seemed strangely out of sorts and quite unlike her usual placid self. By Christmas, when she was certain she was pregnant, she no longer thought of Cicely at all.

But the baron did and his image of her was very different from Ysabel's. Watching her with the eyes of love, he had early recognised the kinship of their souls. In her he continually saw echoes of his own vulnerability; she was too easily wounded by the sight of cruelty or callousness for his peace of mind. There had been the time she brought home a fox cub and been inconsolable when one of the men knocked it on the head. Her grief had been out of all proportion to the death of vermin. But he had read the signs aright, he thought, seeing the shielded, withdrawn look she wore now when the kitchen boys baited curs or held a cockfight. With such a tender heart, what mattered it if discipline were lax? So loving a spirit should be allowed to grow unfettered. And he would find an easy husband for her when the time came. It should not prove difficult; it was already clear that she would be a beauty.

It was early in the new year that he felt a stirring of disquiet. He spent a third part of the first month locked away in his chamber, sick of an ague, with only Ned to wait on him – he would not have Cicely or Ysabel near lest they breathe the miasmic humours and sicken too. Finally though, the fever had left him and he got up, thinner and of

187

a bad yellowish colour, and a little unsteady on his legs, but certain now that death had passed him by.

Ysabel had had screens placed near the fire, for the wind blew from the east and there was an evil draught, and a feather hassock put in his great chair. Here he sat feeling pleasantly weak and comfortable, and played with the ears of his favourite hound who had crept into that cosy spot and fallen into a twitching doze. Presently, Cicely came in and certain of her welcome sat beside him on the hearthstone, watching him with a look at once solemn and eager.

'I am right glad to see you well again, sir,' she said, and then, 'Did anyone tell you that Dickon died this last night?'

'Dickon?' he said, running over in his mind the names of her pets.

'Dickon, the stable lad.'

He raised his head. 'Ah. . . . So death did come. I had a feeling.' He shivered suddenly. 'Did he have the ague too?'

'No, he was well yesterday but this morning he was dead. I saw him in his corner. Will you come and see, sir?'

He frowned, unwilling to leave the comfort of the fire. But he would have to go eventually, they would do nothing without his word. Cicely must have come directly to him to have arrived first with the news. He looked at her sharply but her round-eyed gaze told him nothing.

'Fetch me my fur cape,' he said. While he waited he tried to remember which of the scullions bore his own name. Once he would have known them all, down to the meanest underling. But . . . surely the only Richard was that forsaken brat they had found on the manor all those years ago. Horribly bruised he had been and skinny as a fledgling bird with innumerable scars on the small body to testify to the manner he had been used. Ugly as Satan, too, with a squint so bad it was a wonder he could see. He had flinched and sprung away when any spoke to him, and he no more than a five-year child.

The men had been for turning him away for he was none

188

of their parish, and it was only by chance that the baron had been passing and had been moved to pity because he was something near the age of Cicely. 'Let him stay in the kitchen,' he had said. 'Feed him; he will grow and later work.' At the back of his mind had lurked the thought that so might Cicely have ended had he never returned from the wars. She, too, might have fallen into the hands of evil men to be brutalized and disfigured.

Not only did he squint but he had a shock of black hair like a brush and a skin so swarthy that the house servants were convinced he was a heathen. If he had a name, he did not know it, so they got him baptised to drive the devil out and gave him the name of his benefactor. But the older Richard sometimes had cause to regret his kindness for the boy was affliction as much to the household as he had been to the mother who abandoned him. They had never got him house-trained. And now his brief sad life was over.

He was still lying in the corner of the stables where he had lived. Pulling on his hand, Cicely drew the baron after her towards the spot; he heard the horses whinny anxiously in their stalls and smelt the strong ammoniac smell of horse-piss. The beasts sense death, he thought.

With conscious solemnity Cicely lifted the sack that covered the body and stared down. 'Poor Dickon,' she said. 'Poor Dickon, you are so cold, as cold as stone.' The facile pity in her voice struck the baron unpleasantly, as did the look she gave him. She is saying what she thinks is expected of her, he thought.

He gazed broodingly at the dead child, showing nothing of his inner revulsion. There were no marks of contagion on him. He had vomited before he died, lying on his side, knees drawn up, as ugly and as utterly unlovable as he had been in life. In that pathetic sight, the baron thought, lay all the sorrow of the world. Not because a child was dead for that was a common thing, but that he had died alone and none to weep for him.

189

He felt Cicely touch his hand, warm and alive – and yes, uncaring – and flinched inwardly. Yet why should others care when you did not? he asked himself savagely. You took him in and made yourself his lord, and there it ended. You gave him bread for your own sake, not his nor Christ's. . . . You fed him and thought it enough. In his head rang the words, 'If ye offend against these little ones. . . . Better a millstone be tied about a man's neck and he be cast into the depths of the sea!' Yet when he saw her hand go out he spoke hastily. 'Do not touch him! There may be unseen contagion.' It is all for her, he thought, all the love that's in me, none left for others.

He felt the wind whistle round the corner, piercingly cold. 'Come,' he said, 'it's too cold in here for either of us.' But his mind continued, Because we still live and breathe and feel – though she feels nothing more than a child's relish in the gruesome, that's plain. And a cold finger seemed to touch him as he saw her unmoved stare.

'Come,' he said, and took her hand.

'Why did he die?' she said.

'He had done all he had to do in the world. God called him.'

'To Heaven?'

'Yes,' he said firmly.

'He was a scurvy little knave, Cook said. He told lies and bit people. I cannot think that such as he would enter Heaven.'

The baron's stride lengthened so that she had to hurry to keep up. He did not seem to notice his bad leg. She peered up, trying to read his face, but could see no more than that he was paler than usual. Panting, she proceeded to tell him all the reasons why so ugly and wicked a boy could not inherit Paradise.

During the weeks that followed, the baron was much tormented by heretical thoughts. Always prone to question the

190

workings of Providence, he had found in himself since Dickon's death a growing sense of insecurity. Why, if God so loved his creatures, had He denied to one of them every natural grace, every attribute which could have inspired love in others? That He might number among the Blessed those who took pity on him? Too pat, that priestly answer, too indifferent to his sufferings.

He heard Mass twice a day for a week in the hope that it would drive away the devil who was putting such thoughts in his head but he was reminded every time he passed the mound of pinkish earth that covered Dickon. Finally he decided that only an enquiry into the death would lay that unquiet shade. It was his duty, anyway, since he was held responsible for the lives of everyone on his manor.

But the servants he questioned looked at him with curtained eyes and remembered nothing; it came to him then how much they had hated the stranger within the gates. His people were suddenly strange to him, hard and alien, barely touched by Christian attitudes. He had always sensed they had secrets, a hidden life he knew nothing of; now he suspected it was not as innocent as he had believed.

And Cicely – what of Cicely who was ever in their company? All at once he saw their baleful influence behind her quite untypical lack of feeling for that unfortunate boy. His undefined worries were instantly translated into anxiety for her.

Why had it not struck him earlier that she would be hardened and coarsened by contact with the lowest kind of folk? It could not continue. She must be given entirely into Ysabel's care; she must be Norman as befitted her blood. And she must be betrothed, he could not rest easy now until he was sure she was no more a part of their close-knit alliance against— Against what? He was not sure but his distrust of the English was strengthening.

He believed now that Dickon had been poisoned but saw it was useless to seek for proof. So he would record that the boy had died of eating toadstools in case any came questioning – not that it was likely, but the King's justices were beginning to poke their noses into all sorts of matters this last year or two, matters which were none of their business in his view. It was beginning to seem that Henry Plantagenet would be the master in his realm, indeed.

Beta said nothing when he told her that Cicely was to be placed under Ysabel's tutelage. 'I have no fault to find with you,' he told her carefully, 'but she must be fitly trained in all accomplishments and deportment if she is to fill the place I have in mind for her. The place,' he continued firmly, seeing her doubtful look, 'of a knight's lady.' He sank back, noticing (for the first time in a long while) that Beta was still a comely woman. He covered her hand with his. 'Come to me tonight,' he said.

Ned was still dressing his leg when she scratched at the portal that night but he kept his eyes discreetly lowered and made himself scarce pretty quickly. The baron smiled at her. She did not often visit his chamber now and he saw that she had done her best to make herself fine for him. Her soft light hair was loose about her shoulders and shone from recent washing. Her air of shy expectancy touched him suddenly. He took her face between his hands, meaning to kiss her gently, not as a lover but in gratitude for all she had given him.

There was a pricking on his hand. He pushed back the hair that fell around her face and saw the pendant sapphires in her ears. 'Where did you get those?' he said in wonder, lifting one on his finger.

Her expression made him pause and look harder at her; something moved faintly in his memory. 'Did I give them to you?'

Her eyes wandered away from him. 'Yes – a long time ago.'

'I have never seen you wearing them before.'

'No. I told you then they were too fine for me.'

192

'Well. . . .' Hesitating and unsure what to say to that, he took refuge in embracing her. But when he had done with her and she was dressing ready to go, he noticed them again and asked idly, 'Why do you not give those jewels to Cicely?'

She was lacing her bodice and her hands suddenly stopped their quick deft movements. After a moment they resumed again but stiffly and slow. He watched her curiously. Perhaps the jewels, so long hidden away, meant more to her than he had realised. 'Do not if you wish to keep them,' he sad.

But she unfastened them swiftly and put them in his hand. 'You give them to her. They are more fitting for her. And she would not take them from me.'

Staring down at them, he wondered why not. There was no understanding her, any more than the rest of the common folk. She was gone when he looked up to ask her.

They were very pretty gauds and worth a tidy sum, he thought, but he could not for his life remember where or why he got them. Not that it mattered. They would suit Cicely very well. They were exactly the colour of her eyes.

Sir Richard Fitzurse sat upon a settle in the great hall of Dunster Castle, balancing a goblet of wine on the knee of the leg that was propped on a three-legged stool before him. He was waiting for Baron de Mohun. The hall was empty and silent but for the dogs who sniffed suspiciously around him until one, friendlier than the rest, sidled up and licked his hand. He scratched the top of its head with a wordless murmur until the rest lay down and the sudden soft thump of their tails told him he was accepted.

He did not look well for he had been too much within doors this winter. His face was pale and pulled down, a network of lines had grown at the corners of his eyes, and the skin was tight upon his cheek bones and sagging at the jaw. The old wound that would not heal troubled him constantly. He had been borne hither in a litter for the pain, and he was ashamed of it, and sour-tempered in consequence.

Yet he must control his tongue for he was here to ask de Mohun's favour and he was an irascible man. One thought ill-phrased and they would be at odds. So Sir Richard sat and sipped his wine and considered how best to frame his plea.

At last he saw the man he awaited coming down the hall; he had been at Mass in his chapel and wore an impatient look. Sir Richard made to rise but de Mohun shouted at him to remain seated, and in the same breath called for wine or ale, or both; his thirst was raging, he said. He flung himself heavily down beside his guest and began at once to complain of the slowness of his priest – aye, and the impudence too; he had stopped several times when he thought his lord's discussion of his affairs waxed too loud for reverence.

'I'll be rid of him, the saucy rogue,' declared de Mohun. 'Do you know a likely young clerk, Fitzurse, who would fill my bill? One just priested and,' he laughed, 'of a deferential humour?'

When Sir Richard shook his head, he leaned back and looked at him. 'You're looking ill, Fitzurse,' he said. 'Is it my physician whose services you've come to beg?'

'I'm well enough,' returned Sir Richard, 'apart from this accursed leg of mine and I doubt that even your physician has lotions that will cure it. I am here on another matter—'

'Have you tried poultices of mouldy bread?'

'Aye, mouldy bread, graveyard earth – but that is not why I am here.'

'Perhaps it was not applied at the right phase of the moon.'

Sir Richard sighed, took a deep breath and plunged abruptly into the subject uppermost in his mind. 'I am here about your ward – de Forz's heir. It's true – he's in your

194

wardship?'

'True.' De Mohun's eyes had narrowed. 'What would you? He's under age to inherit but I shall see his lands are farmed. His father owed me fealty. I'm for selling the wardship, Fitzurse.'

'His marriage will be in your gift.'

De Mohun laughed. 'You're early in the field. The lad's but eight years old. It was his mother's marriage I was considering.'

'He's of an age to be betrothed and such matters are best settled when they're young. I have a daughter ten years old and I would keep her near me. My other daughters married into the North country – I would not lose them all.'

De Mohun was picking at a pulled thread on his sleeve; he did not raise his eyes. 'This is your bastard child?'

'It is.'

'The price will be high – and in silver only.'

'Whatever you ask.'

'His mother may object – oh, not at the bastardy, she's a woman of the world, but at the villein blood.'

'Villein blood has mixed with royal ere now. What do you say? Half to be paid on the betrothal, half on the marriage.'

'Yours is not the only offer; we cannot bring it to any conclusion so soon.'

'Perhaps not. But you can give me a price.'

De Mohun shook his head. He looked ill at ease but determined. 'No point. I will speak with his mother on the matter. Leave it in my hands.' His colour was rather higher than usual when he looked directly at Sir Richard for the first time. 'See my physician while you're here – I'll send for him. Let him look at your leg, at least.'

'No,' said Sir Richard. 'No, I'll not trouble him.' He stood up. The pain was intense as the blood ran down into the leg.

De Mohun saw his expression and sprang forward, all solicitude. By the time Fitzurse had reached his litter, leaning on de Mohun's shoulder, affronted pride had turned to active hatred.

He saw the strange horses, not yet stabled, directly they entered his own gates and swore violently under his breath. After that snub from de Mohun, he was in no mood for visitors. And to be arriving thus – on a pallet like a woman!

So his expression was very dour when he was helped within to find none other than Will de Tracy and a skinny, dark-haired fellow whom he could not recall, yet who greeted him with a familiarity that betokened some sort of connection between them. Then he recognised the lineaments of the de Bret family, that house his eldest daughter had lately married into. He asked eagerly for news of her but it appeared they had none; they had come from Canterbury and were riding hard for Devon. He sucked in his lip, eyeing them; there was an air of repressed excitement in their bearing. Well, he would hear what they had to say later.

As Ned was changing his clothes it struck him that they would have the latest news of the Archbishop's doings. But what was le Bret doing in Canterbury? He was none of the Archbishop's household.

At dinner he had them sit on either side of him that they might give him word of his son whom he had forgotten to ask after earlier. Reynold, though, was not uppermost in their thoughts either; it was of greater affairs they wished to speak. And so they did, telling the whole company of all that happened in the great upset between King and Archbishop. Throughout the recital the baron's face grew grimmer, as much because of the attitudes implicit in the way they spoke of the Archbishop as of the story's content.

Pretty soon they were all disputing the pros and cons for when Robert said that it was the Archbishop's place to guard the Church against the rapacity of the King and the barons, Sir William Reigny who was also there cried angrily that it was the King who would protect the people from the rapacity of Churchmen – to wit, these wicked men clothed as religious who were nothing but wolves clad in a sheep's skin. He thought it only right that all men should live under the same law.

They discussed the matter in some heat until Will urged le Bret to recount the tale of his master's harsh treatment at the Archbishop's hands when he had refused to allow him to marry the Countess of Warenne. That touched them all more nearly for there was not a man present who did not resent the Church's interference in matters of marriage and dowers and property in general. Even as le Bret told them, his chin began to shake and his mouth to grow square, and quite suddenly he put his head down on his arms and unashamedly wept.

'Lord William died three weeks ago,' Will said in a hushed voice, 'of a broken heart. They say the King is raging afresh against the Archbishop because of it. That's why le Bret goes with me to Devon. He's masterless now.'

'But you are not,' said the baron pointedly. 'And what is Reynold's view of all this? Will you renounce your fealty?'

'I go to put it all before my lord my father,' said Will, but he had heard the disapproval in Sir Richard's voice and fell silent for a full two minutes. When le Bret sat up and started wiping his eyes on the board cloth, the baron asked him what he would do now. 'Apply to the King,' answered le Bret. 'He is my dear lord's brother; and he may be very sure that if I am ever given a chance to be avenged on him who caused lord William's death, I shall take it.'

The baron's eyebrows rose slightly but he made no comment. They're all talk, the young, he thought. And as for this lord William's broken heart – it's the first time I ever heard that such a wound proved mortal.

William de Reigny was bristling again at something Robert had said. 'The Church has her finger in too many pies,' he shouted. 'A man can't call his soul his own!' The

197

baron bit his lip and spoke hastily to le Bret before Robert could voice the too obvious retort. 'What will the King do now, think you, if he is dissatisfied with the Pope's answer to his embassy?'

'He has sent another, Master John of Oxford and Geoffrey Ridel this time, I heard. Perhaps they will have better luck. I reckon the Pope will have to bow to his will in the end.'

'Not if it's against Christian conscience, he won't,' said Robert with an obstinate look.

'Well,' said le Bret who was growing tired of Robert, 'you think as you like. I've lived in courts and I'm of the opinion the Papal court's no different from the rest.' That silenced Robert.

'Where's the Archbishop now?' asked de Reigny.

'In Canterbury, imposing penances on himself to beat anything the Pope can do. And the townsfolk murmuring against the King on his behalf as they are meant to. "See how the King hath treated me," is what he's saying – and the fools lap it up.'

The baron listened, saying nothing. He was remembering other quarrels, other times, more dangerous than these. What was it all about, anyway? The Archbishop had overstepped his place, no more that he could see. And Henry FitzEmpress had lost his famous temper a time or two. Would the world end because of it? He did not think so. However enraged, kings do not lead armies against archbishops. He closed his mind to it and began to fume again against de Mohun.

VIII

March–April 1164

Henry had not been at Berkhamstead above an hour when word came that his embassy to the Pope was hard on his heels and would be with him shortly. They had been following him for three days but he had not rested anywhere long enough for them to come up with him.

He clenched his hands. 'What news?' he cried impatiently. 'What news? Has the Pope granted the Legateship?' He checked himself, knowing these heralds could not possibly give him an answer. He would have to contain himself until Geoffrey Ridel and John of Oxford arrived.

It was a long day he waited, stamping up and down, refusing food so that everyone else must go hungry too, or creep away to the kitchens to filch what they might. But at last the straggling procession came crawling into sight on the dusty road.

Henry would wait no longer; he had them in immediately, Geoffrey Ridel, thin, red and foxy, and John of Oxford, an exceedingly ugly youngish man with a large head sunk so low upon his shoulders that he appeared to have no neck. Both were clever, both sprung from humble origins – mere cadets of the petty nobility – and both enjoyed the King's fullest confidence. It was Geoffrey Ridel who now performed all the offices of Chancellor though without the title, and it was to him that Henry had given the Archdeaconry of Canterbury when he took it from Thomas. Henry was coming more and more to rely on 'new men' like these, a whole class of minor officials who had no other ties than dependence on the King himself.

'Well?' he said, eyeing them with a fierceness that ill concealed his anxiety.

'The Pope has granted the legateship to the Archbishop of York' – began Geoffrey, then hesitated a moment as the King smote his thigh with a cry of triumph – 'providing only that the Archbishop of Canterbury agrees,' he concluded hastily.

'Ah—' They heard Henry's breath come out with a rush. Abruptly he turned his back on them.

John looked longingly at the bench and shifted the weight upon his aching thighs. The King swung round so suddenly that he jumped. 'Did he put his signature to my Constitutions?'

Dumbly they shook their heads.

'Oh, sit down, sit down!' snapped Henry. 'Tell me the worst then. Was it all useless?'

'No – no, indeed. His Holiness was quite prepared to accept six—'

'Six of sixteen! And they the least important, I have no doubt!' Henry began to tear his thumbnail with his teeth. 'I see that the granting of the legateship is a mere sop that means nothing. Do you think that Canterbury will agree that the Papal Legate shall dominate him? Of course he will not. And the Pope knows it.'

They did their best to tell him of the subtleties of their discourse and of the sums they had laid out to gain the adherence of various cardinals; of all the plots and counter-plots that had gone on between them and the Archbishop's own envoys. Henry was too angry to listen.

'Well, leave me, then,' he bellowed suddenly. 'Don't sit there mumbling – get you gone!'

They got out of the chamber with a speed that belied their weariness but once outside, their steps slowed to a shuffle. Geoffrey wiped his brow which was unaccountably damp. 'That's well over,' he said.

John nodded. 'I fear the lord King has made a mistake in committing the customs to writing.'

'And in bringing them to the Pope's attention at all. Now his Holiness can no longer tacitly ignore them. And what's the King gained by it?'

'Nothing,' said John. 'He should have followed his own dictates and kept English quarrels in English hands.' His chin sank even lower on his chest so that his voice came out a rumble. 'I'd not be in Becket's shoes next time they meet for all the silver in his Treasury.'

After his envoys had left him, Henry began to regret the abruptness with which he had dismissed them. Disappointed rage had driven out good sense. Had he been prepared to listen to the arguments they had used in his behalf, he might have found another means to bring the Pope round to his own way of thinking. But he was still too angry to think about it.

In the background of his thoughts something told him that the first Henry would have behaved differently. It disturbed him. As far back as he could remember his grandfather had been his model; the awe and admiration with which men spoke of him had seen to that. Jealousy had crept in later and with it, a determination to surpass him. When he was gone, he had thought, he would leave a name behind him; the second Henry would be greater than the first. But that dream had been only half-conscious till now when the risk of failure seemed greatest.

What would the old lion of justice (so Henry thought of him) have done in his position? He had got the Pope of his time to confirm the customs and usages of England more than once, but at the very beginning of his reign he had been faced with just such a crisis as this when Archbishop Anselm had refused either to do him homage or to consecrate the bishops he had created. And the old lion had craftily separated the two components of the quarrel, making a great to-do about giving up that which he cared least for – the investiture of bishops – in order to retain the important thing, which was the homage of clergy. It had taken years of negotiation but compromise had been reached at last.

Henry wondered if he could bring himself to compromise and concluded sorrowfully that he could not. He dared not. As he saw it, his royal power hung on this definition of his rights. Where was law unless illegality were clearly defined? Anyway, the old usages were not the root cause of his troubles. The fault lay with the ingrate Archbishop he himself had made. Well, perhaps he could yet gain his ends with cozenage and guile – by baiting a trap that would take that proud and haughty cleric.

His mind made no connection between his grandfather's relinquishment of investiture and his own fiat imposing a doubtful Thomas upon the unwilling Canterbury monks. Dismissing the whole wearisome business, it had leapt ahead to different things entirely. Annora waited for him at Woodstock.

Henry was tired. After love he liked to turn his back and sleep immediately, but Annora would talk. When they had been first together, he had found her whispered confidences endearing and even now he would not admit to himself that they were an irritation, but he did wish she would confine them to the earlier part of the evening. That was the advantage with whores; their duty done, they always departed as silently as they came.

She pressed closer to him and twined her fingers in the hairs on his chest. What would he give her if she should bear a child? she asked. He grunted. 'Why – a husband, I would think. What else?'

His lids began to sink until the quality of the silence made him peer at her. She was looking away, towards the glimmer of the night candle; the light haloed the edge of her cheek with soft gold.

'*Are* you pregnant?' he said.

'I am not sure.' There was a little silence while he watched her. 'Henry, I want no man than you—'

He frowned, almost impatient. 'You have me – and no husband.'

'I want you only,' she said on an obstinate note.

'You do not know for sure that you are with child, do you?'

When she did not answer he said, 'It is too soon to worry. Go to sleep.'

She spoke suddenly then. 'Would you marry me if you were free to?'

He thought about it. Then he thought of his children and knew the answer. 'No,' he returned shortly. He felt her sudden movement, and taking her chin in his hand, turned her face toward him. 'You know as well as I the impossibility,' he said as gently as he was able. 'A king cannot marry with one of his subjects.' But he knew that was not the reason. A year ago he might have given the idea more consideration.

Afterwards, when her even breathing showed she slept, he wondered if her brother had put her up to asking the direct question. He did not believe this tale of pregnancy. She had none of the fluctuations of mood, none of the capricious appetites of that state. It could even be that she was barren. . . . Eleanor, for all her faults, was still capable of childbearing. And he was having difficulties enough with the Holy See without complicating matters further by demanding a divorce. Recognition of the Constitutions was of far greater importance.

His mind began to pace the treadmill of vexation once again, enumerating all the worries he had thought to leave behind. Sleep would not come. He flung himself about and finally rose up, exasperated beyond endurance that she was deep in slumber. Looking down at her, though, he softened. They said she was the most beautiful woman in England and he could believe it. But, oh, he thought, if she were only dumb. . . . If all women were dumb life would be easier.

May 1164

Ysabel was now great with child; she moved with laboured awkwardness, stopping often and holding her hand to the side of her belly, and sometimes when she thought herself unobserved, pressing down her clenched fists upon the table with rigid arms while she gasped for breath. The baron watched her secretly with growing concern; he had noticed that despite the happiness that glowed on her face, it was thinner and paler than before.

There came a day when she spent long hours in the dairy, overseeing the churning and skimming. Sir Richard, who had been more than ever tied to the house of late by the pain in his leg, was checking the stores with Herluin the bailiff; they had come out from the undercroft and were crossing the yard, Herluin striding ahead and the baron following more slowly behind him. He was almost past the wide half-door of the dairy when from the corner of his eye he saw her leaning on the low stone shelf where the flat pans of cream were ranged. The expression on her face was so odd that he stopped and stared until she gave a little shiver and saw him.

'Come, mistress,' he said in a curter tone than he intended out of his sudden shocked surprise, 'Take Herluin's arm and he will help you to the hall in my default.' He forced a smile lest she see his dismay at her appearance. 'We two are in like case in that neither can aid the other—' He broke off abruptly as without a sound her eyes rolled up and she slid along the shelf, sending the pans crashing to the stone floor along with her in a cascade of cream.

All was pandemonium for a minute or two but at length the baron's shouting and banging with his staff produced results and Ysabel was carried into the hall. When she regained consciousness after what seemed to Sir Richard far too long a time for a simple faint, she insisted that she was perfectly well except for the aching of her ankles, but nonetheless the baron ordered her to her couch to rest, and that without argument, for in her gown's disarray he had seen her feet swollen like fool's bladders.

Afterwards he came to see her, looking at her a long while without a word. She shifted uncomfortably under his scrutiny until she saw the kindness and reproach in his blue eyes. Gently he lifted her hand and examined it carefully; her wedding ring had almost disappeared in puffy flesh.

'Why did you not speak of it?' he said, 'I would have procured a physician – or there is a woman in the vill who has knowledge of such ills and how to cure them.'

'I would not cause you trouble,' she murmured, and then with a sudden look of fear. 'Is it not usual? I am not so young, I know—'

'I am not versed in these matters either. . . . But Robert shall send down for Marget – she is the one they call upon in case of difficult births.' He patted the poor swollen hands. 'Don't worry, she will make a physic for you.'

In the doorway he turned and glanced back at her; there were little beads of sweat on her forehead and she had clenched her lower teeth on her upper lip; it made her look like an old woman and his heart sank.

He had sent a man out to find Robert and it was with relief that he heard him ride in. He called and Robert came with anxious questioning look. At that moment a series of shrill screams from the tower rent the air and Robert saw the baron's jaw muscles stand out suddenly.

'Is it my lady?'

'Nay – nay, ignore her. Your wife is poorly – stay, not so fast' – for Robert had turned immediately on his heel. 'We shall send for Marget – all will be well. She has not started on her labour but she is swelling up in feet and hands. We must have more care of her.'

Robert stared at him, thinking: all this concern is for the child – the heir he wants from me. Once that is born he'll care no more for Ysabel than for my lady. He had found it eased his own feelings of guilt to attribute base motives to his father. He said aloud, 'The babe should not be born for six weeks yet – is this in the common run of women's troubles?'

'Marget will know. She shall stay here tonight and watch her. Now do you go and see her – but do not let her know we are troubled.'

So when Robert came into the little chamber he sat and talked long and cheerfully to Ysabel of plans for the child, but she hardly answered him, lying distant and still as though all her being were concentrated elsewhere. Only when he was leaving she said suddenly, 'I feel so strange – it is as if a black shadow lies over me. . . . Is that Marget now I hear?' She turned her head to listen and when he saw her hollow cheek and the stick-like arm against the grotesque hump of her belly, a terrible dread seized him.

'Jesu Mary,' he prayed while still he forced himself to smile, 'Holy Mother, grant the child live and she be safe, and nevermore will I wait by Carpenter's yard!' Yet even as he made the vow, bending his head and pinching his eyelids shut, he knew deep inside he would not keep it, and when old Marget came in, swollen with self-importance, and sent him off, he went with a curious sense of fatality.

Thereafter, Marget slept on a pallet at the foot of Ysabel's couch by night and physicked her with nauseous draughts by day while Robert, banished to communal life in the hall, hung around in everyone's way until Beta complained to the baron and he was set to ride to Dunster Castle to beg the loan of de Mohun's physician. The baron was thankful now indeed that he had held his tongue two months earlier and given no offence to that touchy magnate. But it made no difference anyway for Robert came back without him, the old man having inconsiderately died and left de Mohun angry with everyone.

Ysabel was worse when he returned and the house in turmoil. She had begun to have convulsions, due as much, the baron swore, to Marget's filthy medicaments as to her condition. Robert looked on her and came away with pale, hard face; Beta cared for her now and he had got the rough edge of her tongue. There would be no forgiveness for his wantoning with Carpenter's wife from that quarter. Useless to tell Beta of his vow, useless even to hope – it was too late to bargain with God. He went out and saddled up his horse again and rode forth. It was plain that God along with Beta had turned His face against him because of his sin and now he remembered his early, passionate love for Ysabel and that, but for him, she would have been a nun, quiet and content in her convent – and an Abbess by now, perhaps.

'No one will tell me what to do then,' he recalled her saying – and how pretty she had looked when she said it. She was not pretty any more and so he had stopped loving her – or showing it, which was perhaps the same thing. He had got his child upon her out of duty in the end, and she must have known of his reluctance. . . . But at least it had made her happy – happier than she had ever been, he thought with stricken heart. All her life she had been bidden and chidden as was woman's lot; when he had married her, she had only exchanged one servitude for another.

For hours he let the horse pick its own way, neither knowing nor caring that it was through lush combes and valleys he rode or across the desolation of Exmoor. His head was bowed and his look faraway for he was considering his past life; only now and then his lips would twitch and he would press the back of his hand to them. Once he checked the horse for he thought he heard the wailing of a new-born child; then he knew it for the distant, empty crying of the gulls. He had come past Doniford to the sea.

He dismounted when he reached the shore and heard the sea suck softly at the shingle. It had withdrawn from the slaty slabs of rock and he could see the circular, whorled imprints of the Devil's footmarks clearly. Under a dappled sky the world was drained of colour, muted, silken, mother-of-pearl; grey-gold, grey-green, grey-blue. He sat on the rocks, staring at the horizon a long time while his horse, un-tethered, grazed the meadow that rolled down to the beach where Doniford stream met the sea, nor did he move until the cloud dispersed and the westering sun half blinded him. He rubbed his eyes then, frowning a little. He must go home. But it would be different now.

He came back in a golden, long-shadowed evening when the sky was full of the black arrow heads of rooks returning nestwards, and in the west there glowed the evening star. The stillness of the house struck him before he crossed the bridge and when he came to the stables the ostlers would not meet his eyes. Slowly he went into the hall; only the baron was there, sitting upon the locked chest with back and arms that was his chair.

Robert stood and looked at him.

His father said, 'She died an hour ago – and you not by. . . .'

There was a silence while the shadow of some violent emotion passed across Robert's face. Tentatively the baron stretched out his hand towards his son in the first open overture he had made to another for more than half his lifetime, but Robert did not see it and when he spoke, the baron drew back his hand as from hot iron and laid it in his lap.

'Take me not to task!' Robert said loud and harsh. 'Look to yourself! But for your clamourings for an heir, she would be living still.' His shoulders hunched and he made a sound that was half a sob and half '*Miserere*!' But the baron sat stiff and still and did not offer him any comfort.

As darkness fell Robert sat alone on the bench by the outside stair where the women sat to spin in summer. He had tried to pray and got no solace from it. There was only one place where he might find healing and he would not go there with Ysabel scarcely cold within the house. Besides, he had vowed not to go again. . . . But she had died anyway. He stood up suddenly and put his hand on the rail of the stair, then snatched it away again as he remembered why he could not face his father. 'O God!' he said, 'God have mercy on me!' Then he walked swiftly towards the gate.

When he neared the cottars' huts his footsteps slowed and finally stopped. Some of the doors still stood open; he could hear voices and see the faint yellow flickering of rushlights within. He waited till they were doused one by one, all the time telling himself he would not signal her, that he would go in a little while. Just the same, when everything was quiet, he hooted twice softly like an owl. A minute later he hooted twice again. He was about to leave when she finally came, materialising beside him so suddenly out of the darkness that he jumped.

'I thought he would never fall asleep,' she whispered, taking his hand and drawing him towards the undergrowth. Once in the bushes she lay down and pulled up her skirts. 'Come on,' she said, 'Aren't you ready?'

He stood beside her in silence with hanging head, seeing her white legs glimmer in the faint light from the sky. She shifted impatiently and suddenly he flung himself down on her, bruising his mouth on the hardness of her teeth. Then he found that he was crying helplessly.

'What's wrong? Get off, you're crushing me,' she complained, pushing at his shoulders. But he continued to weep into her neck, blubbering her with his tears, feeling her tangled hair creep into his mouth.

She gave a mighty shove that sent him rolling sideways and sat up. 'What's the matter with you?' she demanded. 'It's your wife, is it? We heard she died.'

209

He nodded, still catching his breath at intervals.

'Well,' she said, 'I'm sorry – we all are. She was a fine lady. And you've lost your little baby too. That's sad.' But her voice did not sound as though she thought so. 'No use to grieve,' she said, 'there's but one cure for the loss of a woman and that's another.' She put her arms round him and began to kiss him.

'No,' he said, 'not tonight. I can't.'

''Course you can,' she murmured, odiously encouraging, ''Course you can. Come on.' She began to caress his body with a practised touch. 'Put your hand there,' she whispered.

When at last she realised it was all to no purpose, she flung aside from him in a fury of disappointment. 'What did you come for then?' she spat at him.

He did not answer, knowing too well he had been a fool to think he would find comfort here. She moved away until she was only a faint shadow by the trees. 'Call yourself a man,' she hissed. 'You were never any good. Ain't an Englishman in this place but's a better man than you, you soft-cocked Norman bastard!'

He stood there rooted as she flayed him with the short, guttural English words whose meanings he had learnt in another sweeter context, closing his eyes as she ripped his pride to tatters, blind to everything but that deliberate, merciless, goading voice.

He came at her so suddenly that she gave a little shriek, and a louder one when his fist caught her on the cheekbone. 'Damn you!' he whispered hoarsely. 'Damn you, you slut! I'll kill you—' He got her by the throat but somehow she eluded him, scratching and kicking, until he wound his fingers in her long black hair and hauled her back. He shook her to and fro while she pulled and struggled frenziedly away from him, and then she tripped and fell slackly in the undergrowth with him on top of her. It knocked the breath out of both of them. He felt her move and saw her face marked and bloodied by the blows; a savage desire possessed him, a hot urgency beside which nothing mattered – not grief, not love, not self-respect.

Afterwards, when he stared down at her, rage was gone with the rest. He felt only a cold emptiness. She moved and winced, and giggled softly. 'That was worth it all,' she said, 'wasn't it?'

He spat beside her into the new, young ferns. 'Yes,' he said, and walked away. But with every step doubt grew stronger. He feared the price of his escape from shame and self-disgust had been too high.

June 1164

The King pulled up his horse at the top of the steep rise that led down to Corfham Castle and waited for the rest of the party to catch up. The day was far advanced because Henry, upsetting all previous arrangements, had decided all at once to leave Ludlow for Wenlock Priory. Now, but a few miles into Corvedale, he had changed his mind again. Wenlock Priory could wait; instead he would pay a surprise visit to the castle.

Down here in the peaceful, sheltered valley, the air was still and warm. Behind the humped, forested shoulders of Brown Clee and the thrusting summit of Titterstone, the sky was blue; that way lay England. But heaped white cloud was gathering and spilling over the great cliff of Wenlock Edge; weather and discord alike had their origins in Wales.

He could hear the others coming now and turned the horse back towards them, shouting to let them know he wished to take the other road. No need to tell them why. They were too used to his sudden impulses and changes of plan to read any special reason into this one. But he had a reason, for all that.

Corfham Castle was held for him by Walter de Clifford, a minor marcher lord of whom he had heard little until he had ridden into Salop this last week. Not so now – the shire was ringing still with the news of his slaying of Cadwgan,

211

son of Maredudd, in ambush. For years, apparently, Walter had feuded with the Welsh of Powys and Gwynedd over his castle of Llannymddyvri in their heartland. Normally Henry cared nothing for that; even secretly commended Walter's fierce determination to hold his own, but just now he wished to keep the peace with the wild chieftains who lived beyond his borders. He was not yet ready to carry war to them again and he had no wish to see them boiling out of their hidden valleys, raiding and destroying his prosperous lands. Remembering the trouble that had ensued when Roger de Clare had engineered the murder of Rhys ap Gruffyd's nephew, Einion, two years ago, he decided to see for himself how much likelihood there was of this latest killing leading to open warfare.

When they rode in he noted with satisfaction the stunned looks of the men-at-arms who kept the gate. His glittering eye roved about, taking in the well fed horses in the stable yard, the garners neatly kept and the small pleasaunce where Arabian roses bloomed. The Welsh had never happened on this place, it would appear. And doubtless de Clifford kept his women here, safe out of harm's way.

It amused Henry to enter a strange place unannounced. He liked to go in first, standing a moment in the doorway to savour the reactions of the surprised inhabitants. This hall was small, rush-strewn and dim after the brightness without. It was a second or two before his eyes accustomed themselves and he could see anything. The dogs set up an instant barking and several men were on their feet, startled and apprehensive at this unheralded invasion. He saw their expressions run the gamut from fear through shock to wonder tempered by some sort of misgiving.

De Clifford had been doctoring a hawk and it mewed and struggled on his wrist; he soothed it with soft clicking sounds as he hurried forward. When he placed it on its perch, it spread its great wings once, then sank to somnolence.

Henry allowed de Clifford to kiss his hand and lead him

forward while he still gazed curiously around. He had seen a number of women in the hall, some of them young. He looked them over idly, only half listening to his host's declarations of delight in his presence, until his eye fell last of all on a downbent fair head not a dozen feet from him. Something in the turn of the head, the curve of the cheekbone— Time stopped.

He was abruptly conscious that de Clifford was silent, staring at him. They were all staring at him but he could not drag his eyes away from that fair head with the curling shoulder length hair. He willed her to look up. When she did, he let his breath out with an audible sigh; she was not really like Hikenai at all. It had been only a trick of the light and her posture and that hair. But his glance kept stealing back to her.

When the introductions were finally effected he discovered that she was one of de Clifford's daughters, the youngest of three. Lucia, Amicia and Rosamund. She was Rosamund. There were three sons too, Walter, Richard and William. He memorised the names with characteristic care.

The ladies soon retired to their own quarters and he spent the rest of the day with the men, but he did not bring up the matter that had brought him here. There would be time enough for that. He had already decided to spend at least three days at Corfham.

A week later he was still there but if he had any doubts about what kept him after convincing himself that the marcher lords of the area could hold the Welsh, his host had not. He and his lady had intercepted too many of the long, soft looks the King bent on their daughter for that.

'But what,' cried Walter de Clifford, throwing his arms wide, 'what can we do? We cannot ask the lord King to leave!' He turned his worried eyes in desperation on his wife. He was not a man to stand willingly by and see his daughter lose her virtue, even to the highest in the land, and he proceeded to lay down the most careful instructions for

213

her safe-keeping.

'Ah well,' returned his lady whose soft plumpness indicated her comfortable temperament, 'I cannot find it in me to worry overmuch. Do you remember how the girl has been set on entering religion since she was small. I doubt that she has even seen the way he looks at her, much less construed it as you have.'

Sir Walter grunted dolefully. 'He has a way with women.'

'She's but a child – scarce fifteen. And pure in heart.' His lady heaved herself up from her seat. 'I will take care she sees him not alone. But if she did – I think he'd only frighten her. For myself I'm only thankful it's not Lucia he looks at so hungry.'

'Oh? And why is that?' demanded her husband, 'What do you mean by it? Why Lucia? Come, woman, explain yourself!'

And as she grew more muddled and evasive, he grew hotter, raging at women's carelessness of their daughters' honour until she retired to her bower in floods of tears and proved him all too right by completely forgetting everything he had ordered for Rosamund's protection.

Only Henry, closely watching after dinner, saw Rosamund go out alone to the pleasaunce in the moth-haunted June dusk, and he was careful to take a couple of companions when he turned out for a last breath of air. It was easy to drop them once outside, and he went on swiftly and silently to the little box-enclosed rose garden. She was standing staring at the sky where the first stars trembled.

She swung round when she heard him brush against the low hedge, eyes wide and mouth slightly open like a child. There was still something about her that reminded him of an earlier love so that his voice was uncommonly gentle when he spoke. 'What do you here alone in the owl light?'

Flustered, she blushed and tried to curtsey but he took her arm and lifted her to face him. He had never been so close to her and his eyes devoured her features, seeking the likeness that eluded him. Her face was a perfect oval, her mouth small with a faint droop to the underlip, and the hair grew from her high brow in a strong springing curve. He thought her eyes were blue but in the deepening twilight could only be sure they were not dark. 'I – I came to see my flowers – and to see the stars come out.'

'Oh – not to see a gallant?' His voice was teasing but he saw the small mouth close primly and tried again. 'They are your flowers, are they? I thought them woman's work. How did you get them to grow in England?' He talked to her persuasively, trying to lead her to a more personal approach that he might uncover her habit and disposition. But she only answered in monosyllables with hanging head so that at last he gave up and stood smiling down at her, content merely to watch the changing play of her expression.

'I must go,' she said, and then on a nervous rush, 'If you will excuse me, my lord King—'

'Not yet,' he said. 'A moment more, I pray you.' And he put out his hand, longing yet half afraid to touch her.

She did not, or would not, see it. 'Oh, sir,' she said, 'my mother—'

'I see you fear your mother's displeasure more than your king's.'

She stared at him, stricken.

'Run along then,' he said. 'Your parents have taught you well a daughter's duty.' And he turned away.

She stood and bit her lip while he watched her from the corner of his eye, certain now that her half-hearted attempts to flee were but a trick to lure the hunter on. He knew how to play that game.

When he began to laugh she moved a step closer. 'You are not angry?' she whispered, looking into his face.

'No,' he said. 'Of course not.' When her eyes fell, he said carefully, 'Do you come often to your pleasaunce?'

Her voice was eager. 'Every day at dusk.'

God's blood, how young she is! he thought. A wave of

tenderness swept over him but she was so plainly on tenter-hooks still that he felt obliged to let her go. He would see her alone again tomorrow – he could not have misread that artless invitation.

When she had gone he remained for a moment watching the pale flowers glimmer under a darkling sky. The resemblance he had seen had been reflected from her sweet soul, he thought, from her essential spirit. He had not thought in all the world to find another such. Rosamund. . . . He reached out his hand and snapped off one of the roses at the neck; for a second he held it against his cheek, then tucked it out of sight in the bosom of his tunic. He was still faintly smiling when he rejoined his fellows.

In the hall Sir Walter sat with his face set hard as stone. He had seen his daughter come in and he knew well now why the King had craved for air after supper. When Henry came in to drink a last cup of wine with him, he wasted no time but started in at once to talk about his children, telling of his arrangements with regard to his daughters' marriages and dowers, and stressing in particular Rosamund's un-wavering desire for the life of a religious.

'Though she's so young,' he said, 'I've no fear she'll alter. It has been so with her since she was a little maid. And it shows plainer every year that she's no taste for men. There have been some,' he added darkly, 'to whom such modesty was challenge. They were sent empty away.' He peered side-ways at the King who was remarkably quiet. 'I but tell you this,' he continued, 'that you may not think her wanting in respect do you notice her avoidance of – your party.'

Henry looked into his cup and then obliquely at Sir Walter. A faint flush had risen to his cheeks. So what he had taken for an unpractised maiden's beckoning withdrawals had been retreat in truth. Well, she need have no fear that he would force unwelcome attentions on her – though surely she could have made the position plain without run-ning to her father! The memory of his earlier feelings completed his mortification. He covered it with bitter self-derision. What was he doing, mooning about in rosegardens at his age? The consummation of such dreams was their destruction anyway – as well he knew.

He stood up, hoping the heat in his face was not visible. 'I wish you well with all your plans,' he said. 'I'll retire now though, for I must be up betimes. Tomorrow I ride for Wenlock Priory and thence to Shrewsbury. I shall charge you to make my farewells to your ladies.'

Sir Walter saw that his glance had passed over him and beyond as if he were already thinking of the next thing he should do. Since that was the very thing he had wished for he was somewhat puzzled by his own annoyance.

Henry could not put enough distance between himself and Corfham; he would not be easy until he was out of Salop altogether. Never – never since his early teens had he suffered such an emotional humiliation. But as the slow hours passed he saw that it existed more in his own mind than in fact. Who but he could know of his foolish hankerings after the unattainable? Assuredly she had not – and her father had merely feared to have his virgin spoiled.

He thought of his wife at Marlborough but dismissed the idea of visiting her. A night's sporting with a good whore would cure him more effectively. Thank God for honest lust.

Feeling his normal spirits returning, he reined in to allow the small group of his intimates to catch up. But he rode on again when he caught the tenor of their conversation, keeping just enough distance that he might overhear. They were discussing the Archbishop's latest manoeuvres. He had taken to publicly reading picked passages from the Fathers which accorded with his own ideas and refuted the King's, and now they had heard that he was proclaiming from Gratian's *Decretum* that bishops were the only lawful judges of ecclesiastical persons.

Henry was seized by so sudden and intense a gust of rage

that he heard the humming of his own blood in his ears. That disobedient vassal's rebellion against him was common talk all over England. If Thomas had been before him at that moment, he would have smashed his fist into that once loved face. He felt himself begin to shake and gripped the saddle more tightly with his thighs. His forehead was wet all round the hairline.

He thumped his heel in the horse's side and waved his arm at them to follow with all speed. It was impossible to tattle at a gallop. And the sooner he found a harlot the better. That would exorcize all his demons.

Once at Woodstock, he immersed himself in state business. It was in the afternoon of the second day that the Chamberlain came in, looking rather ruffled. 'My lord the Archbishop of Canterbury has arrived and craves audience with you,' he murmured.

Henry's head came up and his eyes narrowed; for a moment his face wore the expression of a hunter when he sees the means to take his quarry. Then his lids came down and he waved his hand as at an annoying interruption. 'I am busy. He must wait,' he said.

But it was not more than five minutes before his officials found themselves dismissed and the Chamberlain was ordered to show in the Archbishop. Henry sat with one leg cocked over the arm of the chair and his lips pouted forward. He said nothing until Thomas bent one knee before him, and then only, 'My lord Archbishop?'

He did not know what he expected but it was certainly not the request Thomas was now making. 'To visit the Pope?' he said incredulously. 'For what purpose? That you may persuade him to put an interdict on my lands? Do you take me for a fool?' He flung his leg over the chair arm and sat up. His face had reddened. 'No! You shall not leave England. Have I not made it clear enough that I will not permit foreign interference in English affairs? Say no more! And who gave you leave to rise?' he shouted suddenly as

Thomas stood upright. He sprang up himself so as not to allow the Archbishop the advantage of looking down at him, and was infuriated to find that, two steps higher as he was, Thomas faced him eye to eye.

'The fact that I have consulted the Pope is no concern of yours. It gives you no leave to do the same. Go away!'

Thomas opened his mouth to say something, hesitated and closed it. Henry's blazing, widened eyes glared into his. 'Hear me, Thomas of London,' he said softly, 'this I swear. I will bring you low and put you back where I found you. Now go away.'

Thomas went without another word.

August 1164

Long after they could see it was useless they argued with the sailors who only continued to shake their heads with silent obduracy; all except the captain who kept crying in a loud, excited voice that they knew very well who the intended passengers were, and nothing should make them so risk the King's anger. 'For you are the Archbishop's men from Romney,' he said, 'and that' – jerking his chin at Thomas who stood by muffled in cloak and cowl – 'that's the Archbishop himself! We know him by his height. You do ill indeed to try and deceive poor men so. Do you think we did not hear of your last attempt wherein you were driven back by contrary winds? You will find none now to take you off from this coast.' And pushing away the bags of silver they were proffering, he strode up the gangplank and ordered the sailors to draw it up.

'Come,' said Thomas wearily, 'come, I shall return to Canterbury. It is plainly not God's will that I should leave England.' But as he walked towards the horses he wondered what he could do now. His household was all dispersed, his knights returned to their homes and his bishops fled. Even the Pope was half-hearted in his defence, fearful lest Henry turn from him to the schismatics.

Over the last months fear had crept upon him too. He had met Henry only twice throughout the spring and on each occasion the King had almost ignored him. Thomas, still buoyed up at that time by his penances, had refused to allow it to unsettle him. It was the attitudes of his own friends towards the rupture that began to dismay him most. John of Salisbury wrote despondently from Paris of the gloomy view King Louis took of the situation, and with concern of the large sums of money – 'which Rome has never despised' – that Henry was laying out at the Papal Court.

And hints of the precariousness of Thomas's position were clear between the lines of letters from John Belmeis. He reported regularly on the gossip at the Curia where he kept agents on Thomas's behalf – it was through them that he had heard of the Anti-Pope's death in April. But that gleam of hope had quickly faded with the further news that the Emperor had caused another to be elected, thus prolonging the deadly split at the heart of Christendom and keeping all effective power out of the hands of the Papacy.

On several occasions John had counselled Thomas to cultivate the Abbot of Pontigny – 'it may be that I shall be glad to take refuge there myself should the need arise,' he had written. And he had commended certain cardinals as trustworthy – why, unless he thought it advisable for Thomas to take sanctuary in France until Henry's wrath abated? So he had asked Henry's permission to go and the interview had shown him clearly the peril in which he stood. Flight had seemed the only answer.

But that course was denied him. Only this little knot of faithful friends remained. And if he were prepared to admit to himself now that he was very badly frightened, admitting it to Herbert was another matter; he appeared to feel no fear at all – if anything, the scent of danger hardened his resistance. Yet the risk to him was almost as great as to Thomas for his outspokenness against the King increased in proportion to the lessening of support for the Archbishop. There had been many times when Thomas had to warn him to guard his tongue lest his inflammatory remarks be carried to the royal ear. Sometimes, indeed, Thomas thought that his passionate partisanship jeopardised rather than helped the Church's cause.

Enemies had the King's ear now, men like Geoffrey Ridel, John of Oxford, Roger of York and Gilbert of London. Urged on by them, Henry was putting the Constitutions into practice, seizing clerks suspected of crime and punishing and maiming them without reference to their bishops. The future looked black indeed.

All the way back to Romney Herbert pressed him not to return to Canterbury, to an empty palace and a cold hearth. 'That is my place,' Thomas said grimly, 'There I shall go and there remain. But you and Alexander and the rest may stay at Romney if you so desire.'

Riding hard along Stone Street he knew they were behind him but would not slacken his headlong pace to let them catch up. It was growing dark already; from a bright, fair morning the sky had later become overcast and dull and now a chilly breeze had sprung up. Autumn would come early this year.

Night had fallen when he reached Canterbury; he had to hammer on the gate a long time to rouse the guard and they were sulky and ill-tempered at being dragged away from their dicing and their ale. When they realised who it was though, they kissed his hands and asked his pardon and his blessing but he shrugged them off, impatiently. It was only when he heard the heavy bar thump down across the gate that he remembered he had forgotten to warn them the rest of his party was following.

Five minutes later he looked at the front of his palace with a sinking heart. As he stared up it seemed to be leaning. He stepped back quickly, then saw it was the ragged cloud, pale against a darker sky, that moved. Here and there a few

221

stars twinkled.

He went into the corner of the doorway and leaned his back against the stone. After a while he slid gently down and huddled himself together in the angle of the wall, his knees drawn up and his head sunk upon his crossed arms.

Some hours earlier William Bouhert and his page had ridden into Canterbury, seeking the Archbishop. Finding none to tell them where he might be, they had entered the palace which, though deserted, was unlocked. They had roamed about, growing more and more uneasy at the evidence of hurried departure, a sanding box upset across a table, a heap of pallets flung all anyhow, and everywhere the squalid odds and ends discarded by those who do not expect to return.

William set his boy to light a fire while he foraged in the kitchens. All he could find was a heel of old black bread and a very dubious looking lump of beef. He pumped the water up himself; it ran brown and rusty for quite a while before it cleared.

After they had made a scanty meal he led the way to the Archbishop's chamber. It smelt close and unaired but there was nothing here to show that the occupant did not mean to come back. 'We'll sleep here,' he decided. 'Go you and fetch another pallet from the hall for yourself.' When the lad had gone he walked to the window and stood staring out into the grey evening, tapping his fingernail on his teeth and wondering where the Archbishop was.

The boy had been asleep an hour when William suddenly remembered the outer door was still unlocked. He leaned across and shook him. 'Go down, Bernard,' he said, 'and put the bar across the portal. We'll sleep safer so. Here, take the lamp.' He gave it into the lad's hand. 'Be quick now!'

Holding his chausses up with one hand, Bernard took the lantern with the other and scuttled through the silent, eerie hall. He hesitated a moment at the portal, then pulled it open just enough to insert his head in the gap, and peered outside. The town was dark and sleeping, the bushes whispered in the wind and a gibbous moon raced ghostly overhead through shredded cloud.

The creaking of the door roused Thomas. Seeing the pale tearstained face hang disembodied in the corner, Bernard let out a howl of terror, dropped the lantern and tore back through the hall as though all the fiends of Hell were after him.

William heard his screeching and started up in a sudden sweat, groping wildly in the darkness for his sword. Before he found it Bernard hurled himself on him, gibbering. 'Master! Sweet Christ, a ghost! The Archbishop's ghost! Oh, he is dead and come to haunt us— Holy Mother, help us—'

The boy was clinging like a leech to William's sword arm and gabbling as though demented. Through it all William heard the great outer door slam shut. What had entered? He felt the hair rise on his scalp.

Then he heard the slow footsteps. He flung Bernard off. 'Be quiet, fool!' he hissed. 'Do ghosts wear boots?' With a shaking hand he lit a candle end and grasped his sword.

There was no mistaking the figure in the doorway. He hurried forward. 'Oh, thank God, my lord! That boy' – he indicated Bernard, trying to burrow inside the pallet – 'thought he had seen your ghost. Come out, you dolt,' he continued roughly. 'It was the Archbishop himself you saw.'

Thomas walked across and sat beside the cowering boy. 'Look, lad,' he said gently, 'I'm no ghost. Feel my hands. They're cold, it's true, but solid flesh and bone. I had thought the door barred; that's why I waited on the porch. I'm truly sorry I frightened you.' He glanced around and then enquiringly at William.

William had the grace to colour faintly. 'I – I hope you will pardon us, my lord. We felt safer here—'

Thomas made a reassuring gesture. 'It is nothing.' He

223

leaned forward suddenly, closing his eyes. 'Is there anything to eat?'

Bernard rolled off the pallet. He still sniffed and caught his breath jerkily but his eyes, when he looked at the Archbishop, were eloquent of relief. 'Let me go, lord,' he said, 'I'll run to the monks at Christ Church. I'm not frightened any more. I'll fetch someone back with food and light.'

'Hurry up then,' said William. He swung the Archbishop's legs up on the couch and began to pull off his boots. He wanted to ask him why he was alone and out of doors at dead of night but he was constrained still by the embarrassment of being caught in his bed, and even more so by the Archbishop's reddened eyes and tearstained cheeks.

Thomas felt the silence stretch. Bouhert's face mirrored his questions as plainly as if he had asked them – good, simple Bouhert who, finding the Archbishop fled, had sought consolation by sleeping in his bed and now rubbed his legs like any servant. But he was too tired for explanations. He lifted his arm with an effort and touched Bouhert's cheek. 'Thank you for being here,' he said.

In desperation Thomas had come to see the King again. The last week, spent almost alone in his palace, had unnerved him more than anything that had gone before. Perhaps Henry would be in an easier mood this time. Even if he were not, Thomas could no longer sit idle, waiting for whatever blow might befall.

Henry was in the midst of a group of his lords; Thomas saw the seneschal edge through and speak to him. He looked up and across at Thomas and said something to his companions, and they all turned to stare. Then he pushed them aside and came a few steps forward, beckoning the Archbishop to approach. The expectant hush in the hall was very evident so that small noises were magnified; Thomas heard the rustle of his own feet in the strawing, the low growl of a dog, even the muted cooing of the doves outside.

Henry stopped when they were still several yards apart, waiting for the Archbishop to come to him. He was dressed for riding and he swung a small whip to and fro, a faint self-satisfied smile lurking at the corners of his mouth. Thomas blinked at the breezy good humour of his tone as he said, 'Well. Isn't my kingdom big enough for the two of us now?' A faint titter rose from the watchers and Thomas felt his heart give a great thump, but the King began at once to talk of trivialities though without, Thomas noticed, ever once meeting his eyes.

He made no further mention of his Archbishop's attempted flight except to remark very lightly, when speaking of important letters from Normandy gone astray, that the guard on the ports was now so strictly kept he had no doubt they would soon turn up. Yet somehow, none of it – his bonhomie or the content of his conversation – rang quite true.

And as Thomas became increasingly aware of the side-long glances of the onlookers, the realisation came that Henry was not going to accord him a private audience. He was to be made to stand here like any petty official and state his business before them all.

The dignity of his status forbade it. He said smoothly, 'I am sorry to have interrupted you at such a busy moment' – he looked pointedly at the lounging lords – 'but being in the vicinity, I would not pass without offering my duty to you, my lord King. I will not detain you any longer, however—'

'Yes,' said Henry. He smiled coldly. 'I am very busy. There are matters of justice to which I must attend. I am sadly undermanned in that department. Indeed, I scarcely know what I should do without the willing help of one whom you recommended to me years ago – Master Map. You remember him?'

'Of course,' said Thomas. He lifted his chin a little. Henry should not see how that shaft had gone home if he could help it. But his lips would not frame the pleasantries about Walter the occasion demanded. Instead, ignoring all the others there as they had ignored him, he bade the King a curt farewell and withdrew.

September 1164

From inside the bower where she was laying fresh tutsan leaves under the feather bed, Ilaria could hear Beatrice's high, scolding voice and Reynold's short, gruff rejoinders. They were quarrelling violently again and she knew how that would end. Sure enough, there came a slapping sound, a shriek and a torrent of words she did not hear because she crouched lower over the couch, almost burying her head in the pallet.

The door banged open and Beatrice rushed in with a face like thunder and a livid weal across her cheek. Ilaria said nothing. She had learnt a long time ago that it was inadvisable to notice anything that went on between them. But her heart moved in her breast with inarticulate rage against her kinsman. She wished that he would go away. If he would only do as Beatrice wanted and renounce his fealty to the Archbishop, the King would find something for him to do – something that would take him off on official business, with any luck. Life was so much pleasanter without him.

In his absence she and little Maud shared the great bed with Beatrice. Warm, unformulated feelings stirred her as she thought of it – the same feelings as when she brushed Beatrice's hair, but intensified by the proximity of her soft flesh. She shivered a little, recalling with delight the brush of a naked arm against her own.

Beatrice saw her then. Her thoughts were almost the same as Ilaria's, at least as far as wishing Reynold away was concerned. The quarrel they had just had was the last of many, all on the same subject, but Reynold, as ever, must follow Hugh de Morville's lead in everything, and Hugh apparently

226

was not yet ready to desert the Archbishop. Even now – she ground her teeth in rage at their stupidity – when all of Kent was agog at the Archbishop's unsuccessful attempts to escape from England. What could they hope to gain by remaining in his service? They would be dragged down with him and lose everything. . . .

Furiously she exclaimed, 'I told him that ill will come of it if he cling still to the Archbishop.' She put her hand up to her burning cheek and then examined the palm as if she thought it might be bloody. 'O Jesu, that great ox! If Hugh de Morville asked him to exchange heads, he would race out and get his lopped!'

'Never mind,' said Ilaria. 'Never mind. Come, I will put a wet cloth on it—'

'Oh, that!' answered Beatrice contemptuously. 'It's nothing. I kicked him in the shins. But he is such a *fool*!' She glanced at the bed. 'You are not still bothering with those old leaves? They have never yet prevented me from conceiving. What I need is a charm that will enable me to bear a living son.'

Ilaria lowered her eyes humbly. She felt it must be her fault the tutsan leaves did not work their reputed magic. Perhaps there was a special way to lay them. . . . It was true that a spell for a successful conclusion to pregnancy would be best for Beatrice but she did not know of one. Her dark, heavy face wore a glowering look but Beatrice knew her too well to be deceived by it.

'I'm not blaming you,' she said crossly. 'It simply does not work for me, that's all.' She compressed her lips. Ilaria was unaware of it but she had long accepted that she was accursed by reason of her one-time truck with the devil who possessed Hugh de Morville. She knew this was so because her first-born, little Maud, conceived when she was a virtuous wife, grew and thrived mightily while of her subsequent children not a one had lived. Since Reynold's return from Normandy. in 1160 she had brought forth four still-born

227

babes. It was plain enough that Hugh's devil, having once effected entrance to her womb, had blasted it. She was twenty-four years old and it was a bleak future she faced, even without the prospect of the worldly ruin she saw before her.

Then she thought of the news Reynold had told her before they began to quarrel and arranged her face carefully as she said, 'De Morville has another daughter. They will give a feast here in celebration because he will not ride as far as Yorkshire at this time.' She remembered what Reynold had called her when she objected and brushed away Ilaria's eager questions. 'Do you see to the arrangements. I must rest.'

When Ilaria had gone she sat quite a long while wondering why the demon had no power over Hugh de Morville's wife.

After the feast Hugh stayed on at Barham with them, and to Beatrice's relief, paid almost no attention to her; he spent most of his time deep in talk with Reynold and the other knights. The small snatches of conversation she overheard had to do only with his children and she ceased even trying to listen when she caught Hugh's dark, unblinking regard fixed on her once or twice.

She was forced though, to listen at meal times to his smooth, deep voice replying to Reynold's questions about his family, and it was only by keeping her eyes steadfastly on her dish that she was able to deal with the emotions his presence roused in her. Bitterness was there in plenty, but underneath old longings were rising. She dared not look at him, knowing the spell his beauty cast – and, she feared, would always cast – on her.

That lasted about a week until one day she came quietly through the dark passage between the kitchens and the hall to see Hugh bending over little Maud. Her heart gave a great jump in her chest, and without a thought of his reaction, she ran forward and gathered up the child. She had not realised until that moment by how much fear of him outweighed any other feeling.

But where her child was concerned, love cast out fear. For as Maud had grown and developed, Beatrice had come by gradual degrees from indifference to a passionate absorption in her daughter. Intensified though it was by her losses, its roots lay deeper. Physically a Fitzurse every inch (or more truly, a de Boullers) underneath Maud was all Beatrice, and even at six years old the acumen in that little head was considerable.

She wriggled in Beatrice's arms. 'See, mama, what Uncle Hugh has brought me.' Beatrice glanced down at the wooden puppet in the child's hand, then up at Hugh.

Hugh smiled at her. 'How she has grown! And how like her father!'

For a second Beatrice could not speak. In her view, Hugh could have offered no direr insult to her daughter, and she read into it, besides, a deeper meaning.

'You are too kind,' she said at last and turned to go. He put his hand upon her arm. 'Beatrice!' he said, swift and urgent. She stood quite still, clutching the child as though she were drowning.

'You're pinching me, mama,' whined Maud.

Stiffly she set the child down and watched her stump away on her fat little legs, solemnly addressing the doll and bidding it be good or be straitly punished. Beatrice was suddenly very angry.

'What do you want with me?' she hissed. 'Have you not done enough? If you pester me I will tell Reynold everything and he will kill you!'

She saw his face change and felt a deadlier fear.

'Oh no, my dear,' he said softly, 'it's you he'd kill – and he'd be well within his rights. You tempted me, you see.' He laughed. 'I'm no longer tempted, I might add. You're older now. I was about to tell you of my own little girls, but we'll not bother with politeness, you and I, if that's the way you'll have it—'

She felt his fingers biting into her arm and shook him off. 'Stay away from my child,' she cried on a thin, shrill note.

'Oh, I will,' he said, 'I will, for the time being. She'll be more interesting in ten years or so. And remember, Beatrice, that I, too, can tell tales to Reynold—' He put his hands on her arms again and as she stood transfixed, leaned forward and kissed her lingeringly on the mouth.

When he had gone she took a few steps as though to follow him, then halted with her hand across the lower half of her face. She felt as light and empty as a wraith, as if all her being were concentrated in the lips that he had touched. For the first time in her life she did not know what to do.

A movement in the shadows at the end of the passage recalled her to herself. When she looked harder, she saw it was Ilaria. How long had she been standing there, almost invisible in her dark gown? There was a stiffness in her pose that suggested she had seen something. With an effort Beatrice produced a smile. 'You made me jump,' she said, 'I was far away in thought and you startled me.'

She had come abreast of Ilaria now and the older woman put out her hand and grasped Beatrice's wrist. 'What were you up to with that man?'

'Nothing,' Beatrice mumbled. 'What do you mean?'

'I saw him kiss you.'

Beatrice tried to pull her hand away.

'Why did he kiss you like that? It was as though – I thought you did not like men. You always speak as though you do not.'

Beatrice frowned, her mouth began to shake and she leaned forward so that her head rested on Ilaria's bosom. Ilaria held Beatrice away from her and looked into her face. 'He frightened you, did he? He's after you and that husband of yours sees nothing? Don't be afraid, my darling, I'll

230

look after you.' She drew Beatrice into her arms and stroked her hair.

Beatrice leaned on her in silence. She did not know what to make of Ilaria's enigmatic behaviour. After a while she whispered, 'Please don't tell Reynold.'

Ilaria's hand stopped its stroking. 'Tell Reynold? Nay, indeed, I will not.' She laughed shortly. 'Oh, he's my kin I know, but he means nothing to me. I'd not raise a finger to help any man. It was you I stayed for. Come, come and lie down, my dearest.'

Beatrice lay with closed eyes on the couch in her bower. Puzzlement had been replaced with wonder. 'I love you,' Ilaria had said. 'You are everything in the world to me. I love you.' How pleasant it had been to lie here and accept the gentle fondling and caressing that asked for nothing in return. And no pain or pregnancy to follow. Nor guilt.

Ilaria bent over her. 'I will never leave you, Beatrice,' she said, 'Never – whatever happens.'

It's true, Beatrice thought. She does love me. How very odd. But she did not dwell long on Ilaria's feelings because her busy, planning brain had already leapt ahead to more tangible matters. With what Ilaria possessed and what she could salvage, they could manage yet, even without Reynold. And it might be better so. . . .

IX

October 1164

Archbishop Thomas's progress towards Northampton was slow, in part because he was hardly recovered from the illness which had struck him down in September, but also, some of his companions thought, because he was reluctant to go at all. 'And no wonder,' they muttered among themselves, 'when the King had not even the courtesy to address his writ personally to the Archbishop but only to order his presence in the general writ to the sheriff of Kent.'

Though it had angered him, the insult had not surprised Thomas after his refusal to attend the King last month at Westminster. Sickness had prevented him anyway – that old kidney complaint which always returned in times of stress – but he could not accept that the King's court had jurisdiction in the matter for which he was summoned. He, to be arraigned by a man like John Fitzgilbert, who finding himself failing in a suit against the Archbishopric, had sworn he could not get justice there and betaken himself to the King's court! He could never have done such a thing without the help of those accursed Constitutions of Clarendon. And it must be with Henry's connivance in view of the evidence Thomas had sent of John's swearing a false oath.

Well, John had been marshal to the Empress and one of

her most fervent supporters; perhaps Henry had stretched a point because of that. And Thomas did not really fear the outcome of the case because the facts were plain and he knew Henry to be incapable of perverting justice; what he really dreaded was arousing his anger again.

But it was too beautiful a day to dwell upon the future and he gave himself up to the simple pleasure of riding free from pain. Cattle were grazing on the stubble in the cultivated fields; it was too early yet for winter ploughing; indeed, the trees for the most part were still clad in heavy summer green. Yet though the mellow sunshine was still warm, the indefinable bloom of autumn lay over all; even the nearer bushes wore a shining nimbus of misty light and farther off the great fields shimmered under a pearly haze that thickened with distance until it met and merged with the glowing sky.

Out of the corner of his eye he saw a horse sidle up alongside and a freshfaced page shyly held out a cap filled with small half-ripe blackberries; when he smiled Thomas saw his teeth stained purple with the juice. He took a handful out of politeness but as he feared they were woody and very sour. Before he spat them out he glanced back to be sure the lad was not looking.

They reached Northampton about mid-afternoon to find the herald who had gone ahead waiting with the news that William de Courcy, one of Henry's knights, had occupied the lodgings reserved for the Archbishop.

Thomas's mouth tightened. He could scarcely lay this further insult at Henry's door but certainly de Courcy would never have dared such an impertinence a few years ago. He kept his voice calm however. 'Doubtless the Prior of St Andrew's will find us quarters for the time being. And I am sure the lord King will order Baron de Courcy to vacate our apartments. Do not worry about it.'

The herald addressed his feet. 'The Lord King has not

arrived.'

Thomas turned away. 'We must settle where we can,' he said briskly. 'When the King comes, he will right the mistake.'

No one else said anything but Thomas could see the uncertain looks on the faces of his household. He understood their feelings all too well. Nor was the Prior of St Andrew's in much better case. He fluttered here and there, caught between embarrassment for the Archbishop and fear of de Courcy, but under his profuse apologies for the meanness of the accommodation he could offer, Thomas sensed the querulousness of a quiet man who has been dragged unaware into another's quarrel.

Somehow they were lodged and fed, and all squeezed into the warming-house after Collations for a short period of conversation but it was difficult to hear much for the shouting and carousing of de Courcy's men in the guest house across the Court. It was during Compline that the noise died down, and Thomas, pricking up his ears, heard other noises – the clattering of horses' hoofs and shouts of greeting. So the King had come at last. Thomas guessed he had been hawking en route and prayed that it had put him in a good humour. He resolved to wait upon him early on the morrow and talk to him mildly, even about the loss of his lodgings.

So the next morning, after he had said Mass and recited his Hours, he rode out with his clerks to attend upon the King. It was still and misty and their breath steamed in the chilly air as they came past the great curtain wall of the castle; the tufty grass along its base was so thickly furred with dew that it was as grey as the stone. Looking up its towering height, Thomas saw the sky was a clear milky blue. It would be another lovely day.

Early as it was, there were knots of people in the streets to see the Archbishop ride by; they called on him for his blessing, even pushing up to his stirrup to try and touch him.

There was little doubt, thought Herbert, whose side the common folk were on. They had taken Thomas to their hearts from the outset. And the Archbishop smiled at last as he held out his hands over them.

But the smile died and the withdrawn look returned as they rode in through the castle gates. The party dismounted and went on foot through the bailey towards the council hall. There they were told that the King was hearing Mass in the adjoining chapel. They sat in the ante-chamber in silence; Herbert did his best to make conversation but no one answered and after a while even he gave up.

When they heard the sound of many feet approaching they all stood up. The King entered in the midst of his lords; he was looking cheerful but somehow wary. Thomas caught a glimpse of Leicester and Cornwall and Hamelin, the King's bastard brother; he was half conscious too of the presence of at least half a dozen bishops but his mind was too concentrated on Henry to pay them any attention. Henry looked straight at him and he took a pace forward, bending his head a little to receive the kiss of greeting. But the King only continued to stare at him narrowly with an expression Thomas could not interpret, then he nodded coolly and passed on.

The bishops waited for Thomas to lead them in. He thought they looked as crestfallen as he felt but doubted whether it were on his behalf, more likely they feared the King's acrimony would be visited on them.

However Henry greeted him formally once they were all in their places and listened without apparent annoyance to Thomas's complaint against William de Courcy. He even smiled as he gave the order for de Courcy to vacate the quarters he had seized. But the smile remained when he again denied Thomas permission to visit Sens to confer with Pope Alexander about Archbishop Roger's refusal to profess obedience to Canterbury.

Thomas bit the inside of his lower lip. His voice rose just a little as he stated, 'I am come hither, my lord King, to answer your summons in the case of John the Marshal, yet I cannot see him present. Is he not to answer my own court's charge against him of a fraudulent oath, in that he swore upon a tropary he had secreted about his person instead of upon the Gospels?'

Henry waved his hand airily. 'He is not here at the moment, being busy on my affairs at the Exchequer. When he does arrive, I shall certainly hear the case. But since you must wait upon his coming, you are dismissed for the time being.'

Thomas heard Herbert's sudden intake of breath beside him and sat down abruptly. Truly Henry meant to humiliate him. But such treatment might rally his bishops round him for in insulting him, Henry insulted the Church. He would not rise until he had got control of his face and sat with lowered head until the heat in his cheeks receded.

Henry looked up as he withdrew. 'Wait upon us on the morrow,' he said, 'It may be that John the Marshal will be here then.'

Thomas did not arrive so early the next day. He came prepared to be humiliated again (for the Church's sake, he told himself) but with his determination to withstand the King unimpaired. If Henry thought he would yield to him for the sake of personal pride, he was wrong. He would be meek under insult, submissive to discourtesy; only for God's honour would he affront the King.

This time he looked more closely at the rest of the company. Not since Henry's coronation had such an array of great nobles, lay and ecclesiastical, been gathered together. Of the English bishops who were hale, only Walter of Rochester was absent, and he saw faces among the magnates he did not recognise. Every one of these, Herbert had told him, had been summoned by individual writ; only to himself had the indignity of inclusion in a general writ of lesser tenants been offered. Yet still he did not see John the Marshal.

Once the proceedings opened the reason became clear; they had nothing to do with his petty case over the manor of Pagham. As Thomas listened to the charge of contempt against the Crown's majesty levelled against himself, he saw the ambush into which he had walked so confidently. Henry meant not merely to humble him but to destroy him: '—in that you did not only fail to appear on the fourteenth day of September but offered no essoin—' The words dropped like stones.

When it had been read he stood up to give his answer. He did not recognise the Constitutions of Clarendon, he said, and therefore could not accept that the King's court had any right to try the case. The Pope had not approved the Constitutions—

He could barely make himself heard above the hubbub that broke out, and fell silent. One of his clerks, hoping to mend matters, was crying that the Archbishop was ill at the time and unable to rise from his bed. 'Be quiet,' Thomas hissed. 'You but cloud the issue. My illness is beside the point.'

Henry said out of the corner of his mouth to Leicester, 'He *was* ill, then?'

'It seems so.'

'Yet he'll not plead it as an excuse. He prefers to defy me and set himself above my laws.' Leicester heard his teeth grind together and fixed his eyes imploringly on the Archbishop. Could I but see him alone! he thought. But if I do and it comes to Henry's ears. . . . When they voted he raised his hand with the rest to declare Thomas guilty and in the King's mercy.

But some of the barons, seeing the mood the King was in and realising the Archbishop's goods – Church goods – were now forfeit to him, became uneasy about their own position. While never averse to the abating of clerical pride, most of them had a good deal of respect for the Church's powers and they were far from eager to pronounce sentence. As peers of the accused, that was the bishops' job, they argued.

But the bishops stiffened and shook their heads; they were not prepared to range themselves with Thomas against the King but neither were they ready to strike him down with their own hands. Even Foliot and Roger of York refused and Hilary of Chichester kept his eyes steadfastly lowered in case the King should remember old scores and think to attack him as the weakest link in the chain.

Thomas had forgotten all his resolve to be meek; he glared along the bench of bishops, daring them to yield to the barons' pressure. Finally it was young Roger of Worcester, so lately consecrated by Thomas's own hands, who spoke. 'This is a secular judgment in a secular court,' he said, 'and we sit in our capacity as barons. If you insist on taking our Order into consideration, then you must also consider his. As bishops we cannot pronounce judgment on our Arch- bishop and lord.'

Henry began to hammer his fist on the table. 'Enough! Enough!' he roared. 'The lord Bishop of Winchester will pronounce sentence at once. At once, you hear!'

Anyone but Winchester, thought Thomas in despair, anyone but him, O God! For the first time he looked at Henry with actual hatred.

Henry saw it and it took his breath away. You, he thought, whom I raised from nothing! You who accepted everything I gave as your due! By God's eyes, but you shall pay for your presumption! Do you imagine that the touch of the holy chrism raises you higher than a King? Do you not realise that kings are anointed too?

After the Bishop of Winchester had pronounced sentence – that the Archbishop should forfeit all his moveable goods

238

to the value of £300 – he urged Thomas in a hurried undertone to accept the judgment quietly. Thomas shrugged and did not bother to lower his voice. 'It is a new kind of judgment, this; perhaps according to these new canons promulgated at Clarendon.'

'There is no law which justifies refusal to accept sentence in the King's court,' whispered Winchester anxiously.

'Then must I accept it, but under protest.' Thomas looked about him with burning eyes. 'Never has it been heard of that an Archbishop of Canterbury should be tried in the King's court for such a cause. The Church's dignity forbids it, and the dignity of his own person for he is the spiritual father of the King and of all the realm. And it is unheard of, too, that an archbishop should be judged by his own suffragans. Nonetheless, I do submit and agree to pay the fine.'

'I will have guarantees to that,' said Henry.

Thomas ignored him and sat down while the bishops rustled and whispered; at last old Henry of Winchester announced that they would all stand surety, except the Bishop of London who wished to be dissociated from them in this.

Thomas looked across at Gilbert Foliot who returned his glance with a hard and distant gaze which he could by no means outstare. When his eyes fell he thought with a sort of wonder, so he does hate me then – though why I know not – and for a moment felt as he had when as a little boy he had first met unreasoning dislike.

Then, with a jolt, he heard again the King's loud, hectoring tones and the words, 'Eye and Berkhamstead'. Henry was demanding the return of a further £300 which Thomas had received from those honours in revenue when he had been warden. When he rose again his knees trembled; yet his voice was strong as he proclaimed himself not liable as he had been discharged of all dues – 'and if I were liable, yet

239

did I spend all or more than I received on those same castles or on the Tower of London.'

That was not by his order, the King assured the barons, and Thomas said heavily that he would pay for he would never allow money to be a cause of dispute between the lord King and himself.

'Ah,' said Henry, 'will you not? And where will you find the money? For if I am not mistook, you have spent it all long ago and I must remind you that all you have is already escheated to the Crown.'

There was a great deal of restive movement along the barons' benches by now; even some outright murmuring in which words like 'spite' and 'persecution' could be heard. Henry looked that way and scowled while Thomas stood with hanging head, then there was a scuffling as three men stood up, foremost of them, John, Count of Eu.

''I shall give surety of £100 for the Archbishop,' he said. 'And I the same sum,' said William, Earl of Gloucester, behind him.

A deep voice that sounded familiar chimed in with a challenging note. 'And I the same.' Thomas looked up dazed. The last to speak had been William de Ros of Eynsford.

After the Archbishop had left, followed by a good many of the barons and knights. Henry retired to the upper chamber with the rest of the higher nobility. The *volte-face* he had just witnessed in some of his lords had disturbed him more than he would have admitted. He considered now whether to treat these others to one of his famous fits of screaming rage, and then decided to reserve it for a later occasion if they seemed to be wavering in their allegiance. He knew he could cow most of them by this means and since he seldom lost control entirely, he derived a sadistic pleasure from the exercise. Occasionally he went too far – he never remembered much about it afterwards when that happened – but he thought he knew the boundary now and was careful not to overstep it. That there might be danger to himself in public displays of uninhibited fury never crossed his mind. He was concerned only with the effect upon others.

All the same, someone here must pay for the slight that had been put on him by those traitors who had dared to back the Archbishop. If they thought their petty guarantees would save him, they would soon discover their mistake. There was not enough silver in the kingdom to protect Thomas of London now.

His eye ran over the assembled company. These fools, it seemed, had not the wit to realise their king had been successfully defied. There sat Hamelin, his father's bastard, laughing and drinking with Cornwall, his grandfather's bastard. His own close kin – and not a whit concerned that others of their blood had forgotten where their duty lay. He shouted at them suddenly and they turned round, mouths foolishly open. He ordered Cornwall to approach. Hamelin drifted thankfully off. Henry let him; his loyalty was not in question.

He waited, therefore, until Hamelin was out of earshot before he addressed Cornwall. 'It seems that the sons of one who was famed for his fidelity to our house have inherited none of it,' he began abruptly. Slow as he was, Cornwall realised immediately that Henry was referring to the Earl of Gloucester and the Bishop of Worcester, both sons of Earl Robert who had, with himself, upheld the Empress throughout her long struggle with Stephen. He also realised that Henry knew of his own partiality for the Archbishop.

He sat silent a moment, then being a plain-spoken man answered that the Archbishop's honesty being indisputable, some had misliked seeing it called into question. He thought of saying that loyalty should not be called upon to cover injustice, but at that point he looked up and caught Henry's eye and came to a full stop.

'So you *are* his ally,' said Henry softly.

Cornwall's fleshy face tightened. It was evident that his royal nephew, like another and greater before him, felt that those who were not with him were against him. Swiftly he weighed the duty he owed the Archbishop and the Church against his vows of allegiance. It was not really a difficult choice. He renounced the Archbishop with a surprising sense of relief. Blood was thicker than water after all, and a man who seems bent on self-destruction is not the most comfortable acquaintance. 'I was his friend once,' he said, 'No more!'

Henry's eyes bored into him. 'When you were his friend did he ever speak slightingly of me?'

Cornwall's mouth, which had come open, closed slowly. 'Never,' he said. 'Never in my hearing. Why, he would not – you cannot think—' His leathery old face sagged suddenly. 'I thought him honest always. Do you tell me—'

Henry shrugged impatiently. 'How may I know? Men come to me with tales. How much they twist the truth I know not. But this I know – since he is archbishop, he is changed towards me. The pride of him! He thinks that to be archbishop is greater than to be king.'

'He serves another master now.'

Henry's head came up and his eyes met his uncle's in a long stare. He knew that here was the nub of the matter though he had never expected to hear it from Cornwall's lips. He knew something more too, which many had forgotten: that in days of old it was the King who stood next to God, answerable only to Him for his people; and they were better days, to his mind.

The more power the Church gained, the more she wanted. Would she rule all in the end? – pope instead of king, cardinals and archbishops in place of earls? He looked down at his hands; they were stiff from clenching and he flexed them slowly, seeing the long reddish hairs on the backs of the fingers and the torn cuticles lined with dirt. These are the hands that will hold England and Normandy, he thought, not the soft white paws of bishops.

'I shall put down his pride,' he said harshly. 'Hear me, uncle. The Church shall not rule in my lands. Warn your nephew of Gloucester and those others that they must choose between king and archbishop.' He stood up then because Gilbert Foliot was approaching. Cornwall was glad enough of the excuse to go.

By next morning most of the barons (and the bishops too) had heard a garbled version of Henry's remarks and were waiting anxiously for the outcome. Rumour was flying thick and fast – he would imprison the Archbishop, said some, or drive him into exile, and even mutilation did not seem unlikely to others.

The atmosphere in the hall was alive with expectation as they awaited the King. He came late, passing through the press of eager watchers swiftly, so that he was in his seat before Thomas, lost in gloomy foreboding, realised he had arrived.

Thus Henry saw him sitting with his chin sunk on his breast and his shoulders slumped, to every outward appearance a beaten man. A little weakening pang of pity touched him. He reminded himself that the love he once had felt for this man was dead, and at that moment, Thomas looked up and he knew it was not true. He loved him still, in spite of all. Thomas, conceding, acknowledging the Crown's ascendancy, could melt his heart. Did he know it?

Then he saw Thomas's face harden, light blue eyes grow cold; he turned his own eyes away lest the truth be read in them. He began to rehearse in his mind all the most bitter, cruel things he could say to him.

'What has happened,' he demanded, directly the opening ceremony was over, 'to that sum of one thousand marks you borrowed during the Toulouse campaign?'

Taken by surprise, Thomas protested that the money had been a gift and had anyway been expended in the King's service. But Henry pressed remorselessly on, questioning his good faith, refusing to accept his unsupported word, asking him to account for sums of money for which he had long been given quittance – revenues from vacant bishoprics and abbacies he had forgotten about entirely. In vain he pointed out that such accounting was impossible without notice, and then, realising at last that Henry was not even listening to his answers, checked himself and stood stiffly with his chin high, his mouth set and a flaring patch of colour on each cheekbone.

The look on that shuttered face maddened Henry. If he had seen one flicker of pain, one small sign that he still possessed the power to wound, he might have desisted. But he saw nothing but an untouchable hauteur that drove him on to lacerate Thomas with words, to flay him with a spite that made old Cornwall chew his lip and look sidelong at Leicester beneath his hand. 'This is Foliot's work,' he muttered. 'He was dripping venom last night for hours.'

'By God's eyes,' Henry was screaming, 'I will have an account of every penny! And if you will not settle, I will have security for thirty thousand marks!' He raged on, reciting all the insults and evasions he had endured at the Archbishop's hands until his voice grew hoarse and bubbles foamed at the corners of his mouth.

Inwardly he bled. Something inside him howled at Thomas to submit, to kneel, to beg for mercy, and knowing that he would not, wailed like a child, inconsolable.

Down on the benches someone was calling that he would give security but Henry was blind and deaf to any but the man before him and none of his ministers would attempt to draw his attention to the lone voice, and thus, perhaps, to themselves. In any case no one could possibly guarantee such a sum.

Thomas stared at Henry's crimson contorted face and saw in it the gates of death. With just such a face his ancestors had pillaged. Horror and disgust drove out fear, leaving him icily calm. But his mind was racing, seeking a way out. It seemed to him that his only hope was to represent the King's personal attack on him as an invasion of clerical privilege – it could be considered so in view of the fact that he had already been stripped of his own possessions. All that was left belonged to Canterbury. But to do so he must have the whole bench of bishops ranged solidly behind him.

'I must be allowed to consult with my clergy on so grave a charge as this,' he said in a frozen voice.

'Not here – not during the hours I have set aside for business. I'll wait no more on your convenience. If you want help from your bishops, do your pleading in your own time,' shouted Henry. 'Can they help you explain what you did with the £500 you borrowed from the Jews? Answer me, damn you, or before God, I'll have your balls!' He let forth such a volley of foul-mouthed abuse that Thomas turned away his head.

Manasser Biset, the King's steward, looked questioningly at Leicester. 'How does he think the bishops can help him now?' he muttered. But Leicester, watching the ruin human nature makes of human plans, only shook his head. 'Pray God he is not thinking of trying to separate the spiritual from the lay lords,' whispered Manasser. 'More lay lords than bishops are with him now but if he makes them think this is a quarrel between Church and State they will desert him and range themselves alongside the King.'

Cornwall, listening, said nothing. His choice had been made yesterday but by his head, not his heart. It did not stop him thinking bitterly of those who would choose to do the same.

* * *

245

The next day being Saturday, the King transacted no business. Thomas stayed in the peaceful little Priory outside the walls, quietly saying his Mass and his Office and praying for strength. He was at the prie-dieu when Herbert entered, unwontedly furtive.

'What is it?' he said instantly for his mind was not on his prayers; he had been listening rather to the doleful weeping of the rain.

'A fellow is below asking to see the lord Archbishop.' Herbert approached his lips to Thomas's ear although they were alone. 'He showed me Leicester's badge beneath his cloak.'

Thomas slid his eyes sideways towards Herbert without turning his head, then he stood up quickly. 'Bring him hither. Stay – who saw him come?'

'Only the gatekeeper. And he asked for me by name.' He went out.

He showed in a small, bald man, brown as a nut; then he went out again and they heard his heavy tread going down the stair, but Thomas knew he would sit on the bottom step to keep watch for the bishops.

The man took off his rain-drenched cloak and held it a moment uncertainly; Thomas noticed that he did not drop it on the floor when no servant came running as one used to the ways of the great would have done but folded it meekly and put it over his arm. He thought, Leicester sends a lowly messenger for fear one better-known would be recognised.

He smiled kindly to cover the fellow's awkwardness and at his gentle look the man moved swiftly forward and knelt to kiss his ring. 'My lord,' he said, 'I bring a message from my lord of Leicester.'

Thomas nodded. 'Quickly then,' he urged, 'there is not much time. Soon the bishops will arrive—' he hesitated— 'and I fear not all of them are friends.'

The brown man looked at him obliquely. 'Aye, that we know. We – that is, the poor folk – hear more than's commonly believed. We would not see you harmed, my lord; no more than would my lord of Leicester.'

'Give me the message,' Thomas said.

The man told him then of Leicester's fears for his safety, even for his life, and that while he could not openly help him, he would do all he could for him by stealth. He was to tell him, too, that the holy man, Gilbert of Sempringham, would shelter him if he should need to flee.

Thomas shook his head. 'The King—' he began.

'Pox take the King!' said the man roundly, and then seeing Thomas's face. 'Is not the King under God too?' He knelt again. 'Give me your blessing, my lord Archbishop. And remember your people love you.'

Herbert came in then to say some of the bishops were arriving, and hustled the man off. As he went he whispered that horses would be waiting by the hazel coppice outside the Priory every night for the Archbishop's use; Herbert looked at Thomas sharply at that but made no remark beyond the fact that the Bishop of Winchester had come and others were in sight along the road.

They had all arrived within the hour and Thomas ran his eye over them trying to decide who would back him and risk the King's disfavour. Hardly Roger of York sitting there with his pink jowls lapping his collar like a well scrubbed and complacent pig, nor Hilary of Chichester, an opportunist to his finger tips. As for Gilbert Foliot, his face was implacable. Thomas felt his courage fail. Those three were his enemies, he knew. He had been a fool to think he might win them over.

He rallied to concentrate on the others. Perhaps it would be enough if they would throw their weight behind him. . . . Winchester and Worcester were certainly his allies, and surely he could gain the support of Bartholomew of Exeter and his old tutor, Robert of Melun? But Norwich and Salisbury had been badly frightened once already, and Chester and Lincoln were plainly not the stuff of martyrs. Facing the fact that his chances of success were slim, he set himself to the task, pointing out that their only hope lay in preserving a united front.

When he had finished he looked around at their doubting faces, wondering if he had moved any of them. One or two cleared their throats, then Gilbert Foliot rose to reply. Cold anger came up in Thomas as he heard the opening words.

'It is not the King but your resistance that threatens to ruin the Church and all of us. You ought to recall the lowly state from which he raised you and remember with gratitude the gifts he heaped upon you instead of blaming him—'

He was so angry that he missed the next bit, then he heard Gilbert say – 'you will see you should resign! If you can bring yourself to humility the King may even restore everything he has taken from you.'

'We can all see you taking such advice were our positions reversed,' Thomas snapped. 'For pride you have no equal here!'

Henry of Winchester too came back at Gilbert sharply, demanding to know what sort of example that would set for any future primate. 'For then it would be impossible for any prelate to oppose the King. What of the effect on canon law?'

But Gilbert refused to believe that any principle of ecclesiastical freedom was at stake at all, insisting that this was merely the King's natural determination to protect himself against dishonest officials.

'Whose dealings he trusted for a decade,' interposed Roger of Worcester, his lip curling in contempt.

'In any case, the Archbishop was released from all financial obligations at his consecration,' thundered Winchester above the lesser arguments raging among the rest.

'In a case like this, some compromise must be made with the letter of canon law—'

'This persecution is personal, not general – better for the Archbishop to suffer than the whole English Church—'

'In a choice between execution and resignation, I cannot see what good the Archbishopric will do him if he is no longer alive.' That was a plaintive cry from Chester: woolly minded as always, thought Thomas, allowing himself a brief, wry smile.

Winchester raised his voice again to suggest that the King's motive might be avarice. His desire for money almost equalled his lust for power. That silenced them a moment and the few weak protests died away unheeded as he offered all his vast personal wealth for the Archbishop's disposal. Confused by the fear that he might weep, Thomas maintained an impressive dignity as he accepted, but he was painfully aware of the ostentatiously turned backs of York, Chichester and London.

The rest began to argue then about the wording of the proposal offering 2000 marks to the King as a gift. Even after it had been despatched the arguments went on, but Thomas said very little now. He had no hope of Henry accepting such a sum in settlement, nor indeed any sum of money at all. All these threats and accusations had but one end in view, to break his will, to force him through fear to accept Henry as the final arbiter in all matters. But that he could not do for as the ultimate judgment was God's, so the last judgment on earth must be spiritual. Anything other would lead to tyranny. And to yield now would bring only more aggression. . . .

So his thoughts ran on as the bishops bickered, scarcely seeing and not hearing them at all. Only the sharp jangling of the bell for dinner roused him, and then their resentful looks when he did not rise immediately to lead them to the Frater. At the antagonism on their faces he knew that he had failed to make them see what was so plain to him, that the King would have all power if he could, passing the power of the Pope, passing the power even of God.

He made one more effort to explain it to them and ended with an appeal. 'I thought to have had you with me in such a cause' – he looked towards Exeter, Lincoln and Hereford who stood together – 'or at least, some of you. . . .'

Bartholomew of Exeter shook his head heavily saying, 'We must render unto Caesar that which is his' – and Lincoln, staring at his feet as if he had only just discovered them, muttered something about fulfilling their duty to the King.

'You do but lend his arrogance wings to fly,' returned Thomas wearily and turned towards the door. Even there he stopped and tried again. 'Your obligation to him is temporal, to me you are bound in spirituals.'

But they answered nothing, only staring at him with unbending hostility until Winchester gave him a gentle shove and he found himself leading them through the Cellarer's Hall, past the raised trapdoor where baited lines dangled into the stream below, and so into the Frater.

Thomas picked miserably at the food. Only Winchester sat close and Thomas could not help remembering his high standing with Henry; he had little to fear from him. The others had edged down the board away from them. They still wrangled among themselves in low voices; he heard Hilary's rather high voice: 'Surely a discreet submission is better than a forced retreat from an extreme position.' He could not catch Lincoln's reply but then Exeter's voice came clearly, 'These are evil days! I fear this storm will be weathered only by compromise.' He turned to Worcester: 'What is your view, Roger?'

Thomas strained his ears for the answer and it seemed to him that Roger spoke unwillingly. 'I will give no advice to anyone,' he said. 'It is against my conscience to counsel the

Archbishop to resign, yet neither can I advise him to continue as he is doing; to do so would place me at the bar alongside him.'

Thomas had just put a piece of bread into his mouth; now he found he could by no means swallow it. Yet neither could he for politeness remove it so he sat there with the half-masticated lump sticking to his tongue, praying that none would look his way. What he had just heard had dispelled his last illusory hope of understanding from the men who should have been his support in this hour of trial.

They received the King's flat refusal of the money during the afternoon. Hilary of Chichester sprang into the attack at once. 'Now it is plain you must resign. You know him better than anyone here so it is for you to act. After all you served him for years as Chancellor so he will surely listen if you show yourself humble and penitent. Has he not said there is not room in England for you as Archbishop and him as King? Otherwise – *Di meliora!* – he may imprison you for embezzlement or lay violent hands upon you, which would bring harm to the Church and disgrace to himself. Try for once to put others' good before your own.'

Thomas had been downcast before Hilary's outburst; now all the colour left his face and he sat stunned. Even his lips were white. 'Judas!' he breathed and hunched forward.

Roger of Worcester spoke up, crying loudly and angrily that it would harm the Church far more for the Archbishop to put his personal safety before principle and that there were precedents for such a case; none of the Archbishop's predecessors had given way before persecution.

But his support came too late for Thomas. He put by Winchester's hand which rested on his arm and rose. 'I have no more to say,' he announced, 'but what I have said already. I put it to your consciences.' He tried to go on but only swallowed once or twice and bowed his head, muttering something that only Winchester heard. 'It is in God's hands now.'

Long after he had retired they quarrelled; as bitter in contention with one another as ever King and Archbishop were. Yet when the early dusk came down, no one had changed his mind; rather each clung to his own opinion the more firmly for the battering, as a drowning man will cling to a spar even when the tide sweeps it farther out to sea. Gilbert Foliot's certainty that the Archbishop was nothing but a hypocrite was backed by York and Chichester, clever men both, while Winchester and Worcester were as firm in their belief that before them stood a noble soul, wrongfully used. The others, not so personally involved, may have seen more clearly, or perhaps they were not prepared to see anything but the risk to themselves.

Thomas got little sleep that night so he retired early on Sunday. 'See I am not disturbed till dawn,' he told his servant. The man put his pallet outside the door to keep watch but it was not much past midnight when he heard movements in the Archbishop's chamber and raised his head to listen. Being weary himself, he drifted almost immediately into sleep again, only to wake with a start a short while later. He thought he heard his master groaning and lay for a moment uncertain what to do. But concern for the Archbishop whom he dearly loved soon overcame fear of his displeasure. He opened the door very quietly and peered within.

He heard the moaning clearly now and hurried across to the couch. 'What is it, my lord?' he whispered, taking up the guttering night candle. Thomas rolled over towards him. 'The same old pain.' He tried to smile but another spasm took him and he closed his eyes, breathing shallowly until it passed.

'I'll warm the bran pillows. Don't worry, my lord, we'll soon have you better—'

'O God!' Thomas writhed on the bed. 'O God, why

now? I dare not absent myself from the Council tomorrow—' Another groan burst from him as the agony returned. When it receded he tried to sit up. 'The King will never believe this is not a trick.'

'If he doesn't believe it, he can send someone to see,' returned the man. He watched the Archbishop anxiously. 'I'll send for Master Herbert. One thing's sure – you'll not face the lord King tomorrow, nor this week, I'm thinking.'

'It's his own fault, anyway,' he muttered under his breath as he packed pillows around Thomas's back, 'All this upset! Threatening God knows what – why should he be surprised do it make folk ill.'

At dawn the attack was at its height and a message was sent to inform the King of the Archbishop's illness. Thomas was in too much pain by then to care about Henry's reaction; he could only set his teeth and hang on grimly to the knowledge that it would pass. Either that or he would die, and just now he had no particular preference in the matter.

But by the third hour the throes were lessening. They had brought Thomas a bowl of pottage when they heard the sounds of men and horses in the great court. Herbert went quickly to the window; his chin was up and jutting so that they knew he was ready to repel any unlicenced invasion.

'It is Leicester and Cornwall,' he said. 'Not enemies, at least. I will go down to them.'

'I will see them,' said Thomas. 'Bring them here.'

Herbert's face expressed the disappointment of a warrior denied battle. He sighed heavily as he went.

Leicester stopped in the doorway a moment with Cornwall peering over his shoulder before he entered, then he came swiftly across to the couch and stood staring down grave-faced at Thomas. 'We are come from the King,' he said somewhat unnecessarily. Under cover of an altercation at the door where Herbert was refusing entrance to the men who had accompanied the nobles, he fixed Thomas with an urgent, interrogative look.

Thomas nodded as though in answer to his statement. So Leicester was unsure of Cornwall. . . . And indeed Cornwall's air of acute discomfort made the truth plain. He had thrown in his lot with Henry. He caught Thomas's eye on him, coughed, and true to his orders, demanded to know whether the Archbishop were ready to present his accounts.

Thomas held his breath as he felt the pain returning but it was not so bad this time. When he opened his eyes, Leicester said sharply, 'Surely it is plain this is no feigned illness. I think we may carry word to the lord King that his suspicions were incorrect!'

Thomas spoke with an effort, 'If you will ask the King to grant me a respite for this one day, I swear that I will appear tomorrow – yes, even if I must be carried thither. And' – he drew a deep, painful breath – 'I will answer as God wills.'

'I pray you take care,' began Leicester, and then Cornwall, discarding his official personality all at once, shouted for stools that they might speak with the Archbishop in some degree of comfort. 'And clear off, the rest of you!' he roared. 'The Archbishop is safe enough with us.'

When the three of them were alone, he hitched his stool nearer the couch and removed the pottage bowl with his own hands. Once holding it though, he did not seem to know what to do with it and sat nursing it on his knees. 'I would not say this before anyone but him,' he said, jerking his chin at Leicester, 'but it's as much sin to hold my tongue as to speak. The King means you mischief, Archbishop. This I know and do you not ask me how. First it was to be your eyes put out and your tongue cut off, then he would have your very life.' He stared down into the pottage bowl as though he thought he might read omens in it, sighed and placed it on the floor. 'Well, I have warned you,' he said, 'and if that be treachery, then am I a traitor.'

'Well,' said Leicester, 'Well. . . . All those are rumours current in the Court. I have heard them too.' He looked at

Thomas doubtfully. 'Shall you be well enough to ride tomorrow?'

'If not, I shall come by litter,' said Thomas.

That night he sent for his confessor and laid the facts before him. Prior Robert wrung his hands. 'Will you flee?'

'No,' said Thomas, 'I gave my word to face the King tomorrow and I shall do it.'

The Prior had always had a great devotion to the Holy Martyrs and it struck him now that he might be in the presence of one destined to join them. He felt a holy exaltation. 'If you are determined on that,' he said, 'I would advise you to say the Mass of Saint Stephen tomorrow before you go. It will be pleasing to God and heartening to yourself.'

About that same time two Canons of Sempringham were shown into my lord of Leicester's chamber. He was alone and sitting by the fire but he rose with eagerness when they came in and led them to the settle himself, nodding to dismiss the servant. After the door was firmly shut he said, 'Well? You got my message?' They agreed that that was so.

'And you will help the Archbishop?'

'If it lies within our power – or yours, my lord.'

'He will face the King tomorrow. After – well, I know not. But if it lies within my power as you say, he shall be smuggled away to you. You have a habit for him?'

They nodded and he began to pull at his moustaches, pacing up and down. 'I will not ask where you will ride – best that I do not know. But you must come at the coast by circuitous means, for when the King hears of his escape – *Deo volente!* – that is the first place he will look. I leave it in your hands.' He looked at them sharply but evidently liked what he saw for he went across to a small hutch by the wall. 'Here's silver.'

He put into their hands some heavy bags. 'Do not stir

255

from St Andrew's Priory tomorrow – none can say at what time he may have need of you. But you cannot go before dark.'

When they had gone and he was alone again, he thought – so much for Cornwall's treason! – what is this that I have done? But since he was a man well on in years and could remember times when half the realm was accounted in treason by the other half, it did not worry him overmuch. He was sorry though that he had forgotten to ask the canons to housel him before they went.

Thomas saw the pale sun rise on Tuesday, the thirteenth day of October and wondered if it were the last time he would ever see it. Long pink bars of cloud lay along the horizon; above them was a marbled pattern of gold. Blue washed the zenith. His attack of renal colic was over, and with it had gone the heavy weight of dread. The suddenness of its onset had shown him something he had overlooked: that recoil from it as all men must, death is not ultimately to be evaded. And to die striking a blow for God could be the greatest privilege of all. He would look gently on His own.

After all, he thought, I never feared death in battle; indeed, I always believed it the finest way to die. Was not this dispute with the King also a battle? It came to him suddenly that those months he had spent as a warrior (which at the time had seemed the consummation of his life) had truly been but a rehearsal for this moment, a testing time to try his mettle. If he were right, then God had led him – gently, softly, by degrees for many years, towards this confrontation. . . .

The notion freed him finally from the deadening hand of fear and he watched the sky, uplifted, until the first dazzle pierced the clouds and the distant chanting of the monks drifted through the open window. Surely a foretaste of Paradise – to gaze on glory with a background of angelic choirs.

But the mood was shattered when he went below. Already the bishops were waiting for him, to hammer him with words, with expostulations, with pleas to think of them. He would be condemned for treason, they cried, he must throw himself on the King's mercy.

Thomas raised his hand. He had grown very thin these last months but the hollow eyes flashed fire as he faced them. 'The world may rage against me as it will,' he cried, 'but the saddening thing to me is that my own brothers are fighting against me. Even if I were to submit today, future ages would remember how you deserted me, how you twice judged me. Although a sinner, I am yet your Archbishop and father. And now you think to go and judge me once again in a secular court. I will not have it. By virtue of your Obedience and at the peril of your Orders, I forbid you henceforth to sit in any judgment on me.'

He was astonished to find himself shouting. They were astonished too; their eyes fell away from him in doubt and fear. 'And if the barons raise their hands against me,' he continued, 'you will defend me by ecclesiastical censure!'

That really frightened them. Excommunicate the barons! He saw their ashen faces and the way they clung together and finished on a note calculated to strengthen himself as well as them. 'My body may tremble because the flesh is weak but with God's help I shall not wickedly yield nor abandon the flock committed to me.'

Alone of his adversaries Gilbert Foliot had preserved his outward dignity. He stepped forward. 'I, my lord, shall not accept your order. Because the oath you ordered us to take at Clarendon is still binding, I shall appeal against you to the Pope—'

Thomas did not pay Foliot the courtesy of listening; he dismissed the bishops and was halfway to the door with Henry of Winchester when Gilbert finished, going with great strides as though to put as much space as possible between himself and them. Nor did he look back to see if

257

any would come to hear his Mass, though after he was in the church and robed, he took a swift survey of the congregation. Worcester and Winchester were there, and his faithful clerks, but the bulk of the crowd was made up of Henry's spies and informers, come to keep watch on him.

He drew a deep breath when he prepared to speak the Introit and raised his voice. '*Sederunt principes, et adversum me loquebantur, et iniqui persecuti sunt me; adjuva me, Domine Deus meus, quia servus tuus exercebatur in tuis justificationibus.*' 'Princes sat and spoke against me and the wicked persecuted me; help me, O Lord my God, for thy servant was exercised in Thy justifications.'

A satisfaction that was almost savage filled him as he heard the rustle run round the church. Let them carry that to Henry! It might give him pause in his headlong plunge to perdition; it was no more than the truth of the situation he had forced on his Archbishop. Yet he could not keep a tremor from his voice when he recited from the Gospel the words of Jesus to the Pharisees. 'That upon you may come all the just blood that hath been shed upon the earth, from the blood of Abel the just even unto the blood of Zacharias the High Priest whom you killed between the temple and the altar—' He was reading facing the congregation and he could see how many of Henry's men were withdrawing, all eager to carry the exciting news of the Archbishop's challenge to the King.

Back in the vestry he waved aside the acolytes who came to disrobe him and bending down, unlaced his shoes. Barefoot, he took his Cross from Alexander and walked outside. The crowd of clerks and Templar knights stared blankly when he came out. 'Well, I am ready to go into the King's presence,' he said. 'Will you attend me?'

'You do not mean to walk – and barefoot?' Their horror and perturbation were evident. Pleading with him to change his mind, they pointed out that the King would be angered out of all reason if he appeared thus; it might mean the difference between life and death. 'The fear of death shall not prevent me,' answered Thomas, and saw by their faces that his was not the only death they feared. 'Oh well, so be it then,' he conceded reluctantly; for a mere gesture he would not have them on his conscience.

So he suffered them to remove the cope and cover the rest of the vestments with a heavy cloak, to replace his shoes and help him mount, but when they were ready he saw how the number of clerks had dwindled; of the forty or so who had been waiting, not more than a dozen remained.

He looked at Herbert and jerked his head significantly backward; Herbert took a glance and said in a loud, scornful voice, ' "The wicked flee when no man pursueth, the righteous are bold as a lion".' He turned to William Fitzstephen, 'Is it not so written in the Scriptures, brother?' William kept his voice low. 'Aye brother, and also – "the wrath of a King is as the roaring of a lion," ' and lower still, 'Also – "ira principis mors est".'

Thomas saw Herbert's mouth open to reply and called peremptorily to Alexander to lead on. And when they rode out of the Priory gate into the golden autumn sunshine, he was cheered and astonished to see a great multitude of townsfolk waiting. They surged forward in a mass to try to touch him, calling their good wishes through their tears.

They believe I ride to martyrdom, he thought, and then with a great jolt, Do I believe it? – truly believe that this day I shall die? A sense of unreality invaded him. All at once he knew he did not; the fact that he would no longer be was inconceivable, the promises of Heaven an illusion and all his former self-communings nothing but sham. He felt his heart knock and his fingers curl and pick. He was much more frightened than he had expected to be. Then he looked at Herbert and knew that, sham or not, he must go forward.

And since he must face what came, he would do it well. In the bailey of Northampton Castle he took the heavy Archiepiscopal Cross from Alexander despite the protests of

259

his companions, and holding it aloft, walked to the door of the hall with measured tread. He heard the rattling of the chains and keys as they locked the great gate behind him. Strangely, the knowledge that he was trapped strengthened him. He was far past the point of no return; whatever happened now, none should say he died craven. The sunlight on the shaft of the cross so near his eyes was dazzling; he blinked and looked past it at the door. Gilbert Foliot stood in the porch with several of his followers. They were staring at him in amazement.

'My lord Bishop,' exclaimed one of Thomas's clerks indignantly. 'Will you stand by and allow him to carry his Cross himself?'

Gilbert's voice was acid. 'My good man, he always was a fool and always will be!' He glared at Thomas. 'Give me that, you madman!' He grabbed at the shaft of the Cross and for a moment they wrestled in an angry, hard-breathing silence until Thomas, younger and stronger, shook him off.

Gilbert fell back, his face a harsh and ugly red. 'Suppose the King now flaunts his sword,' he hissed. 'A brave show you will make, each threatening the other!'

Thomas spoke through pinched, white lips. 'I do this to preserve the peace of God, both for my own person and the Church of the English.' He heard one of Gilbert's men snort contemptuously and added with venom, 'If you were in my place, it would be a different tale.' He pushed past with a violence that made the clerk step back abruptly on Gilbert's toe. The sudden gasp of pain filled Thomas with a quite disproportionate satisfaction.

Once he was seated with Herbert on his right hand and William Fitzstephen at his feet, he took a look around. Only the King's marshals were in the hall with them; Henry and the other bishops had withdrawn to the upper chamber on hearing their arrival. Footsteps overhead announced their presence there. Hearing voices at the door, he glanced over to where Gilbert still waited. Roger of York had just arrived. Why were those two not already with the King? In order, Thomas wondered, to try subsequently to convince men that they had taken no part in any plot for his destruction? He flushed angrily when Roger entered, carrying the Cross of York. Undoubtedly Gilbert had put him up to it, but he had no right to carry it outside his own diocese. He barely acknowledged them as they passed through and went on up the inner stair.

Into the lengthening silence Herbert whispered, 'My lord, if they try to lay impious hands upon you, excommunicate them at once.' William looked up. 'Far be it from him,' he said clearly. 'The holy apostles and martyrs of God did not so when they were seized and ill-treated. If it happens, he should pray for them, forgive them and possess his soul in patience.'

Herbert, unaccustomed to rebuke, preserved a haughty and offended silence. William watched him for a moment, then turned his eyes to Thomas's drawn face. 'Holy Writ teaches us, my lord—'

'Quiet!' called a marshal and walked quickly towards them, his rod levelled like a sword. 'The King has ordered that none may speak with the Archbishop.'

William pressed his lips together but after a while he glanced up at Thomas again, and by dint of raising his eyes to the figure on the Cross and placing his hands palm to palm, indicated that he should pray. Thomas nodded, bowed his head and closed his eyes.

Squeezed together in a corner upstairs, Reynold Fitzurse, Hugh de Morville, Will de Tracy and Richard le Bret watched the King harangue the bishops. When they had finally brought themselves to tell him of the Archbishop's ban on their taking any part in his trial, he had screamed and raved and flung the parchments on the table at them; he had clawed out handfuls of his already thinning hair and torn the front of his fine jerkin so that it hung in a huge triangular flap. Now he strode up and down, kicking the rushes aside and swearing in a dull, monotonous undertone between sudden shouted attacks on the bishops as he re-hashed old scores against each of them.

Le Bret, as one of the King's own men, had smuggled the others in; among so many they would not be noticed. He warned them to keep their heads down, though, and make no remarks that might be overheard. So, peering between the crowding heads, they listened in fascinated silence to the exchanges of the principals in this great quarrel, Reynold and Will with worry about their own futures uppermost in their minds; le Bret with an open and Hugh with a secret eagerness to see the Archbishop smashed and broken.

Henry was waving his arm towards the barons now. 'Go down, go down and ask him whether he means to persist in this defiance. And see if he is yet prepared to present the accounts of his Chancellorship to me.'

Thomas's knights went down too in the midst of the thrusting, jostling press, making for the darkest corner. It was difficult to hear anything the earls said to the Arch-bishop from there because of the pushing and whispered asides of their fellows but the crowd quieted as soon as the Archbishop began to speak.

He remained seated, holding his Cross; his knuckles show-ing white with the effort to keep it steady. But the jewels in it, which caught the light, betrayed the movement of his hands. At the other end of the hall, the Cross of York was raised as if in opposition.

'Men and brethren,' he began, 'earls and barons of the lord King, I am indeed bound to the King, our liege lord, by homage, fealty and oath—' Someone shifted in front of Reynold and he craned sideways to find his view blocked by another. 'I decline this suit,' he heard, and then someone nearby began to whisper vehemently to his neighbour and he caught snatches only for a time – enough though to realise that the Archbishop was insisting he had been given free to the Church – 'quit and loosed from every secular suit of the King although he now angrily denies it. This many of you well know, and all the clergy of the realm.' Reynold nodded to himself, he knew it too. But he could not see how that sort of argument would sway the King who was well known for forgetting old promises when it did not suit him to remember them.

The calm voice was coming to him clearly now. 'I cannot give sureties for rendering an account. I have already bound all the bishops and friends of mine who could help me here; neither should I be compelled thereto, for it has not been so judged against me. Nor am I being impleaded concerning this account for I was not summoned for that cause, but for the case of John the marshal. As for my prohibition to the bishops, I have forbidden them to judge me in any secular suit arising from the time prior to my assumption of the Archiepiscopal dignity. I still forbid it and I place both my person and the church of Canterbury under the protection of God and the lord Pope.'

There was dead silence for several seconds after the Archbishop ceased speaking. Then a loud, jeering and familiar voice yelled, 'King William, who conquered England, knew how to tame his clergy. He arrested his own brother, the Bishop of Bayeux.' It was Ranulf de Broc, well known for his hatred of all churchmen. Someone else shouted, 'He condemned Stigand, the Archbishop of Canterbury, to life imprisonment.' 'And what about our King's father?' Ranulf came back, 'He gelded the Bishop-elect of Séez and some of his clerks. And had the evidence brought to him in a bowl.'

The younger knights were all chiming in now, their taunts becoming coarser and more explicit by the minute. The noise was so great that le Bret had to nudge Reynold in the ribs to get his attention. 'We have heard him condemn himself.' He was grinning broadly. Reynold could make nothing of that; he looked at Hugh and Will for guidance.

Will's brow was furrowed, but whether with worry or puzzlement he could not tell. And Hugh gazed at the Archbishop, rapt, intense, as on a lover, his breath coming soft through parted lips. Then the long lashes hid his eyes, he breathed deeply once and put his hand across his mouth. He smiled brilliantly at le Bret. 'All heard the blasphemy proceeding from his mouth!'

Reynold watched the great earls and the bishops making for the stair to carry the Archbishop's answer to the King. 'Shall we remain here or go up?' he said. He saw Hugh and le Bret look at each other and felt an unaccountable irritation. They both seemed to have heard something he had missed, or were privy to a secret they had not shared with him. 'Shall we go up and hear what the King will do?' he repeated.

'No, we will stay by the Archbishop,' said Hugh. Le Bret tittered. 'Close by,' he said. Reynold shrugged and looked away from them towards Will. Though they all four were cronies, he was beginning to feel that le Bret was pushing him out of his privileged position with Hugh. On a sudden qualm of angry jealousy he said, 'Well, I am going up. I will have the King know whose part I take in this. Are you coming, Will?'

'Stay!' Hugh put his hand on Reynold's arm. 'When swords are drawn the King will know.'

Reynold stared. 'Swords? Do you think—?'

'He will be condemned,' le Bret said harshly. 'And afterwards – outside – he will not escape! The King will thank us later – even reward us. Thus will no blame attach to him, but he will be free of the fellow. Hark! Hark, even now he is swearing he will have his life!'

Someone had left the door of the upper chamber open and the King's bellowed curses were clearly audible below. The knights had stopped deriding the Archbishop to listen. Then it slammed shut with a crash and a second later the

264

Archbishop of York and his clerks appeared on the stair, descending slowly as if unsure of their knees. The Archbishop's normally florid face was the colour of whey. They got into some semblance of a procession at the foot of the stairs, and as the knights and marshals drew aside to make a way for them, York called over his shoulder rather more loudly than was necessary – 'Let us go from here! It is not fitting that we should watch what is going to be done to the Archbishop of Canterbury!'

'You see,' hissed le Bret, 'they know his hour is come. God grant me a chance to avenge my master.'

One of Roger's clerks, bolder than the rest, was crying, 'I shall not leave until I see what is God's will. If he should spill his blood fighting for God's justice, what finer end to life could there be?'

Bartholomew of Exeter had followed York down; he pushed past and fell on his knees before the Archbishop. 'Father and lord,' he pleaded, 'spare yourself and us. The King has said he will treat all who oppose him as traitors.' The Archbishop stared at him stonily. 'Go,' he said, 'you do not understand the will of God.'

There was another sudden bustle on the stair and all eyes turned that way. The bishops were returning, a number of them weeping and making little effort to hide their tears. They swarmed about the Archbishop's chair and Chichester's shrill tones rose above the rest. 'We have much to complain of against you, my lord. You have shut us up in a trap by your prohibition; you have placed us between the hammer and the anvil, for if we disobey you we are ensnared in the bonds of disobedience, and if we obey we infringe the Constitutions and trespass against the King.'

They could not make out the words after that, only the complaining voice running on. Reynold did not try to listen anyway; he was prepared to accept le Bret's assurance that the Archbishop would be convicted and his mind was too taken up with a wild and mounting excitement to think of anything else. At least they had let him into the plot. For after the behaviour of the fighting men, he could not doubt that they were all in it. The King's gratitude would be unbounded – and such a stroke would silence Beatrice's complaints of his ineptitude once for all.

He scarcely noticed the comings and goings thereafter and only discovered that the King had in fact excused the bishops from sitting in judgment on their lord when Will poked him, whispering, 'Here's Leicester, come to pronounce sentence,' and he saw that all the clergy sat apart from the other barons. Leicester was looking as unhappy as they; he hummed and hawed a great deal, and at length began to recapitulate the old business done at Clarendon, as though all of them there did not know enough of it already. There was much sighing and groaning amongst the audience until one, though keeping himself well hidden, shouted most insolently to Leicester to come to the point. So Leicester stopped, and after drawing a deep breath, announced that the Archbishop must now hear the sentence.

Thomas stared at him. During the hours he had sat here, the fear that had threatened to swamp him had gradually receded. It was still there, he knew, a tiny kernel that could flower into monstrous growth if once he loosed his guard upon it, but the ugly taunting of the King's knights had raised in him a burning anger that caged it more effectively than any prayer could do. He had endured the indignity with the same Christian forbearance he had returned to the marshals' petty pricks and malevolent glares, to the treachery and cowardice of his own suffragans. But Leicester – his comrade, his peer, his friend. . . . Forbearance would stretch no further.

He said furiously, 'What is this you would do? Have *you* come to judge me? You have no right. Judgment is a sentence given after trial and this day I have said nothing in the way of pleading. And such as I am, I am your father; you are magnates of the household, lay powers, secular personages. I will not hear your judgment!'

He stood up, and seeing the look on his face and the sudden fierce jerk with which he lifted high his cross, the converging crowd fell back a pace or two. The dangerous glitter of his eyes informed them that here was no acquiescent victim for the sacrificial knife and it came with shock to more than one mind that that heavy cross could scatter brains as effectively as any mace.

Their hesitation was all that Thomas needed. He was half-way to the door before anyone moved, and even then the most they dared was to hurl rushes and other refuse after the few who followed him.

Close to the central hearth a bundle of faggots lay ready for kindling. In his furious progress Thomas did not see it; he caught his toe, tripped, staggered, and almost fell. Ranulf de Broc, circling the hearth behind Hamelin, the King's half-brother, yelled, 'Perjurer!' 'Traitor!' bellowed Hamelin. He was almost upon the Archbishop.

Righting himself, Thomas turned and faced him. His voice rang out, cold and deadly. 'Were I still a knight, you bastard lackey, mine own hands would give you the lie!' Hamelin found that he was staring transfixed into eyes that spoke murder as plainly as any he had seen in battle. His legs had carried him three steps backwards before he was aware of having moved.

Almost weeping, le Bret with Reynold and Hugh de Morville in tow, forced through the press towards them. 'Follow him, follow him,' he was bawling but Hamelin had turned away. He had quite suddenly lost all his taste for the front rank.

The daunting of the vanguard held back the baying mob behind them for the few precious moments it took Thomas and his companions to get through the door and slam it behind them. The bailey was empty; the gate, though locked, unguarded.

'Mount, my lord, while we find the keys,' urged Herbert.

'That door will not hold them long.' Then from the gate came William's voice, tremulous with thanks – '*Laus Deo!* Here be the keys on a nail.'

Through the pounding on the hall door and the rattling of the huge iron keys as William and Alexander tried and discarded them, Herbert forced the Archbishop up into the saddle of the nearest horse. 'Go, my lord!' he cried as the gate creaked open. 'We will follow.'

Outside, a crowd of citizens blocked the entrance and filled the road beyond. A great roar of joy went up as they saw the Archbishop; racing forward, they surrounded his little group, miraculously opening up a path for the horses. Through laughter and tears they cried their thanks to God, their gratitude to the saints for his safety in the midst of enemies. As the horses slowed in the press, they forced forward sufferers from scrofula, begging the mercy of his touch, as if that power had passed from the King to him.

Back in the upper chamber, Henry heard their shouting even over the noise below. He stopped his tirade in mid-sentence, and listened. The change in his expression startled his audience. They waited, shifting uneasily, till he spoke in an oddly lifeless voice. 'He has gone. Hearken to the rabble hail him.'

There was a silence and the lesser bishops dared to breathe again as the King stared blankly into space. Then Gilbert Foliot leaned close and muttered in his ear.

Henry heard the words but it was a moment before he took in their sense. But Gilbert's suggestion – that he wait until the town was quiet and the knights dismissed before arresting Thomas and casting him in prison – seemed to be the only thing to do. He stirred himself. 'Shout at them below to cease their caterwauling. None are to follow him. I'll have no blood spilt in the town on his account.'

268

X

October–November 1164

THE CHEERING HOST followed Thomas back to St Andrew's Priory. As they surged on, more and more poured out of their homes to join them until the narrow streets were jammed. Even if it had been attempted, no enemy could have reached the Archbishop in that seething mass.

By the time they came to the Priory rain was beginning in earnest, and a wild wind was lifting cloaks from the riders' backs like banners. Thomas glanced back at the motley crowd. The townsfolk were leaving now; those who remained were the beggars and the homeless. 'Bring them in and see that they are fed,' he said to Herbert. 'It may be the last time that I shall feed Christ's poor.'

They dismounted in silence, but as they went through the door William sighed and remarked, 'Indeed, this has been a bitter day.' 'The Last Day will be more bitter,' Thomas replied shortly.

Throughout their triumphal progress he had been consumed by remorse. But he would make what amends he could. 'Let each of you keep silence and peace,' he said, miserably aware of how his words contrasted with his behaviour. 'Let no harsh words fall from your lips. Let them taunt you and do not answer. It is the mark of a higher character to bear insults, of the lower nature to inflict them. They command their tongues but we our ears. Insults touch us only if we recognise in ourselves the evils they allege.' He felt a little better when he had said it. William, at any rate, would understand the implicit admission.

A goodly number of familiar faces were absent from the board that night at supper but their places were taken up by strangers, among them a small group of Gilbertian canons. Thomas looked them over curiously. It would be unwise to assume they had come to support him, though he now remembered Leicester's assertion that he could find refuge with Gilbert of Sempringham. And just at that moment, like a voice from heaven, the sonorous tones of the monk reading from the *Historia Tripartita* rang out – 'if they persecute you in one city, flee to another.' Herbert had noticed too; they exchanged guarded looks.

But his attention was distracted from Herbert by a noise and bustle at the door. Gilbert of London and Hilary of Chichester were entering and pushing forward as if they brought momentous news. Thomas half rose and then sat down again, keeping his hands, those betrayers of tension, out of sight beneath the board. The monk who was reading fell silent, his mouth half open.

'We have found a means to make peace between the King and yourself,' announced Hilary importantly, to the company at large rather than to Thomas.

Thomas eyed him. 'On what terms?' he said at last.

'It is only a question of money between you and the King. If you will turn over to him two of your manors, Otford and Wingham, as a pledge for the time being, we think he will be satisfied.'

Thomas stared. Was this another trap? 'Did the King send you?' he asked.

No, they said, but they were convinced it was a way to end the trouble. Thomas shook his head. 'The lord King holds one of those manors already, and in any case they belong to Canterbury, not to me. I cannot barter with the

Church's property.'

Gilbert shrugged and looked at Hilary. 'Well, we have done our best – no more can be expected of us.'

Knowing then why they were there, Thomas turned away his eyes from their faces and found himself looking at one of the Gilbertian canons, a big, rawboned man with deep eyes and sunken cheeks. There was affection and respect in those eyes, and he thought, a look full of meaning. It warmed him and he made up his mind to speak to the man later. When he turned back to Hilary and Gilbert, they had gone with as little ceremony as they had come.

After supper the few knights and pages left to him knelt and tearfully requested that he release them from his service. He could do no other, as he knew. The acclaim of the citizens of Northampton had hammered home the last nail in his coffin. That Henry would never forgive, but these innocents must not suffer because of it.

Outside the gale had increased in force. Wind howled around the corners of the old buildings and whistled piercingly through ill-fitting doors; shutters creaked and groaned under the beating of torrential rain. From somewhere nearby came an incessant loud banging, suddenly stilled as whatever caused it was carried away on a roaring tide of air.

The violence of the storm excited Herbert. While his men were taking a sad leave of the Archbishop, he had been talking with the canons and now he brought them over with hardly suppressed exaltation. 'We shall escape the King yet,' he cried, not bothering to lower his voice. But his exuberance subsided by degrees as the realisation that he was not to accompany his beloved master slowly dawned on him. 'For it will not do,' the canons told him. 'The Archbishop is well known and difficult to disguise because of his height; another easily recognisable figure might mean the difference between escape and capture.'

Herbert nodded finally. Later – somehow – he would give the King the slip and get away himself. For the moment he set his inventive brain to making plans for the Archbishop's escape. 'It will be a great deal easier to get out of the church unnoticed than down from your bedchamber,' he said at last, 'and what more natural than a wish to spend the night in prayer? We will place your pallet between the two altars so that the monks may see you resting there when they sing Compline. You will have at least four hours then, until they return to the church again—'

I shall go back to Canterbury, he was deciding, and gather what treasure I can to take to him in exile. The King shall not get his hands on it if I can help it. . . .

When the news of the Archbishop's flight was confirmed by Henry of Winchester who had it direct from Osbern, Thomas's chamberlain, a number of the bishops converged upon the King.

Gilbert Foliot, quicker off the mark than the rest, arrived first. He saw immediately that Henry had been angry but had passed into the calm after the storm; it was plain in the hard, bright glitter of his eyes and the stillness of his pose. Besides, he was alone which was unusual at this hour. Gilbert knew that he had no reason to fear but he was glad, nonetheless, that the news had already broken. He saluted the King with the portentous air and long face of one who sorrows deeply for his master's worries, and when the King told him to sit, eyed him with a grave and silent sympathy.

'So he has escaped,' said Henry abruptly.

Gilbert inclined his head.

'We have not finished with him yet,' said Henry and there was so much pent-up fury in his tightly controlled voice that Gilbert's eyes flickered away for a perceptible moment. When he brought them back, his demeanour had altered slightly; now he was ready to be fired by the injuries

272

done his master. Henry continued in a hissing voice; he would sequestrate the revenues of Canterbury and the goods of the Archbishop's clerks and relatives; he would demand his extradition from France or Flanders or wherever he might be; he would put a price upon his head—

While the King spoke, Gilbert stared out of the window to where the tops of the trees swayed against the pale blue of the sky; only a few yellow leaves still clung to the branches after the storm and even as he watched, they fluttered away on the wind. He let the King talk his anger out and then suggested gently that such actions might give the totally wrong impression of a tyrant thirsting for revenge. This would not be the way to make the Pope see that the blame lay with the Archbishop. It was important that his treachery be plain to other princes.

'God's death!' screamed Henry. He sprang up and at the top of his voice commanded his Maker to commit a number of the grosser perversions upon this Archbishop who had eluded him. Gilbert affected not to hear, prudently recognising that this was no time to take him to task for blasphemy.

Henry ran down at last and sat glaring before him and breathing heavily; when he looked at Gilbert again he seemed ready to recognise the force of his argument. 'I will give orders,' he said abruptly, 'that his people and their property are not to be molested. But' – he ground his teeth – 'I will have all those of his blood out of my realm empty-handed!'

Since Gilbert had no special regard for Thomas's relatives, he let that pass; indeed, his mind had been grappling with only one wild eventuality ever since he had heard of the Archbishop's flight, and all his advice to the King had been designed with that in mind. The mitre of Canterbury hovered again within his grasp. Surely the Pope must see the unsuitability of the man. Surely in the interests of the

273

English Church he would deprive him now.

Thomas strained his eyes across the choppy sea for the last glimpse of England but the scattered roofs of Sandwich had vanished in the pre-dawn mist. Behind him, the two canons laboured at the oars; it was unsafe as yet to hoist the sail. And to be taken now after the discomforts they had endured on the indirect journey from the Danelaw to the Kentish coast would be too much.

Soon though, he could tell they were in the open sea by the increased buffeting of the waves on the little boat's hull. The timbers creaked dismally. It would be strange if he had eluded Henry's wrath only to be food for fish.

The mist was lifting now with a rising off-shore breeze and the light grew stronger by the moment. Thomas's man, Roger, had taken over an oar while the big canon struggled with the sail. Thomas looked at him questioningly but he shook his head; he was a Fenman, brought up on water, and almost insulted at any offer of help. He got the sail up at last and sat down to regain his breath while the boat began to bowl merrily along at a spanking rate.

'Not much like our stilly waters,' he said with a faint smile, indicating the racing waves, 'but we shall make good speed today. And a good day for it.' He pulled up his cowl over his head and began to tell his beads, staring into the distance with the far-sighted gaze of a man who spends little time within walls.

Thomas nodded. All Souls' Day had just dawned. They had spent a week in travelling by devious routes from Northampton to the manor of Eastry near Sandwich, for they had ridden north to Lincoln on the first lap of the journey. That was a night Thomas was never to forget — the furtive departure from the Priory into a wild tumult of wind and rain, the urging on of horses which continually

274

floundered and slipped in mud and water, the anxious waiting in a copse for imagined sounds of pursuit while the gale snapped great branches above their heads like so much kindling. Twice more they had stopped on that furious ride – to cut a strip off the hem of Thomas's cloak, so weighted was it with water. When they arrived at Lincoln, seventy miles away, it was as short as Henry's own. There they had taken refuge with a fuller named James, and Thomas had put on the Gilbertian habit and become Brother Christian.

The next day had seen them rowing down the Witham to that house of the canons known as the Hermitage, in the heart of the fens. In that lonely spot among the bird-haunted reedbeds Thomas had rested a few days while couriers went ahead to prepare other houses for his coming. And so at last they had come to Eastry which belonged to the monks of Christ Church, Canterbury, and was a safe haven. Another whole week they had lingered there, waiting for the weather, sweating out the hours, never knowing whether treachery or loose tongues might betray their whereabouts to the King.

Now, on the untenanted sea, it was a time of pause for Thomas, a time for taking stock. He lay in God's hand, as empty of thought for the future as of hope. But watching the grey waste of water round them, he was reminded of other times he had crossed the Channel as the most important passenger on the finest ship of the fleet. They had been big ships with figureheads and pennants, well found, strong and watert-tight, with awnings on the deck and cabins below.

How far had he fallen to be fleeing the land he loved in this leaky hulk. A bitter shame and shrinking rose in him and he turned his face quickly that the others might not see his tears.

They reached the Flanders coast in the late afternoon, and avoiding the ports, landed on the wide, flat beach near Gravelines. Not a soul was in sight, the sands stretched empty as far as they could see. Thomas's knees shook after the long hours of sitting in the little boat and his numbed feet would not obey him; hampered by the trailing monastic gown and clumsy shoes, he slipped and fell full length repeatedly. The last time he continued to lie there, gazing at his scraped and bleeding hands. He was at his lowest ebb. 'It is no use,' he whispered, 'I can no more. Leave me and go. If God wants me, He will send help.'

Roger was staring up the beach. A lone figure was approaching. 'There's a boy coming this way,' he said. 'Gathering shellfish by the look of it.' He staggered off towards him.

Afterwards Thomas remembered little of the rest of the journey. His companions got a horse from somewhere – a sorry nag without saddle or bridle, but it carried him to an inn at Gravelines. He slept all night and most of the next day.

When he awakened at last, Roger was sitting beside him. For a moment he could not remember where he was and started up in sudden fear. 'Don't worry, my lord,' said Roger softly, 'you are still safe. The landlord is a good man — he knows who you are but he has sworn on his hope of Heaven that he will never betray you to the Counts of Flanders or Boulogne.' He went to the door and shouted to someone below to bring broth and bread.

While Thomas was eating it, he talked in a hurried undertone of their need to move on. 'We can take sanctuary with the Cistercians at Clair-Marais.' He looked sideways at the Archbishop. 'Do you remember anything of the man with the merlin?' Thomas shook his head blankly. 'We thought you were not yourself. We met him on our way here and you insisted on discussing hawks with him – it seemed to us that he was suspicious of your identity. He kept staring at you.'

Thomas put aside the bowl. 'We will go tonight,' he said. 'You are quite right, I cannot endanger the good people

276

here. Remember this place. One day I will reward them for their kindness.'

Strength had flowed into him with the broth. He would regain his power and position. He would win this battle – God's battle – and teach Henry a lesson he would never forget. Not only Henry either; it would be an object lesson for all kings in times to come.

Richard de Luci, the Justiciar, had been for nearly half a year out of England. He had hoped for many years to travel to the Holy Land before he died but always the King had needed him. Then the thought to make a pilgrimage to St James of Compostella had come to him; it was not to be compared with Jerusalem but he was no longer young and perhaps God would take the arduous journey as expiation for his sins. So he had gone to the great shrine and said his prayers and gained his cockleshell.

Spain had been hot and arid and little news from other lands had reached him. It was only when he came up through Burgundy and Blois and into Flanders on the way home that he heard details of the great events that had taken place in England. The Archbishop driven away in disgrace – and here near St Omer! He found it hard to believe. Never had he thought things would come to this pass. He fought a silent battle between his personal distaste for Thomas of London and his unswerving devotion to his King. Duty won. He would do what he could. He turned for Clair-Marais where rumour had it the Archbishop was staying.

He was shocked when he saw Thomas. Gaunt and bony, his old colleague was a shadow of his former self. They talked alone in a cold and quiet little chamber in the monastery. But it seemed to him that the Archbishop was singularly lacking in the humility that befits a Christian man, speaking of the King in terms which could only be called disrespectful at best. He frowned a little and tried again. 'If you will return to England with me—'

The Archbishop interrupted him. 'You do not understand the position. Have I not told you of the King's vile threats?'

'I cannot believe—'

'*You* cannot believe! You were not there! God has guided me to this spot—'

De Luci kept a tight rein on his impatience. 'Well, if you will not accompany me, will you return later with my assurance of your safety?'

Thomas stood up abruptly. 'I do not know why you think you know the King better than I. I tell you my life is at stake.'

'Yet you intend to continue opposing the King?'

'That is God's will.'

De Luci stood up too. 'Then I must tell you that the King's enemies are my enemies.'

Thomas glared at him. 'You have no right to speak to me like that. You are my vassal.' It was true; de Luci held lands of Canterbury.

He recognised it and his face grew grimmer. 'I take back my homage,' he said shortly.

Thomas could never resist the opportunity to score the last point and he had long forgotten his predecessor's gentle teaching concerning the custody of the tongue. The scorn in his voice cut like a lash as he said, 'I was unaware that I received it as a loan.'

De Luci's eyes narrowed and his lips thinned as he regarded the Archbishop for a long moment. All his dislike of the man had flooded back. He turned on his heel.

Left standing, Thomas smiled grimly. Undoubtedly de Luci would carry the story of this interview to the King and the full extent of his personal failure would be brought home to Henry. Strong with a sense of achievement, he knelt to offer thanks.

Bibliography

Appleby, John T.: *Henry II*, G. Bell and Sons 1962.

Bagley, J. J.: *Life in Mediaeval England*, Batsford 1960.

Barber, Richard: *Henry Plantagenet*, Barrie and Rockliff 1964.

Barlow, Frank: *Feudal Kingdom of England*, Longman 1955.

Barrow, G. W. S.: *Feudal Britain*, Arnold 1956.

Brooke, Christopher: *From Alfred to Henry III*, Nelson 1961.

Brooke, Christopher: *Twelfth Century Renaissance*, Thames & Hudson 1969.

Coulton, C. G.: *Social Life in Britain: Conquest to Reformation*, Cambridge University Press 1918, revised edition 1956.

Duggan, Alfred: *Thomas Becket of Canterbury*, Faber 1967.

English Historical Documents, Volume II (ed. David C. Douglas and George W. Greenaway), Eyre Spottiswoode 1968.

Eyton, R. W.: *Court, Household and Itinerary of Henry II*, Taylor 1878.

Hay, Denys: *The Mediaeval Centuries*, Methuen 1953.

Hutton, William Holden: *Thomas Becket*, Cambridge University Press 1926.

Kelly, Amy: *Eleanor of Aquitaine and the Four Kings*, Cassell 1952.

Knowles, David: *Episcopal Colleagues of Thomas Becket*, Cambridge University Press 1951.

Knowles, David: *Thomas Becket*, Cambridge University Press 1970.

Lyte, Sir Henry C. Maxwell: 'Fitzurse', Somerset Archaeological and Natural History Society Proceedings: 1922. Vol. LXVIII, pp. 93–104.

Quennell, Marjorie and C. H. B.: *History of Everyday Things in England—1066–1499*, Batsford, 4th edition, 1957.

Stenton, Doris Mary: *English Society in the Early Middle Ages*, Pelican History of England III, 1951.

Warren, W. L.: *Henry II*, Eyre Methuen 1973.

Webb, Clement C.: *John of Salisbury*, Methuen 1932.

Winston, Richard: *Becket*, Constable 1967.

WILLIAM I

| Robert
Duke of Normandy | WILLIAM II
(Rufus) | HEN |

| Robert
Earl of Gloucester
d. 1147 | | Regin
Earl of G |

William
Earl of Gloucester

| William
d. 1120 | | I |

Louis VII = Eleanor of Aq
of France

| Marie | | Alice |

| William
b. 1153
d. 1156 | | Henry
b. 115 |